Calypso

Ed McBain was born in Manhattan, but fled to the Bronx at the age of twelve. He went through elementary and high school in the New York school system, and the Navy claimed him in 1944. When he returned two years later, he attended Hunter College. After a variety of jobs, he worked for a literary agent, where he learnt about plotting stories. When his agent-boss started selling them regularly to magazines, and sold a mystery novel and a juvenile science-fiction title as well, they both decided that it would be more profitable for him to stay at home and write full time.

Under his own name, Evan Hunter, he is the author of a number of novels, including *The Blackboard Jungle*, *Come Winter* and *Every Little Crook and Nanny*. As Ed McBain he has written the highly popular '87th Precinct' series of crime novels, including *Shotgun*, *Jigsaw*, *Fuzz*, *Hail, Hail, the Gang's All Here!* and *Sadie When She Died*, all of which are available in Pan.

Ed McBain

Calypso

An 87th Precinct Mystery

Pan Books London and Sydney

First published in Great Britain 1979 by Hamish Hamilton Ltd
This edition published 1980 by Pan Books Ltd,
Cavaye Place, London SW10 9PG
9 8 7
© HUI Corporation 1979
ISBN 0 330 26200 9
Printed and bound in Great Britain by
Hunt Barnard Printing Ltd, Aylesbury, Bucks

This is for Jay and Connie Cronley

1

In this city, autumn is often wasted. There are not that many parks, there is never a riotous flame of leafy colour sufficient to stun the senses. The skies are often sodden and grey with the after birth of tropical storms born in the Caribbean and swept far northward by raging winds. It is not until October that they turn constantly, achingly, intensely blue. It is then that the air comes briskly alive in a season of dying.

This September, as usual, there was rain.

The two men walking through the late-night storm were autumn enough. The taller of the two had a warm café au lait complexion, and he was wearing under his raincoat a yellow silk blouse and red silk trousers. Yellow glowed in the V-neck of the raincoat; red flashed below the hem and in the gap that opened with each long-legged stride he took. He was carrying a guitar case in his left hand. The case swung in counterpoint to his hurried steps. The shorter man had difficulty keeping up with him. His complexion was darker, a rich chocolate brown that glistened wetly in the teeming rain. He was wearing a green ski parka and trousers that almost matched the colour of his skin. When he smiled, as he was doing now, a gold tooth gleamed at the front of his mouth.

'You were sensational,' he said.

'Yeah,' the taller man said without enthusiasm.

'You killed them, baby, I don't know what I got to say to convince you.'

'Yeah.'

'Look at what the crowd was. A three-hundred advance, another fifty at the door. That's a sizeable crowd, George.'

'That's skimpy. For a Friday night, that's real skimpy.'

'No, no, that ain't skimpy. With capacity at four hundred? You almost filled the hall. Nossir, I don't consider that skimpy.'

'None of them knew what I was doing, man.'

'They caught it all, George. You were laying it down, baby, and they were pickin it up. What you think they were yellin and screamin so? When you did the one...'

The shots came from a shadowed tenement doorway.

There was a flash of yellow paler than the tall man's shirt, and then a shocking explosion. The bullet entered the left side of his neck and blew out an exit wound on the opposite side, blood spattering in globules on the falling rain. He groped the rain for support, staggered, dropped the guitar case and turned in time to see the second muzzle flash. The bullet shattered his left cheekbone, and veered wildly through the top of his skull, opening his head in a shower of gristle, bone and blood.

The shorter man's reaction time was slow. He was turning towards the doorway when the muzzle flared yellow again. Lightning flashed above, there was the sound of the explosion and then a thunderclap that made it seem magnified and echoing. He winced in anticipation, and then realized the bullet had missed him. He began running. He heard another explosion behind him, and swerved like a quarterback dodging opposition, a futile reaction given the speed of the bullet. But the aim was wild again, he was still on his feet and running, and beginning to think he would get away clean. The fifth bullet caught him high on the left shoulder. It hit him hard, he felt only the pressure at first, as though someone had swung a sledgehammer at his back, and then he felt the searing pain as the bullet tore through flesh and bone, and suddenly he fell flat to the pavement. Up the street, he heard someone yelling. In the gutter on his right, he heard rushing water. And then he heard something that caused him to feel suddenly faint. Footsteps. Footsteps moving swiftly from the doorway to where he lay bleeding on the sidewalk.

He said, 'O, Jesus, please,' and lifted his head. He saw only the tips of black leather boots below the legs of narrow black trousers. He squinted through the teeming rain, raised his head a bit higher, and saw a black-sleeved arm levelled at his head, a hand clutching a black pistol. Lightning flashed again, he thought at first it was the flaring muzzle, heard the thunder and mistook it for the explosion of the pistol. Instead, there was a click. It reverberated through the hoarse whisper of the rain. Up the street, there was more yelling, a chorus of voices approaching. There was another click, and yet another. He saw the tips of the black leather boots only an instant longer, and then they were gone. He heard the footsteps rushing away through the falling rain, and then more footsteps approaching from the opposite direction, voices above him and around him now, 'Man, you see that?' 'Call the police, man,' 'Somebody git an ambulance,' 'You okay, man?' and then he passed out.

The Police Administrative Aide at Communications Division was wearing a telephone headset with a single earphone, the mouthpiece close to her chin. She was sitting before a console that looked like a television screen with a typewriter keyboard under it. To her right was another console with thirty-two buttons; it was this console that would be activated by a 911 call from any of the city's five separate sections. At twenty minutes to midnight, the ISOLA button flashed, and she immediately said into the mouthpiece, 'This is operator Seventy-Four. Where's the emergency?'

From a phone booth on the corner near where the two men lay bleeding on the sidewalk, a man said in an excited voice, 'There's two guys been shot here. They're layin on the ground here.'

'Where's that, sir?'

'Culver Avenue, near South Eleventh.'

'Hold on, please.'

Her hand flashed to the typewriter keyboard. Her index finger punched first the 'I' key and then the 'Q' key. On the screen above the typewriter, in glowing green letters on a darker green background, a two-hour sector summary flashed:

IQ/3 1A
IQ/3 CULVER SOUTH ELEVENTH
    ASSAULT WEAPON/OUTSIDE
  NO INCIDENTS FOUND

The computer had just told her that the telephone caller was not reporting an emergency already reported within the past two hours. Into the mouthpiece, she said, 'Sir, is there any shooting going on at the moment?'

'No, he run away. Man with the gun run away. They layin here on the sidewalk, the two of them.'

'What is your name and the number you're calling from, sir?'

There was a click on the line. This was the city. It was one thing doing a good turn, it was another getting involved with the fuzz. The aide, unsurprised, hit four digits on her telephone console and began typing as her call went through to Centrex.

'Ambulance Receiving,' a woman's voice said.

'Two men with gunshot wounds, sidewalk on Culver and South Eleventh.'

'Rolling,' the woman said.

There was another click on the line. The aide continued typing. As she typed, her words appeared in bright electronic letters on the console screen

IE/1A GUNSHOT ASSAULT PAST/TWO
       VICTIMS SIDEWALK CULVER
       SOUTH ELEVENTH/AMBULANCE CASE

She reached for the ENTER button on her keyboard and hit it at once. Instantaneously, in another part of Communications, a green light flashed on an almost identical console in the Emergency Dispatchers room The dispatcher sitting in front of the console immediately hit his 'Q' button The message the aide had just typed and entered appeared on his screen. He hit the TRANSMIT button on the console to his right. As he spoke into a microphone hanging over the unit he was already beginning to type.

'Adam Two,' he said, 'are you available?

Affirmative, Central

'Ten twenty-four, two men with gunshot wounds on the sidewalk on Culver and South Eleventh

'Ten-four

On the screen, the words ES ADAM 2 appeared. Adam Two was the emergency service van covering that section of the city. The dispatcher knew that an ambulance was already on the way; the aide taking the call had indicated this was an ambulance case, and he knew she would have contacted Ambulance Receiving at once. It was his guess that the Adam Two van would get there before the ambulance did. If this had been a jumper on one of the city's bridges, or a man pinned under a truck, or a bomb scare, or anyone of a dozen other emergencies requiring heavier equipment than that carried on the van, he would have radioed Truck Two as well, and asked them to respond if they were available. As it was, he knew Adam Two could handle it alone. He hit two digits on his telephone console now, opening communication with one of the Mobile Unit Dispatchers elsewhere on the floor.

'Mobile.'

'Emergency,' he said, 'Ten twenty-four, two men with gunshot wounds on the sidewalk at Culver and South Eleventh.'

'Got it, Frank.'

The radio frequency used by the Mobile Unit Dispatcher and every radio motor patrol car in Isola was not the same one used by the Emergency Dispatcher. In the Adam Two van, the driver and his partner would be monitoring *both* frequencies, but the men in the separate r.m.p. cars would be tuned only to the Mobile Unit band. The dispatcher knew the whereabouts of every r.m.p. car in Isola; there were four other dispatchers on the floor, separately controlling the cars in Riverhead, Calm's Point, Bethtown and Majesta. The Isola dispatcher knew that Culver and South Eleventh was in the 87th Precinct. He further knew that Boy car up there had responded to a 10-13 – an Assist Police Officer – not three minutes earlier, leaving its normal sector to join Adam car at Culver and South Third. Charlie car had just responded to a 10-10, a Suspicious Person call, and had radioed back with a 10-90 – Unfounded. Into the mike, the dispatcher said, 'Eight-Seven Charlie, ten twenty-four, two men with gunshot wounds on the sidewalk at Culver and South Eleventh.'

The man riding shotgun in the Charlie car was undoubtedly new on the job. He said at once, and with obvious excitement, 'Ten *thirty*-four, did you say?'

'*Twenty*-four, *twenty*-four,' the dispatcher said impatiently, distinguishing for the rookie a past crime from a crime in progress.

'Ten-four,' the rookie said, acknowledging. He sounded disappointed.

Five minutes later, in response to a police call-box report from Charlie car to the station house, Detectives Steve Carella and Meyer Meyer of the 87th Precinct arrived at the scene. Five minutes after that, Detectives Monoghan and Monroe of the Homicide Division were standing on the pavement looking down at the dead man in the yellow shirt and the red pants.

'Must be some kind of musician,' Monoghan said.

'A guitar player,' Monroe said.

'Yeah, that's a guitar case,' Monoghan said.

'Did a nice job on his head there,' Monroe said.

'Those're his brains you're looking at,' Monoghan said.

11

'Don't I know brains when I see them?'

'What's the other guy's condition?'

He addressed this question to Carella, who was staring silently at the corpse. There was a pained expression on Carella's face. His eyes – faintly Oriental, slanting downward – seemed to exaggerate the look of grief, presenting a false image of someone who might suddenly burst into tears. A tall, athletically slender white man, he stood in the rain with his hands in his pockets, staring down at the corpse. Near the doorway behind him, the man from the Photo Unit snapped his Polaroids, his strobe flash blinking like a distant star. In the hallway, one of the lab technicians was searching for spent cartridge cases.

'Carella? You hear me?' Monoghan said.

'Meat wagon took him away before we got here,' Carella said. 'Patrolman in Charlie car said he was bleeding front and back.'

'But still alive, huh?'

'Still alive,' Carella said, and looked again at the dead man.

'Hey, Petie, you finished with the stiff here?' Monoghan called to the photographer.

'Yeah, I got all I need,' the photographer answered.

'Did you toss him yet?' Monoghan asked Carella, gesturing towards the dead man.

'I was about to when you got here.'

'Don't get his brains all over you,' Monroe said.

Carella knelt beside the corpse. In the righthand pocket at the rear of his trousers – the sucker pocket, the one any pickpocket could slash undetected – Carella found a brown leather wallet with a driver's licence that identified the dead man as George C. Chadderton. His address was given as 1137 Raucher Street, uptown in Diamondback. The licence gave his height as six feet four inches, his sex as M for Male, and a date of birth that would have made him thirty years old on the tenth of November – if he'd lived that long. The licence also indicated that it was valid only if the bearer wore corrective lenses while driving. George C. Chadderton, lying on the pavement dead, was not wearing eyeglasses, unless they were contacts.

Behind the licence was a lucite-sealed card stating that he was a member in good standing of the local chapter of the American Federation of Musicians – corroboration of the identification, not that any was needed. There was no registration for a motor vehicle in the wallet, but this meant nothing; most motorists kept their registration in the glove compartments of their cars. In the section for cash, Carella found three hundred-dollar bills, a five, and two singles. The hundred-dollar bills bothered him. They did not seem like the denominations a man would be carrying in this neighbourhood – unless he were a pusher or a pimp. Or had Chadderton been heading home after a gig? Still, three hundred dollars seemed like more than any guitar player could reasonably earn in a single night. Was this his pay for a week's work? He rolled the man over on his hip, and reached into the left rear pocket. Only a soiled handkerchief was in it.

'Don't get snot on your hands,' Monroe said cheerfully.

The rain drilled the sidewalk. Carella, hatless and wearing a tan trenchcoat, was flanked by the two Homicide men, who stood like bulky bookends on either side of him, both of them dressed in black raincoats, both wearing black fedoras. Their hands were in their pockets. They watched Carella with something less than interest but more than curiosity. In this city, a homicide was investigated by the precinct detective catching the squeal. Homicide detectives responded as a matter of course, and the later paperwork would be routinely delivered to them. But they were spectators, in effect. Or perhaps referees. Carella, hunched and squatting in the rain, emptied the dead man's righthand side pocket. Chadderton was carrying six keys on a ring, none of them car keys, sixty-seven cents in change, and a subway token. The subway kiosk for the Culver Avenue line was only two blocks away. Had he been slain on his way to the subway? Or had he and the other man been walking towards a car parked somewhere in the neighbourhood?

'What's his name?' Monoghan asked.

'George Chadderton.'

'Nice,' Monroe said, almost to himself.

'Is the ME on his way?' Monoghan asked.

'He should be,' Carella said. 'We notified him.'

'Who said you didn't?' Monoghan said.

'What's the matter with you tonight, anyway?' Monroe asked. 'You seem depressed.'

Carella did not answer him. He was busy bagging and

13

marking the things he'd taken from the dead man's pockets.

'Rain got you depressed, Carella?' Monoghan asked.

Carella still said nothing.

Monroe nodded. 'Rain can depress a man,' he said.

'So how come we don't get umbrellas?' Monoghan asked suddenly. 'Did you notice that?'

'Huh?' Monroe said.

'You ever see a cop with an umbrella? I never seen a cop with an umbrella in my entire life.'

'Me neither,' Monroe said.

'So how come?' Monoghan asked.

'Don't let the rain depress you,' Monroe said to Carella.

'Look what it done to Chadderton here,' Monoghan said.

'Huh?' Monroe said.

'Walkin around with the top of his head open like that, rain *killed* the man,' Monoghan said, and began laughing.

Monroe laughed with him. Carella walked to where the lab technician was still working in the hallway. He handed him the dead man's belongings.

'His pockets,' he said. 'Find anything?'

'Nothing yet. How many shots were fired, do you know?'

'Meyer's talking to one of the witnesses now. You want to listen?'

'What for?' the technician said.

'Find out how many shots were fired.'

'It's raining out there,' the technician said. 'I can find out how many shots were fired right in here, if I locate any casings.'

Meyer and the witness were standing under the open awning of a bakery shop. The shop's windows were grilled for the night. The man Meyer was talking to was a thin, light-skinned Puerto Rican. The neighbourhood here was a mixture of Hispanic and black, the Puerto Ricans along Mason Avenue spilling over on to Culver in the past several years, the friction constant. Carella caught only the tail end of the man's sentence. He spoke with a thick Spanish accent.

'. . . to may dee call,' he said.

'Do you know who made it then?'

'Nobody *wanns* to may it,' the man said. 'We don't wann to geh involve, *comprende*?'

'Yes, but who finally called the police?'

'Some black guy, I don' know who.'

'Where were you when you heard the shots?' Meyer asked.

He was a tall burly white man with china-blue eyes, wearing a Burberry raincoat and a checked Professor Higgins hat that made him look more like an inspector from Scotland Yard than a detective from right here in the Eight-Seven. The hat was a new acquisition. It hid the fact that he was totally bald. The hat was wet now, somewhat shapeless. Above his head, the awning dripped a fringe of rain on to the sidewalk. He waited for the witness's response. The man seemed to be thinking it over.

'Well?' Meyer said.

'We were juss hanging aroun dee pool hall,' he said, and shrugged.

'How many of you?'

'Fi' or six, I'm not sure.'

'Then what?'

'We herr dee shots.'

'How many shots?'

'*Quién sabe?* Plenty.'

'Then what?'

'We come runnin.'

'See anybody with a gun?'

'We see a man run away. Tall man, all dress in black.'

'Can you describe him for me?'

'Tall. Skinny, too. All in black. Black coat, black hat, black shoes.'

'Did you see his face?'

'No, I dinn see his face.'

'Was he white or black?'

'I dinn see his face.'

'Did you see his hands?'

'No, he wass run away.'

'How tall would you say he was?'

'Fi' nine, fi' ten, someting like dat.'

'How much would you guess he weighed?'

'He wass skinny. Like a boy, you know.'

'You said a man.'

'*Si*, but skinny like a boy. *Como un adolescente, comprende?*

'I don't know what that means? What's that in English?'

15

'*El parecía tener diecinueve años.*'

'Anybody here speak Spanish?' Meyer yelled.

A patrolman in a black rubberized rain slicker came to where they were standing. The plastic nameplate pinned under his shield identified him as R. SERRANO. 'Help you?' he said.

'Ask this guy what he just said.'

'*Qué le acabas de decir al detective?*' the patrolman said.

'*Que el hombre que se iba corriendo parecía un adolescente.*'

'What'd he say?' Meyer asked.

'He said the guy who split looked like a teenager.'

'Okay, thanks,' Meyer said. 'Tell him thanks. *Gracias,*' he said, telling the man himself. 'Tell him he can go now. Tell him we're finished with him. *Gracias,*' he said again, and turned to Carella. The patrolman was busily translating to the witness. The witness seemed reluctant to leave. Now that he'd been interrogated by the police, he seemed to consider himself a star. He was clearly disappointed when the patrolman told him he could go. He started an argument with the patrolman. In English, the patrolman told him to get lost, and then went back to stand in the rain where the police barricades had been set up. The cardboard 'CRIME SCENE – DO NOT ENTER' signs tacked to the barricades were beginning to wilt in the steady downpour.

'You heard it, Steve,' Meyer said. 'Tall skinny teenager.'

'How many tall skinny teenagers in this city, would you guess?'

'Jesus, I didn't get that guy's name! Hey! Hey! Meyer yelled. 'Hey, you! Wait a minute!'

The witness, reluctant to leave not a moment before, now heard himself being called with some urgency. He did what anyone in his right mind would have done. He began running. The Puerto Rican cop who'd translated for Meyer began chasing him. He rounded the corner, slipping and almost falling on the wet pavement. The rain was coming down harder now. The lightning and thunder had passed; there was only the steady drilling rain. Monoghan and Monroe came over to stand under the awning.

'Where's the goddam ME?' Monoghan said.

'Don't he know it's rainin?' Monroe said.

'You need us here any longer?' Monoghan said.

'We still need a cause of death,' Carella said.

'Big mystery, *that's* gonna be,' Monoghan said. 'Guy's head is all blown away, whattya *think* the ME's gonna say killed him? A flower pot fallin from a window sill?'

'Maybe the rain,' Monroe said, remembering, laughing again. 'Maybe it rained in on him, like you said.'

'I'd appreciate it if you waited till the ME got here,' Carella said quietly.

The patrolman who'd run after the witness came back around the corner panting. He walked to where the men were standing under the dripping awning. 'I lost him,' he said.

Monoghan looked at his nameplate. 'Good work, Serrano,' he said. 'A promotion is in order.'

'What's your captain's name?' Monroe asked. 'We'll put in a commendation.'

'Frick,' the patrolman said. 'Captain Frick.' He looked worried.

'Captain Frick, remember that,' Monoghan said.

'Got it,' Monroe said.

'We want to get over to the hospital,' Meyer said, 'talk to the other victim. Can you wrap this for us here?'

'What, in the rain?' Monoghan said.

'You can stay under the awning,' Meyer said.

'Here's the ME now,' Carella said, and walked out into the rain towards the kerb, where a black car marked with the city's seal was pulling in at an angle to one of the r.m.p. cars.

'How nearly done are the rest of them?' Monoghan asked.

'Photo is about to leave,' Meyer said. 'I don't know how long the techs'll be. They'll want to mark the position of the body . . .'

'How about your sketches? Have you made your sketches yet?'

'No, but . . .'

'Then why the hell are you planning to leave the scene?'

'Because the other guy may die before we get to him,' Meyer said patiently.

'You're a team, ain't you?' Monoghan said.

'A pair,' Monroe said.

'A couple.'

'*Two* cops, not one.'

'A team,' Monoghan said. 'So one of you can stay here to wrap while the other one goes to the hospital. That's the way to do it.'

'That's the *only* way to do it,' Monroe said.

'That's the way *we'd* do it.'

'That's the *only* way we'd do it.'

'Send us your paper shit,' Monoghan said.

'In triplicate,' Monroe said, and both Homicide detectives walked out into the rain towards where their black Buick sedan was parked.

Meyer sighed.

2

A dying man's declaration is admissible evidence in court, but Ambrose Harding was far from dying. He was, in fact, a very lucky man. Had the bullet entered his back a little lower and a bit more to the right, it might have smashed his spinal column. Even had it missed his vertebrae and the posterior rib cage, it might have passed through a lung to shatter one of his anterior ribs and exit through the chest wall – in which case, he'd have undergone immediate surgery and would at this moment have been in the Intensive Care Unit with a respirator tube sticking out of his larynx, another tube draining his chest, and yet more tubes intravenously feeding him dextrose, water and blood. Instead, and because the bullet had entered his back high on the left shoulder, missing the scapula and then only fracturing the left clavicle on exit, he was now on the hospital's orthopaedic floor, his left shoulder immobilized in a cast, but otherwise only mildly sedated and feeling pretty good, all things considered.

The detective who spoke to him was Steve Carella. They had tossed a coin to see who stayed at the scene in the rain, and Meyer had lost. Meyer sometimes suspected that Carella had a coin with two heads. But even when Meyer called heads, Carella won. Maybe Carella also had a coin with two tails. Or maybe Carella was just lucky. Ambrose Harding was certainly lucky. He told Carella how lucky he was, and Carella – who'd informed him at once that Chadderton was dead – assured him that he was lucky indeed.

'Tried to kill us *both*, that's for damn sure,' Harding said. 'Stood over me with the gun in his hand, aimin for my head. Pulled the trigger three times, standin over me like that. Thing was empty. Otherwise, I'd be dead.'

'How many shots were fired altogether, do you know?'

'I wasn't countin, man. I was *runnin*.'

'Tell me what happened.'

'We were walking along, that's what happened, talkin about the concert...'

'What concert?'

'George done a concert at a hall on Culver and Eighth. We were headin uptown to where I parked the car – what's gonna happen to my car, man? Am I gonna go back there and find a parking ticket on it?'

'Tell me where you parked it, I'll make sure it isn't tagged.'

'It's in front of a pawn shop on Culver and Twelfth.'

'I'll take care of it. When you say a concert...'

'George done a concert.'

'What kind of concert?'

'He sung calypso. You ever hear of King George?'

'No, I'm sorry.'

'That's George Chadderton. That's the name he used. King George. I'm his business manager. *Used* to be, I guess,' he said, and shook his head.

'What time did the concert begin?'

'Eight-thirty.

'And when did it end?'

'Eleven or so. Time we left the hall, it musta been, I don't know, eleven-thirty. Had to get the bread, you know, say hello to some people...'

'How much did the job pay?'

'Three-fifty. I took fifty as my commission, he was left with the three bills.'

'In hundreds?'

'Yeah.'

'Okay, go on. You left the hall at...'

'Eleven-thirty, something like that. We were walkin toward the car, rainin like a bitch, talkin about the concert, you know, when all of a sudden somebody cuts loose from the buildin there.'

'Did you see the person shooting?'

'Not just then.'

'When?'

'When he was standin over me tryin to kill me. I'd already been hit then, I was layin flat on the sidewalk.'

'Was he white or black?'

'I don't know, man. I only saw that gun pointin at me.'

'How about his hand? Did you see his hand?'

'I saw his hand, yes.'

'White or black?'

'Damn if I know. All I saw was . . . first I saw his boots, black boots, and then these skinny pants legs, and then I looked up and saw that gun pointin at me.'

'Was the hand around the gun white or black?'

'I don't know. He was wearin a black coat, the sleeve of the coat was black.'

'And the hand?'

'I don't *know*, man. All I saw was that big mother *gun* lookin me in the eye.'

'*How* big?' Carella asked.

'*Big*, man.'

'Are you familiar with guns?'

'Only from the Army.'

'Would this have been as big as a .45, for example?'

'Big as a *cannon*, man! When a gun's pointin at your head, it's a cannon, never mind what calibre it is. Anyway, why you askin *me*? Can't your own people work that out? Don't you have people can tell what kind of gun it was? The calibre and all that?'

'Yes, we have people who can do that.'

'Cause, man, all I know is I thought it was all over – goodbye, nice to've met you. I was layin there lookin up at that thing and thinkin in two, three seconds there's gonna be a hole in my head. Then *click*, man, the thing's *empty*! He pulled that trigger three times tryin to do me in, but the gun was empty.'

'What happened then?'

'He ran off, that's what. Heard people comin, figured he'd best get out of there, stead of standin in the rain with a gun ain't doin the job.'

'Tell me about the concert,' Carella said. 'How'd it go?'

'Beautiful.'

'No problems?'

'None. Crowd loved him.'

'Nobody heckling him from the audience or . . .'

'No, man, they were *cheerin* him, they loved him.'

'How many people would you guess were there?'

'Three-fifty, cordin to the guy runs the hall. But he's a crook, and maybe he sold more at the door than he let on.'

'What do you mean?'

'We were spose to get a dollar a head. Capacity was four hundred, it sure looked to me like the place was near full.' Harding sighed, and then shrugged, and then sighed again. 'Don't seem to matter much now, does it?'

'What's the man's name? The one who runs . . .'

'Lou Davis.'

'White man?'

'Black.'

'Did you talk to him about the head count?'

'George tole him he was a crook, that's all.'

'What'd he say?'

'Who, Davis? He laughed, that's all.'

'What's he look like, this Davis?'

'Short fat guy.'

'Short fat guy,' Carella repeated.

'Them legs in the skinny pants weren't Lou Davis' legs, if that's what you're thinkin.'

'Tell me more about the crowd.'

'I told you, they loved him.'

'Young crowd?'

'Not for the most part.'

'Any teenagers in it?'

'None that I saw. Kids don't much dig calypso. With calypso, you got to *think*, man, you got to make an effort to *hear* what the man is sayin up there. Kids today, they don't like to do much thinkin. They like it all spoonfed. When George was up there layin it down, you had to use your head. You know what calypso is, are you familiar with calypso?'

'Only Harry Belafonte,' Carella said.

'Yeah, well, that's *canned* calypso. *Real* calypso is you make up your own stuff. Down in the islands, you sing another man's calypso, they look down on you. George made up his own calypso, the way you *spose* to, the way it was in the beginning. You know how calypso started? With the slaves down there, man. They weren't allowed to talk to each other while they were working, so they used to sing out all the gossip, fool Whitey that way. George sang the *new* calypso. Social comment. Protest. Talkin about the scene. He was the king, man, he named himself right. He was King George. Three, four years from now, he'da been a big star. Man, I don't know why this had to happen, I just don't know why the hell this had to happen.'

The room went silent. Carella was suddenly aware of the rain drumming against the window. Somewhere on the street, a horn honked in what was a clearly marked HOSPITAL ZONE.

'When you say social comment...'

'Yeah.'

'And protest...'

'Yeah.'

'Could he have annoyed anyone tonight? Is it possible...?'

'Everybody, man. I know what you mean, and I'm tellin you *everybody*. That's the whole point of calypso. To get people irritated, to start them *thinkin* about a situation.'

'People like who?'

'Everybody from the mayor on down.'

'He sang about the mayor tonight?'

'He sang about the mayor all the time. That was one of his biggest numbers, the one on the mayor.'

'Who else did he sing about tonight?'

'Why?' Harding asked, and grinned. 'Don't you think the mayor coulda been the one who killed him?'

'You see where I'm going...'

'Sure, I see where you're going. George done a song about cops, and he done one about rats and garbage, and he done another one about a neighbourhood pusher, and one about a black girl peddlin her ass to white guys, and he done one about straightening hair and using skin bleaches ... man, he done the whole scene. That's calypso.'

'What neighbourhood?'

'Huh? Oh. Uptown. Diamondback.'

'In this song... did he name a *specific* pusher?'

'I don't know who he was singin about,' Harding said.

22

'Well, you heard the song...'

'If a man says someone's the mayor, then you got to know he's singin about the mayor.'

'How about if a man says someone's a pusher?'

'Then you know he's singin about somebody's a pusher.'

'*Which* pusher?'

'Who knows?' Harding said, and shrugged. 'A pusher, that's all.'

'Could any pusher in Diamondback...'

'I don't know who mighta taken offence or not.'

'*Was* the song offensive?'

'George's songs were social comment. He was telling what it's like to be black in a white world.'

'Would *you* say he was singing about a specific pusher?'

'Not that I know of.'

'Anyone who, for example, might have taken offence and killed him.' Carella paused. 'And tried to kill you as well?'

'I don't know who that might've been.'

'Do you represent any musicians who are addicts?'

'Nope.'

'Was George an addict?'

'Nope. Smoked a little pot every now and then, but who don't?'

'Who supplied him?'

'Oh, come on, man, you can buy pot anywhere in this city.'

'I know. But who'd *George* buy it from? Was he dealing with anyone on a steady basis?'

'I don't think so, we never talked about it. Who talks about buying pot? That's the same as talkin about brushin your teeth.'

'I'm trying to find out whether this song about a pusher...'

'I *know* what you're tryin to find out.'

'Might have identified a specific pusher George was dealing with.'

'To my knowledge, he did not have anybody like that. He wasn't a pothead, he just smoked every now and then, same as everybody else I know. Pot's legal now.'

'Not entirely. And *dealing* pot isn't.'

'Even so, the song was about hard drugs. About a guy pushin heroin to young black kids.'

'George know anybody like that?'

'If you lived in Diamondback, you got to know a *hundred* people like that.'

'Personally? Did he know anyone like that personally?'

'You ever been to Diamondback?'

'Yes,' Carella said, 'I've been there.'

'Well, everybody up there knows who the pushers are.'

'But not everybody sang about them,' Carella said.

'I think you're on the wrong track,' Harding said, 'I don't think George's song put the finger on anybody. Not so's he'd come after George and kill him. Anyway, *I* didn't sing about anybody, and the guy tried to kill *me*, too.'

'He may have thought you'd seen him, and could identify him.'

'Maybe,' Harding said.

'These other musicians you represent. You said none of them are addicts. Were any of them messing even casually with hard drugs?'

'Nobody messes casually with hard drugs,' Harding said.

'Any of them experimenting?'

'You're still on this pusher kick, huh?'

'I'm still on it,' Carella said.

'Why? Cause George was a musician?'

'That's part of it.'

'What's the other part?'

'Money. There's a lot of money in drugs. If George was breaking somebody's rice bowl, that could've been reason enough for murder.'

'I told you I don't think the song fingered anybody in particular. It was about corruptin our kids, that's ail, our black kids.'

'These other musicians you represent...'

'Just one other client.'

'Who's that?'

'A group called Black Monday.'

'Rock?'

'Rock.'

'Any rivalry there?'

'Between George and the group? None. They're rock, he was calypso. That's worlds apart, man.'

'This black hooker turning tricks for white men...'

'That's *all* black hookers.'

'But not a specific hooker who might have been identified in George's song, huh?'

'Not that I know of.'

'Could the person who shot you have been a woman?'

'Could've been, I don't know.'

'But you said it was a man.'

'I figured somebody usin a gun had to be a man.'

'But you don't have any idea who that man might have been.'

'None at all.'

'How close were you and George?'

'Close,' Harding said, and held up his right hand, the index finger and third finger pressed tightly together.

'Would he have told you if he'd received any threatening letters or phone calls?'

'He'da told me.'

'*Did* he mention anything like that?'

'Not a word.'

'Did he ever use any musicians when he...'

'Just himself and his own guitar.'

'Then he wouldn't have owed money to any sidemen or...'

'Never *used* any sidemen. Not recently anyway. He used to have a band one time, but he's been operating as a single for the past six years.'

'What was the name of the band?'

'Don't know. That was before my time. I only started managing George when he went out on his own.'

'Would you know who was in the band?'

'His brother was in it, but if you're thinkin of lookin him up, he's long since gone.'

'What do you mean?'

'Split seven years ago.'

'Where'd he go?'

'Don't know. Maybe back to Trinidad.'

'Is that where they're from originally?'

'George and his brother were born here, but their father came from Trinidad. Maybe Santo went back lookin for his roots. His father split, too, you see. Longer ago than Santo did.'

'Santo? Is that the brother's name?'

'Yeah. That's Spanish. Their mother was from Venezuela.'

'She still alive?'

'She died six years ago. George used to say she died of a broken heart. Santo splitting and all.'

'Was this a younger brother, an older brother?'

'Younger, but I don't know his exact age. You'll have to ask . . . oh, Jesus. Chloe don't know yet, does she? Oh, Jesus.'

'Chloe?'

'George's wife. Oh Jesus, who's gonna tell Chloe?'

3

Chloe Chadderton responded to their insistent knocking in a voice still unravelling sleep. When they identified themselves as police officers, she opened the door a crack, and asked that they show her their shields. Only when she was satisfied that these were truly policemen standing there in the hallway, did she take off the night chain and open the door.

She was a tall slender woman in her late twenties, her complexion a flawless beige, her sloe eyes dark and luminous in the narrow oval of her face. Standing in the doorway wearing a long pink robe over a pink nightgown, she looked only sleepy and a trifle annoyed. No anticipation in those eyes or on that face, no expectation of bad news, no sense of alarm. In this neighbourhood, visits from the police were commonplace. They were always knocking on doors, investigating this or that burglary or mugging, usually in the daytime, but sometimes at night if the crime was more serious.

'Mrs Chadderton?' Carella asked, and the first faint suspicion flickered on her face. He had called her by name, this was not a routine door-to-door inquiry, they had come here specifically to talk to *her*, to talk to Mrs *Chadderton*; the time was two in the morning, and her husband wasn't yet home.

'What is it?' she said at once.

'Are you Chloe Chadderton?'

'Yes, what is it?'

'Mrs Chadderton, I'm sorry to tell you this,' Carella said, 'but your husband...'

'What is it?' she said. 'Has he been hurt?'

'He's dead,' Carella said.

The woman flinched at his words. She backed away from him, shaking her head as she moved out of the doorway, back into the kitchen, against the refrigerator, shaking her head, staring at him.

'I'm sorry,' Carella said. 'May we come in?'

'George?' she said. 'Is it *George* Chadderton? Are you sure you have the right...?'

'Ma'am, I'm sorry,' Carella said.

She screamed then. She screamed and immediately brought her hand to her mouth, and bit down hard on the knuckle of her bent index finger. She turned her back to them. She stood by the refrigerator, the scream trailing into a choking sob that swelled into a torrent of tears. Carella and Meyer stood just outside the open door. Meyer was looking down at his shoes.

'Mrs Chadderton?' Carella said.

Weeping, she shook her head, and – still with her back to them – gestured with one hand widespread behind her, the fingers patting the air, silently asking them to wait. They waited. She fumbled in the pocket of the robe for a handkerchief, found none, went to the sink where a roll of paper towels hung over the drainboard, tore one loose, and buried her face in it, sobbing. She blew her nose. She began sobbing again, and again buried her face in the towelling. A door down the hall opened. A woman with her hair tied in rags poked her head out.

'What is it?' she shouted 'Chloe?'

'It's all right,' Carella said: 'We're the police.'

'Chloe? Was that *you* screamin?'

'They're the police,' Chloe murmured.

'It's all right, go back to sleep,' Carella said, and entered the apartment behind Meyer, and closed the door.

It wasn't all right; there was no going back to sleep for Chloe Chadderton. She wanted to know what had happened, and they told her. She listened, numbed. She cried again. She asked for details. They gave her the details. She asked if they had caught who'd done it. They told her they had just begun working on it. All the formula answers. Strangers bearing witness to a stranger's

27

naked grief. Strangers who had to ask questions now at ten past two in the morning because someone had taken another man's life, and these first twenty-four hours were the most important.

'We can come back in the morning,' Carella said, hoping she would not ask them to. He wanted the time edge. The killer had all the time in the world. Only the detectives were working against time.

'What difference will it make?' she said, and began weeping softly again. She went to the kitchen table, took a chair from it, and sat. The flap of the robe fell open, revealing long slender legs and the laced edge of the baby doll nightgown. 'Please sit down,' she said.

Carella took a chair at the table. Meyer stood near the refrigerator. He had taken off the Professor Higgins hat. His coat was sopping wet from the rain outside.

'Mrs Chadderton,' Carella said gently, 'can you tell me when you last saw your husband alive?'

'When he left the apartment tonight.'

'When was that? What time?'

'About seven-thirty. Ame stopped by to pick him up.'

'Ame?'

'Ambrose Harding. His manager.'

'Did your husband receive any phone calls before he left the apartment?'

'No calls.'

'Did anyone try to reach him after he left?'

'No one.'

'Were you here all night, Mrs Chadderton?'

'Yes, all night.'

'Then you would have heard the phone...'

'Yes.'

'And answered it, if it had rung.'

'Yes.'

'Mrs Chadderton, have you ever answered the phone in recent weeks only to have the caller hang up on you?'

'No.'

'If your husband had received any threatening calls, would he have mentioned them to you?'

'Yes, I'm sure he would have.'

'*Were* there any such calls?'

'No.'

28

'Any hate mail?'

'No.'

'Has he had any recent arguments with anyone about money, or...'

'Everybody has arguments,' she said.

'*Did* your husband have a recent argument with someone?'

'What kind of argument?'

'About anything at all, however insignificant it might have seemed at the time.'

'Well, everybody has arguments,' she said again.

Carella was silent for a moment. Then, very gently, he asked, 'Did you and he argue about something, is that it?'

'Sometimes.'

'What about, Mrs Chadderton?'

'My job. He wanted me to quit my job.'

'What *is* your job?'

'I'm a dancer.'

'Where do you dance?'

'At the Flamingo. On Landis Avenue.' She hesitated. Her eyes met his. 'It's a topless club.'

'I see,' Carella said.

'My husband didn't like the idea of me dancing there. He asked me to quit the job. But it brings in money,' she said. 'George wasn't earning all that much with his calypso.'

'How much would you say he normally...'

'Two, three hundred a week, *some* weeks. Other weeks, nothing.'

'Did he owe anyone money?'

'No. But that's only because of the dancing. That's why I didn't want to quit the job. We wouldn't have been able to make ends meet otherwise.'

'But aside from any arguments you had about your job...'

'We didn't argue about anything else,' she said, and suddenly burst into tears again.

'I'm sorry,' Carella said at once. 'If this is difficult for you right now, we'll come back in the morning. Would you prefer that?'

'No, that's all right,' she said.

'Then ... can you tell me if your husband argued with anyone *else* recently?'

'Nobody I can think of.'

'Mrs Chadderton, in the past several days have you noticed anyone who seemed particularly interested in your husband's comings and goings? Anyone lurking around outside the building or in the hallway, for example.'

'No,' she said, shaking her head.

'How about tonight? Notice anyone in the hallway when your husband left?'

'I didn't go out in the hall with him.'

'Hear anything in the hall after he was gone? Anyone who might have been listening or watching, trying to find out if he was still home?'

'I didn't hear anything.'

'Would anyone else have heard anything?'

'How would I know?'

'I meant, was there anyone here with you? A neighbour? A friend?'

'I was alone.'

'Mrs Chadderton,' he said, 'I have to ask this next question, I hope you'll forgive me for asking it.'

'George wasn't fooling around with any other women,' she said at once. 'Is that the question?'

'That was the question, yes.'

'And *I* wasn't fooling around with any other men.'

'The reason he had to ask,' Meyer said, 'is . . .'

'I *know* why he had to ask,' Chloe said. 'But I don't think he'd have asked a *white* woman that same question.'

'White *or* black, the questions are the same,' Carella said flatly. 'If you were having trouble in your marriage . . .'

'There was no trouble in my marriage,' she said, turning to him, her dark eyes blazing.

'Fine then, the matter is closed.'

It was not closed, not so far as Carella was concerned. He would come back to it later if only because Chloe's reaction had been so violent. In the meantime, he picked up again on the line of questioning that was mandatory in any homicide.

'Mrs Chadderton,' he said, 'at any time during the past few weeks . . .'

'Because I guess it's *impossible* for two black people to have a good marriage, right?' she said, again coming back to the matter – which apparently was not closed for *her*, either.

Carella wondered what to say next. Should he go through the tired 'Some Of My Best Friends Are Blacks' routine? Should he explain that Arthur Brown, a detective on the 87th Squad, was in fact happily married and that he and his wife Caroline had spent hours in the Carella household, discussing toilet training and school busing and, yes, *even* racial prejudice? Should he defend himself as a white man in a white man's world, when this woman's husband – a black man – had been robbed of his life in a section of the precinct that was at least fifty per cent black? Should he ignore the possibility that Chloe Chadderton, who had immediately flared upon mention of marital infidelity, was as suspect in this damn case as anyone else in the city? *More* suspect, in fact, despite the screaming and the hollering and the tears, despite the numbness as she'd listened to the details.

White or black, they *all* seemed numb, even the ones who'd stuck an icepick in someone's skull an hour earlier, they all seemed numb. The tears were sometimes genuine and sometimes not; sometimes, they were only tears of guilt or relief. In this city where husbands killed wives and lovers killed rivals; in this city where children were starved or beaten to death by their parents, and grandmothers were slain by their junkie grandsons for the few dollars in their purses; in this city, any immediate member of the family was not only a *possible* murderer but a *probable* one. The crime statistics here changed as often as did the weather, but the latest ones indicated a swing back to so-called 'family' homicides as opposed to those involving total strangers, where the victim and the murderer alike were unknown to each other before that final moment of obscene intimacy.

A witness had described George Chadderton's killer as a tall skinny man, almost a boy. A man who looked like a teenager. Chloe Chadderton was perhaps five feet nine inches tall, with the lithe supple body of a dancer. Given the poor visibility of a rain-drenched night, mightn't she have passed for a teenage boy? In Shakespeare's time, it was the teenage boys who'd acted the women's roles in his plays.

Chloe had taken offence at a question routinely asked and now chose to cloud the issue with black indignation, perhaps genuine, perhaps intended only to bewilder and confuse. So Carella looked at her, and wondered what he should say next. Get tough? Get apologetic? Ignore the challenge? What? In the silence, rain lashed the single window in the kitchen. Carella had the feeling it would never stop raining.

'Ma'am,' he said, 'we want to find your husband's murderer. If you'd feel more comfortable with a black cop, we've got plenty of black cops, and we'll send some around. They'll ask the same questions.'

She looked at him.

'The same questions,' he repeated.

'Ask your questions,' she said, and folded her arms across her breasts.

'All right,' he said, and nodded. 'At any time during the past few weeks, did you notice anything strange about your husband's behaviour?'

'Strange how?' Chloe said. Her voice was still edged with anger, her arms were still folded defensively across her breasts.

'Anything out of the ordinary, any breaks in his usual routine – I take it you knew most of his friends and business acquaintances.'

'Yes, I did.'

'*Were* there any such breaks in his usual routine?'

'I don't think so.'

'Did your husband keep an appointment calendar?'

'Yes.'

'Is it here in the apartment?'

'In the bedroom. On the dresser.'

'Could I see it, Mrs Chadderton?'

'Yes,' she said, and rose and left the room. Carella and Meyer waited. Somewhere outside, far below, a drainpipe dripped steadily and noisily. When Chloe came back into the room, she was carrying a black appointment book in her hand. She gave it to Carella, and he immediately opened it to the two facing pages for the month of September.

'Today's the fifteenth,' Meyer said.

Carella nodded, and then began scanning the entries for the week beginning September eleventh. On Monday at 3.00 p.m., according to the entry scrawled in black ink in the square for that date, George Chadderton had gone for a haircut. On Tuesday at 12.30 p.m., he'd had lunch with someone identified only as Charlie. Carella looked up.

'Who's Charlie?' he said.

'Charlie?'

'Lunch 12.30 p.m., Charlie,' Carella read.

'Oh. That's not a person, it's a place. Restaurant called Charlie down on Granada Street.'

'Have any idea who your husband had lunch with that day?'

'No. He was always meeting with people, discussing gigs and contracts and like that.'

'Didn't Ambrose Harding handle all his business affairs?'

'Yes, but George liked to meet who he'd be playing for, the promoter or the man who owned the hall or whoever.'

Carella nodded and looked down at the calendar again. There were no entries for Wednesday. For Thursday, the fourteenth, there were two entries: 'Office, 11.00 a.m.' and 'Lunch 1.00 p.m. Harry Caine.'

'What would "Office" be?' Carella asked.

'Ame's office.'

'And who's Harry Caine?'

'I don't know.'

Carella looked at the book again. For tonight, Friday, September fifteenth, Chadderton had written 'Graham Palmer Hall, 8.30, Ame pickup 7.30.' For tomorrow, Saturday the sixteenth, he had written 'C.J. at C.C. 12 Noon.'

'Who's C.J.?' Carella asked, looking up.

'I don't know,' Chloe said.

'How about C.C.? Does that mean anything to you?'

'No.'

'Would it be a person or a place?'

'I have no idea.'

'But you did know most of his friends and business acquaintances?'

'Yes, I did.'

'Were there any recent conversations or meetings with strangers?'

'Strangers?'

'People you didn't know. Like this C.J., for example. Were

there people whose names you didn't recognize when they phoned? Or people you saw him with, who . . .'

'No, there was nobody like that.'

'Did anyone named C.J. ever phone here?'

'No.'

'Did your husband mention that he had a meeting with this C.J. tomorrow at noon?'

'No.'

'Mind if I take this with me?' Carella asked.

'Why do you need it?'

'I want to study it more closely, prepare a list of names, see if you can identify any of them for me. Would that be all right?'

'Yes, fine.'

'I'll give you a receipt for the book.'

'Fine.'

'Mrs Chadderton, when I spoke to Ambrose Harding earlier tonight, he mentioned that your husband's songs – *some* of his songs – dealt with situations and perhaps personalities here in Diamondback. Is that true?'

'George wrote about anything that bothered him.'

'Would he have been associating lately with any of the people he wrote about? To gather material, or to . . .'

'You don't have to do research to know what's happening in Diamondback,' Chloe said. 'All you need is eyes in your head.'

'When you say he *wrote* these songs . . .'

'He wrote the songs down before he sang them. I know that's not what calypso *used* to be, people used to make them up right on the spot. But George wrote them all down beforehand.'

'The words *and* the music?'

'Just the words. In calypso, the melody's almost always the same. There're a dozen melody lines they use over and again. It's the *words* that count.'

'Where did he write these words?'

'What do you mean *where*? Here in the apartment.'

'No, I meant . . .'

'Oh. In a notebook. A spiral notebook.'

'Do you have that notebook?'

'Yes, it's in the bedroom, too.'

'Could I see it?'

'I suppose so,' she said, and rose wearily.

'I wonder if I could look through his closet, too,' Carella said.

'What for?'

'He was dressed distinctively tonight, the red pants and the yellow shirt. I was wondering...'

'That was for a gig. He always dressed that way for a gig.'

'Same outfit?'

'No, different ones. But always colourful. He was singing calypso, he was trying to make people think of carnival time.'

'Could I see some of those other outfits?'

'I still don't know why.'

'I'm trying to figure out whether anyone might have recognized him from the costume alone. It was raining very hard, you know, visibility...'

'Well, nobody would've seen the costume. He was wearing a raincoat over it.'

'Even so. Would it be all right?'

Chloe shrugged, and walked wordlessly out of the kitchen. The detectives followed her through the living room, and then into a bedroom furnished with a rumpled king-sized bed, a pair of night-tables, a large mahogany dresser, and a standing floor lamp beside an easy chair. Chloe opened the top drawer of the dresser, rummaged among the handkerchiefs and socks there, and found a spiral notebook with a battered blue cover. She handed the book to Carella.

'Thank you,' he said, and immediately began leafing through the pages. There were pencilled lyrics for what appeared to be a dozen or more songs. There were pages of doodles, apparently scrawled while Chadderton was awaiting inspiration. On one of the pages, doodled all across it in block lettering and script lettering alike, overlapping and criss-crossing, were the words IN THE LIFE.

'What's this?' Carella said, and showed the page to Chloe.

'I don't know. Maybe a song title.'

'Did he sing anything called "In The Life"?'

'No, but maybe it's just the *idea* for a song, just the title.'

'Do you know what that expression means?' Carella asked.

'Yes, I think so. It refers to criminals, doesn't it? People in... well, in the criminal life.'

'Yes,' Carella said. 'But your husband wasn't associating with any criminals, was he?'

'Not to my knowledge.'

'None of the pushers or prostitutes he wrote about.'

'Not to my knowledge.'

'That's a common expression among prostitutes,' Carella said. 'In the life.'

Chloe said nothing.

'Is that the closet?' Carella asked.

'Yes, right there,' she said, gesturing with her head. Carella handed the spiral notebook to Meyer, and then opened the closet door. Chloe watched him as he began moving hangers and clothing. She watched him intently. He wondered if she realized he was not looking for any of the colourful costumes her husband had worn on his various gigs, but instead was looking for black boots, a black raincoat and a black hat – preferably wet. 'These are what he wore, huh?' he asked.

'Yes. He had them made for him by a woman on St Sab's.'

'Nice,' Carella said. Chloe was still watching him. He shoved aside several of the garments on their hangers, looked deeper into the closet.

'Mrs Chadderton,' Meyer said, 'can you tell us whether your husband seemed worried or depressed lately? Were there any unexplained absences, did he seem to have any inkling at all that his life was in danger?'

Searching the closet, hoping that his search appeared casual, Carella recognized that Meyer had buried his 'unexplained absences' question in a heap of camouflaging debris, circling back to the matter of possible infidelity in a way that might not ruffle Chloe's already substantially ruffled feathers. In the closet, there were several coats, none of them black and none of them wet. On the floor, a row of women's high-heeled pumps, several pairs of men's shoes, some low-heeled women's walking shoes, and a pair of medium-heeled women's boots – tan. Chloe had still not answered Meyer's question. Her attention had focused on Carella again.

'Mrs Chadderton?' Meyer said.

'No. He seemed the same as always,' she said. 'What are you looking for?' she asked Carella abruptly. 'A gun?'

'No, ma'am,' Carella said. 'You don't own a gun, do you?'

'This has got to be some kind of comedy act,' Chloe said, and stalked out of the bedroom. They followed her into the kitchen. She was standing by the refrigerator, weeping again.

'I didn't kill him,' she said.

Neither of the detectives said anything.

'If you're done here, I wish you'd leave,' she said.

'May I take the notebook with me?' Carella asked.

'Take it. Just go.'

'I'll give you a receipt, ma'am, if you . . .'

'I don't *need* a receipt,' she said, and burst into fresh tears.

'Ma'am . . .'

'Would you please *go*?' she said. 'Would you please get the hell out of here?'

They left silently.

In the hallway outside, Meyer said, 'We were clumsy.'

'We were worse than that,' Carella said.

4

In the silence of the three a.m. squadroom, he sat alone at his desk and wondered what the hell was happening to him. He would have to call her in the morning, apologize to her, tell her it had been a long day and a longer night, tell her that sometimes in this business you began looking for murderers under every rock, explain – *shit*. He had treated a grieving widow like a goddam assassin. There was no excuse. He was tired, but that was no excuse. He had listened to Monogham and Monroe making jokes about death and dying, and he had been irritated by their banter, but that was no excuse, either. Nor was the rain an excuse. Nothing could excuse his having played cop with a woman who'd been feeling only intense grief over the death of her husband. He sometimes believed that if he stayed at this job long enough, he would forget entirely what it meant to feel anything at all.

'This is your case,' the manual advised, 'stick with the investigation.' Stick with it in the pouring rain where a man lay with his open skull seeping his brains onto the sidewalk, stick with it in a hospital room reeking of antiseptic, stick with it in a tenement apartment at two in the morning, the clock throwing minutes into the empty hours of the night while a woman wept tears for her man who was dead. Search her closet for the clothes the killer wore. Get her to talk about her husband's possible infidelities. Be a fucking cop.

He should have gone home. The squadroom clock read ten minutes to three now. Technically, it was already Saturday morning, though it still felt like Friday night, and it was still raining. Technically, his tour had ended at midnight, and he'd have gone home then if the Chadderton squeal hadn't come in at a quarter to twelve, just when Parker and Willis were supposed to relieve. He was exhausted and irritable, and feeling hugely like a horse's ass for his handling of the Chadderton woman, feeling not a little self-pity besides, poor public servant forced to deal with the more violent side of life, low pay and long hours, lousy working conditions and departmental pressures for swift arrests and convictions – he should have gone home to bed. But the notebook was here on his desk, sitting with its frayed blue cover and its pages of lyrics written by the dead man, urging scrutiny. He rose, stretched, went to the water cooler, drank a paper cup full of water, and then went back to the desk. The clock on the wall read 3.05 a.m. The squadroom was silent, a poorly lighted mausoleum of empty desks and stilled typewriters. Beyond the slatted wooden railing that separated the squadroom from the corridor outside, he could see a light burning behind the frosted glass door to the locker room, and beyond that the banister post for the iron-runged steps that led to the muster room on the first floor of the building. Downstairs, a telephone rang. He heard a patrolman greeting another patrolman coming in off the street. Alone in the squadroom, Carella opened the notebook.

He had never been to Trinidad, had never witnessed the monumental calypso contests that took place in the carnival tents at Port of Spain each year before Ash Wednesday. But as he leafed through the pages of the notebook now, the words scribbled in pencil seemed suddenly to pulse with the Afro-Spanish rhythms that had been their base, and he might have been there at Mardi Gras, swaying to the music that swelled from the corrugated-iron and palm-leaf tents, the men and women in the audience snapping their fingers and shouting the call-and-response, the performers ingeniously twisting their rhythms and rhymes, singing out their sarcasm, their protest, their indignation:

Now I tell you, my friends, in this here city
They's a mayor he think he sittin real pretty
Livin downtown fat suckin he mama titty
Never givin no mind how the nigger live shitty.

Now this mayor fat mama buy she pretty blue gown
Throw a fancy dress ball City Hall downtown
While the nigger man dance for the pusher uptown
And the nigger lady she chasin rats all aroun.

What the mayor forget is the booth at the school
Come November when the nigger he play it real cool
Close the curtain, pull the lever, nigger man no fool
Mayor's out, Mama's out, they's a brand new rule.

Smiling, Carella wondered if he should go look up the mayor. A song like that was reason enough for murder, ridiculing as it did the mayor's obese wife Louise and the highly touted Champagne Ball she'd sponsored last April. He shook his head, washed his hand over his face, and told himself again that it was time to go home. Instead, he turned to the next page in the notebook.

The rhyme scheme and rhythm in the next song seemed similar to that of the first, but he detected almost at once – before he'd come through the first several lines, in fact – that it was written to be sung at a much slower tempo. He tried to imagine the dead George Chadderton singing the words he'd jotted into his notebook. He imagined there would be no smile on his face; he imagined there would be pain in his eyes. Recognizing the intent of the song, Carella went back and began reading the lyrics again from the top:

Sister woman, black woman, sister woman mine,
Why she wearin them clothes showin half her behine?
Why she walkin the street, why she workin the line?
Do the white man dollar make her feel that fine?
Ain't she got no brains, ain't she got no pride,
Lettin white man dollar turn her cheap inside?
Takin white man dollar, lettin he . . .

The white man who approached her was holding an umbrella over his head. She stood just across the street from the city's main railroad terminal, a long-legged, good-looking black girl in her early twenties, wearing a blonde wig, a beige coat, and black high-heeled patent leather pumps. She stood in the doorway of a closed delicatessen, her coat open over a scoop-necked pink blouse and a short black skirt. She wore no bra under the blouse; the chill wetness of the September night puckered her nipples against the thin satin fabric. It was ten minutes past three a.m., and she had turned eight tricks since beginning work at ten. She was bone weary and wanted nothing more than to go home to her own bed. But the night was young – as Joey often reminded her – and if she didn't bring home no more bread than she already had in her bag, he'd more'n likely throw her out naked in the rain. As the white man approached, she pursed her lips and made a kissing sound.

'Want a date?' she whispered.

'How much?' the man said. He was in his late fifties, she supposed, short little man with almost no hair, wearing eyeglasses that were spattered with rain despite the umbrella over his head. He looked her up and down.

'Twenty-five for a handjob,' she said. 'Forty for a blowjob, sixty if you want to fuck.'

'Have you . . . ah . . . been to a doctor lately?' the man asked.

'Clean as a whistle,' she said.

'Forty sounds high for a . . . for what you said.'

'A blowjob? Is that what you're interested in?'

'I might be.'

'What's holdin you back then?'

'The price. Forty sounds definitely high.'

'Forty's what I'm gettin.'

'You're not getting much standing here in the rain,' he said, and laughed at his own little joke. 'Three o'clock in the morning,' he said, 'you're not getting much standing in the rain.'

'*You* ain't gettin *nothin* 'thout the forty dollars,' she said and laughed with him. 'Think it over. Take your time.'

'That's a nice . . . ah . . . set you've got there,' he said.

'Mmm,' she said, smiling.

'Very nice,' he said, and reached out to touch her breasts.

She turned away shyly. 'No, please,' she said. 'Not here.'

'Where?'

'Place around the corner.'

'Forty dollars, is that it?'

'Forty's the price.'

'Are you very good at it?'

'I'm not Linda Lovelace, but I promise you won't be sorry.'

'And you're clean? You've been to a doctor?'

'Get a checkup every day,' she lied.

'Still,' he said, shaking his head. 'Forty dollars.'

She said nothing. He was already hooked.

'Well, okay,' he said, 'I guess so.'

She looped her hand through his arm, and stepped under the umbrella with him.

Sister woman, black woman, why she do this way?
On her back, on her knees, for the white man pay?
She a slave, sister woman, she a slave this way,
On her knees, on her back, for the white man pay.
On her knees, sister woman, is the time to pray,
Never mind what the white man he got to say.
Let the white *girl do . . .*

'This is my first time with a coloured girl,' the man said.

'Always a first time,' she said. 'Change your luck. You want to let me have the forty, please?'

'Oh, sure,' he said, 'of course,' and took his wallet from his rear pocket, and pulled out a sheaf of bills. 'What's your name?' he asked.

'C.J.,' she said. She waited while he searched for the forty. She once had a john ask her if she could break a C-note. Surprised hell out of him when she dug the change out of her bag. Thought he was going to get a free ride, the jerk. Can you break a hundred? Sure, honey, how you want it? Twenties or tens? This same room right here. Sometimes they let her use a room in one of the massage parlours, when things weren't busy with the regular girls. Go in there, mirrors on the walls, bottles of oil all different colours on the floor, think you were in an Arabian whore house someplace. This room here at the hotel was costing her five bucks for however long it'd take her to blow this dude and send him on his way Double bed and a dresser, sink in the corner, easy chair over by the window, shade on it, no curtains. Five bucks for a half-hour at *most*. She was in the wrong business, she should be a hotel owner someplace.

'You gettin that forty?' she said.

'Yes, yes,' he said. 'Do you mind singles?'

'Singles? Forty dollars in singles?'

'I'm a waiter,' he said, as if that explained it.

'*I'm* gettin to be a waiter, too,' she said, 'waitin for the forty.'

He looked at her again, and then laughed and said, 'Sorry,' and began counting out the forty for her, one bill at a time, on to the palm of her outstretched hand. She listened to him counting it out, thinking the damn fool would spend all night *paying* her, never *would* get down to business here.

'. . . thirty-six, thirty-seven, thirty-eight, thirty-nine, and *forty*,' he said triumphantly. 'I hope this'll be good.'

'It'll be real fine,' she said, 'don't you worry. You want to go wash yourself now?'

'Wash myself?'

'Mm, wash your little ole dick, honey. Way *I* stay clean is to make sure *you're* clean.'

'Yes, good,' he said. 'Very good. Yes.'

'This your first time with a hooker?' she asked.

'No, no.'

'I'll bet it's your first time,' she said smiling.

'No, I've been around,' he said, and went to the sink in the corner.

'But you never been asked to wash yourself before, huh?'

'Oh, sure I have,' he said.

'Wash it good now,' she said, and climbed on to the bed. She was wearing no panties. She opened her legs wide, figuring she'd give him a shot of the beaver when he turned around, maybe talk him into a fuck at sixty. Blowjobs were quicker, though. All percentage, she guessed. Come on, you asshole, she thought. I said *wash* it, not *sterilize* it. He turned from the sink, saw her lying there with her legs wide open, and damn if he didn't blush!

'Come on over here,' she said, smiling.

He had a little white dick, was drying it with one of the hand towels as he came towards the bed. He was still blushing, little bald honkey in his fifties, blinking at her behind his glasses, blushing red all the way from under his chin to the top of his baldy bean head.

'Think you might want some of this sweet pussy instead?' she asked, raising her hips. 'Cost you only twenty more.'

'No, no, that's all right,' he said.

'Mighty sweet pussy,' she said.

'No, no, thank you.'

'Just the blowjob, huh?'

'Yes, please.'

'Just C.J.'s tender lips, huh?'

'Yes, please, just that.'

'Well, fine then,' she said. 'Get up here on the bed. What's your name, honey?'

'Frank,' he said.

Frank, she thought. Shit, your name is Marvin or Ralph. I get more fuckin *Franks*, she thought.

'Will you...ah...take off your clothes?' he asked.

'Sure,' she said, 'if that's how you want it.'

'Yes, I'd like that.'

'You're the boss,' she said.

She stripped silently. He watched her while she undressed. Wearing only the blonde wig and the high-heeled patent leather shoes – always turned them on, you wore your spikes to bed – she went back to him.

'Ready, Frank?' she asked.

'Yes, please,' he said.

Her mouth descended.

Sister woman, black woman, on her knees give head
To a man like he like to see her dead.
Can't she see, don't she see, can't she read in his head?
She a slave to his will, and the man want her dead.
She a nigger for sure, she a slave still in chains,
And the white man'll whip her ...

It was still raining when they came out into the street together. Frank, or whatever his name was, thanked her for her services, and told her he'd look for her again sometime. She said, 'Right, Frank, glad you enjoyed it.' They parted company on the corner outside the hotel. With the umbrella over his head, he walked off into the rain. She pulled the collar of her coat high on the back of her neck, ducked her head against the rain, and began walking up towards the railroad station again. It was almost three-thirty. Turn a few more tricks, call it a night. Fuck Joey. Had no heart that man, sending a whore out on a night like this. Well, it wasn't gonna be for much longer. Warned him, told him you keep treatin me mean like this, I'm splittin for good, you just wait and see. He told her You split on me, baby I'll split your *head*. They'll find you in the gutter with your skull in two halves, you split on me. Sure, Joey, she thought, but you just wait and see. I got me twenty-six hundred in the bank now, money you don't know nothin about, man, got it all in a savings account uptown, Clara Jean Hawkins, *far* from the scene, man, don't want you seein me make no deposit. Twenty-six hundred so far, and more coming. Two hundred every Wednesday night. And tomorrow I'll be talkin to the man again, I'll be sittin down at lunch with him and we're gonna be talkin bout that album again. I'm gonna tell him I'll have the three thou by the end of the month, which is more'n enough to get it done he tole me, and then you know what *you* can do, don't you, Joey? You can take your warnins and your threats, and you can shove them right up your...

There were footsteps behind her.

Light, clicking through the rain.

She turned, thinking it might be a john making an approach. She squinted through the rain, could make out only somebody tall and thin, dressed all in black. She pursed her lips and made a kissing sound.

'Want a date?' she asked.

The shots thundered into the night, four of them in succession. The first bullet missed her, but the second one entered her body just below the left breast and killed her instantly. The third shot ripped into her larynx and the fourth, as she staggered backwards dead, entered her face just to the right of her nose, and blew out an exit wound the size of a half-dollar at the back of her head. Her wig fell off as she collapsed to the pavement. It lay on the sidewalk beside her open skull, the rain drilling its synthetic blonde fibres, the rain pocking the spreading puddle of thick red blood.

Sister woman, black woman, won't she hear my song?
What she doin this way surely got to be wrong.
Lift her head, raise her eyes, sing the words out strong,
Sister woman, black woman ...

5

Carella hated mysteries.

In mysteries, there were never funerals or wakes. In mysteries, the victim got shot or stabbed or strangled or clubbed to death, and then was conveniently forgotten. In mysteries, a corpse ׳ as only a device to set an investigative pot boiling. In real life, the murder victim was a *person*, and this person usually had relatives or friends who arranged for a wake and a decent burial. The dead man, in keeping with tribal custom everywhere, was accorded the same respect and dignity he would have earned had he died peacefully in his sleep. He had once been a person, you see, and you do not sweep people under the rug just so a private eye can keep things moving along at a brisk clip.

The wake for George Chadderton was held in the Monroe Funeral Home on St Sebastian Avenue, in Diamondback. Further uptown, near Pettit Lane, a similar wake was being held for a young black hooker named Clara Jean Hawkins who'd been murdered the night before in Midtown South, while Carella was poring over Chadderton's notebook. Carella did not know about the second murder. This was a very big city, and the Midtown South precinct was a good three miles from the Eight-Seven. The man who'd caught the squeal on the Hawkins murder was named Alex Leopold, a Detective/Third who'd been transferred from a Calm's Point precinct three months earlier. He did not know Carella and had never worked with him. The two Homicide cops who'd put in their obligatory appearance at the scene of the second murder were not Monoghan and Monroe, who'd gone home to bed after leaving the scene of the Chadderton murder, but were instead a similar pair of dicks named Forbes and Phelps. Mandatory autopsies had been performed on both the Chadderton and Hawkins corpses, and recovered bullets had already been sent to the Ballistics Section. But two different men at Ballistics were working the two different cases, at microscopes not six feet from each other, and they had instructions only to report their findings to the two separate detectives working the two cases in different sections of Isola. There had been no witnesses to the second murder – no citizen eager to step forward and say that Clara Jean Hawkins had been slain by a tall, slender man or woman dressed entirely in black. At ten minutes to twelve that Saturday morning, September 16, as Carella approached the doors of the funeral home, neither he nor anyone else in the Police Department had the faintest notion that the murders might have been linked.

It was still raining. He was wearing a soggy trenchcoat and a soggier rainhat, and feeling very much the way he looked after only six hours of sleep on a cot in the precinct locker room. Chadderton's notebook was in a sodden manila Police Department evidence envelope he carried under his arm. He had studied it till close to five a.m., and had found nothing in the lyrics that would point a finger at a possible murderer. From Chadderton's appointment calendar, he had made a list of names he wanted to ask Chloe about. He intended to do that when he returned both books to her – with apologies for his behaviour the night before. A call to the Medical Examiner's Office this morning had informed Carella that Chadderton's body had been picked up at the hospital at eight a.m. for transfer to the funeral home on St Sab's. Presumably the body had by now been drained of its blood and the contents of its stomach, intestines and bladder. Presumably the mortician had already injected by trocar or tube a solution of formaldehyde that would cause coagulation of the body's proteins. Presumably the mortician had worked with wax and cosmetics to repair Chadderton's shattered left cheekbone and disguise the gaping holes in his neck and the top of his skull. Carella wondered whether there would be an open coffin. Mourners usually chose to see their departed loved ones as sleeping peacefully; either that, or they chose not to view them at all.

The funeral director was a short, very dark black man who told Carella that the body would be ready for viewing at two p.m., in the Blue Chapel. He further informed Carella that Mrs Chadderton had been there earlier today, to receive the body and to make all the arrangements, and had left at approximately eleven a.m. She had mentioned that she would not be back until five. Carella thanked the man, and stepped outside into the pouring rain again. He went back in a moment later, and asked if he might use the telephone. The man showed him into an office opposite the Pink Chapel. In the Isola directory, Carella found a listing for George C. Chadderton at 1137 Raucher Street, He dialled the number and let it ring twelve times. There was no answer. He could not imagine that Chloe Chadderton had gone to work on the day following her husband's murder, but he looked up the number of the Club Flamingo, dialled it, and spoke to a woman who identified herself as one of the bartenders. She told him that Chloe was expected at twelve noon. He thanked her, hung up, jotted the club's address into his notebook and then went outside to where he'd parked his car. He had forgotten to close the window on the driver's side, which he'd partially opened earlier to keep the windshield from fogging. The seat was soaking wet when he climbed inside.

Both plate glass windows of the Club Flamingo were painted over pink. In the centre of the window on the left was a huge hand-lettered sign advertising 'TOPLESS, BOTTOMLESS, NOON TO 4.00 a.m.' The club apparently offered more by way of spectacle than Chloe had revealed to him last night; 'It's a topless club,' she'd said, the difference between topless and bottomless being somewhat akin to that between Manslaughter and Murder One. In the other window was an equally large sign promising 'GENEROUS DRINKS, FREE LUNCH'. Carella was hungry – he'd had only a glass of orange juice and a cup of coffee for breakfast. He opened one of the two entrance doors, and stepped into the club's dim interior. Adjusting his eyes to the gloom, he stood just inside the entrance doors, listening to the canned rock music that blared from speakers all round the room. Dead ahead was a long oval bar. Two girls, one on either side of the bar, were gyrating in time to the rock music. Both girls were wearing sequined, high-heeled, ankle-strapped pumps and fringed G-strings. Both girls were bare-breasted. Neither of them wore anything under the G-strings. Neither of them was Chloe Chadderton.

He noticed now that there were small tables around the perimeter of the room. The place was not very crowded, he suspected the rain was keeping customers away. But at one of the tables, a blonde girl danced – if one could call it that – for the exclusive pleasure of a man who sat there alone, nursing a beer. There were four men sitting at the bar, two on each side of it, three of them white, one of them black. Carella took a seat midway down the bar. One of the bartenders – a young redheaded girl wearing a black leotard and black net stockings – walked to where he was sitting, her high-heeled pumps clicking on the hard wooden floor.

'Something to drink, sir?' she said.

'Have you got anything soft?' Carella asked.

'Oh, yes indeed,' she said, and rolled her eyes and took in a deep breath, at once imparting sexual innuendo to his innocuous question. He looked at her. She figured she'd somehow made a mistake and immediately said, 'Pepsi, Coke, 7-Up or ginger ale. It'll cost you the same as the whiskey, though.'

'How much is that?'

'Three-fifty. But that includes the lunch bar.'

'Coke or Pepsi, either one's fine,' Carella said. 'Has Chloe Chadderton come in yet?'

'She's taking her break just now,' the redhead said, and then casually asked, 'You a cop?'

'Yes,' Carella said, 'I'm a cop.'

'Figures. Guy comes in here wanting an ice cream soda, he's got to be a cop on duty. What do you want with Chloe?'

'That's between her and me, isn't it?'

'This is a clean place, mister.'

'Nobody said it wasn't.'

'Chloe dances same as the other girls. You won't see nothing here you can't see in any one of the legitimate theatres downtown. They got big stage shows downtown with nude dancers in them, same as here.'

'Mm-huh,' Carella said.

The redhead turned away, uncapped his soft drink, and poured it into a glass. 'Nobody is allowed to touch the girls here. They just dance period. Same as downtown. If it isn't against the law in a legitimate theatre, then it isn't against the law here, either.'

'Relax,' Carella said. 'I'm not looking for a bust.'

The girl rolled her eyes again. For a moment, he didn't quite understand her reaction. And then he realized she was deliberately equating the police expression for 'arrest' – a term he was certain she'd heard a hundred times before – with what was bursting exuberantly in the black leotard top. He looked at her again. She shrugged elaborately, turned away, and walked to the cash register at the end of the bar. One of the dancers was squatting before the solitary black customer now, her legs widespread, tossing aside the

48

fringe of the G-string to reveal herself completely. The man stared at her exposed genitals. The girl smiled at him. She licked her lips. The man was wearing eyeglasses. The girl took the glasses from his eyes, and wiped them slowly over her opening, a mock expression of shocked propriety on her face. She returned the glasses to the man's head, and then arched herself over backwards, supporting herself with her arms, thrusting her open crotch towards his face, and pumping at him while he continued staring. Just like the legitimate theatres downtown, Carella thought.

The state's obscenity laws were defined in Article 235, Section 2 of the Criminal Law, wherein 'producing, presenting or directing an obscene performance or participating in a portion thereof which is obscene and contributes to its obscenity' was considered a Class-A misdemeanour. A related provision – PL 235.00, Subdivision 1 – stated: 'Any material or performance is "obscene" if (a) considered as a whole, its predominant appeal is to prurient, shameful or morbid interest in nudity, sex, excretion, sadism or masochism, AND (b) it goes substantially beyond customary limits of candour in describing or representing such matters, AND (c) it is utterly without redeeming social value.'

There was no question in Carella's mind but that the girl down the bar, her back arched, her own hand now toying with her vulva for the obvious pleasure of the man seated before her, was performing an act the predominant appeal of which was to a prurient interest in nudity and sex. But as the redheaded bartender had pointed out to him a moment ago, there wasn't anything you could see here that you couldn't see in some of the legitimate theatres downtown, provided you had a first-row seat. Make the bust, and you found yourself in endless courtroom squabbles about the difference between art and pornography, a thin line Carella himself – and even the Supreme Court of the United States – was quite unready to define.

When you thought about it – and he thought about it often – what the hell was so terrible about pornography, anyway? He had seen motion pictures rated R (no one under seventeen admitted unless in the company of an adult) or even PG (parental discretion advised) which he had found to be dirtier than any of the X-rated porn flicks running in the sleazy theatres along The Stem. The language in these socially acceptable films was identical to what he heard in the squadroom and on the streets every single waking day of his life – and he was a man whose job placed him in constant contact with the lowest elements of society. The sex in these approved films was equally as candid, sparing an audience only the explicit intercourse, fellatio and cunnilingus common in X-rated films. So where did you draw the line? If it was okay for a big-name male star to make simulated love to a totally naked woman in a multi-million-dollar epic (provided he kept his pants on), then why was it wrong to depict the *actual* sex act in a low-budget film starring unknowns? Put a serious actress up there on the screen, show her simulating the sex act (but God forbid never actually performing it) and somehow this became high cinema art while *Deep Throat* remained cheap porn. He guessed it was all in the camera angles. He guessed he was a cop who shouldn't be wondering so often about the laws he was being paid to enforce.

But what if he walked down the length of the bar right this minute and busted the dancer there for 'participating in an obscene performance' (screwing a man's eyeglasses was certainly obscene, wasn't it?) and then busted the owner of the joint for 'producing, presenting or directing an obscene performance' – what then? The offence was a Class-A misdemeanour, punishable by not more than a year in jail nor more than a thousand-dollar fine. Get your conviction (which was unlikely) and they'd be out on the street again in three months' time. Meanwhile, there were killers, rapists, burglars, muggers, armed robbers, child molesters and pushers roaming the city and victimizing the populace. So what was an honest cop to do? An honest cop sipped at his Pepsi or his Coca Cola, whichever the redhead with the inventive pornographic mind had served him, and listened to the blaring rock, and watched the naked backside of the blonde dancer across the bar as she leaned over to bring her enormous breasts to within an inch of a customer's lips.

At twenty minutes to one, Chloe Chadderton – naked except for high-heeled shoes and a silvery fringed G-string – stepped up on to the bar at the far end of it. The dancer she was replacing, the one who'd wiped the black man's glasses over what the Vice Squad would have called her 'privates', patted Chloe on the behind as she strutted past her down the ramp leading off the bartop. A new rock record dropped into place on the turntable. Smiling broadly, Chloe began dancing to it, high-stepping down the bar past the black man with the steamy eyeglasses, shaking her naked breasts, thrusting her hips, bumping and grinding to the frantic rhythm of the canned guitars, and finally stopping directly in front of Carella. Still shaking wildly, she began kneeling before him, arms stretched above her head, fingers widespread, breasts quaking, knees opening – and suddenly recognized him. A look of shocked embarrassment crossed her face. The smile dropped from her mouth.

'I'll talk to you during your next break,' Carella said.

Chloe nodded. She rose, listened for a moment to recapture the beat, and then swivelled long-leggedly to where the black man was taking another dollar bill from his wallet.

She danced for half an hour, and then came to the small table where Carella was eating the sandwich he'd made at the lunch bar. She explained at once that she had only a ten-minute break. Her embarrassment seemed to have passed. She was wearing a flimsy nylon wrapper belted at the waist, but she was still naked beneath it, and when she leaned over to rest her folded arms on the table top, he could see her breasts and nipples in the V-necked opening of the gown.

'I want to apologize for last night,' he said at once, and she opened her eyes wide in surprise. 'I'm sorry. I was trying to touch all the bases, but I guess I slid into second with my cleats flying.'

'That's okay,' she said.

'I'm sorry. I mean it.'

'I said it's okay. Did you look at George's notebook?'

'Yes. I have it here with me,' he said, reaching under his chair to where he'd placed the manila envelope. 'I didn't find anything I can use. Would you mind if I asked you a few more questions?'

'Go ahead,' she said, and turned to look at the wall clock. 'Just remember it's a half-hour on the bar, and a ten-minute break. They don't pay me for sitting around talking to cops.'

'Do they know your husband was killed last night?'

'The boss knows, he read it in the newspaper. I don't think any of the others do.'

'I was surprised you came to work today.'

'Got to eat,' Chloe said, and shrugged. 'What did you want to ask me?'

'I'm going to start by getting you sore again,' he said, and smiled.

'Go ahead,' she said, but she did not return the smile.

'You lied about this place,' he said.

'Yes.'

'Did you lie about anything else?'

'Nothing.'

'Positive about that?'

'Positive.'

'Really no trouble between you and your husband? No unexplained absences on his part? No mysterious phone calls?'

'What makes you think there might have been?'

'I'm asking, that's all.'

'No trouble between us. None at all,' she said.

'How about unexplained absences?'

'He was gone a lot of the time, but that had nothing to do with another woman.'

'What did it have to do with?'

'Business.'

'I jotted some names down,' Carella said, nodding, 'got them from his appointment calendar, people he had lunch with or meetings with in the past month, people he was scheduled to see in the next few weeks ahead. I wonder if you can identify them for me.'

'I'll try,' Chloe said.

Carella opened his notebook, found the page he wanted, and began reading. 'Buster Greerson,' he said.

'Saxophone player. He was trying to get George to join a band he's putting together.'

'Lester . . . Handey, is it?'

'Hanley. He's George's vocal coach.'

'Okay, that explains the regularity. Once every two weeks, right?'

'Yes, on Tuesdays.'

'Hawkins. Who's that?'

'I don't know. What's his first name?'

'No first name. Just Hawkins. Appears in the calendar for the first time on August tenth, that was a Thursday. Then again on August twenty-fourth, another Thursday.'

'I don't know anybody named Hawkins.'

'How about Lou Davis?'

'He's the man who owns Graham Palmer Hall. That's where George...'

'Oh, sure,' Carella said, 'how dumb.' He looked at his notebook again. 'Jerri Lincoln.'

'Girl singer. Another one of George's album ideas. He wanted to do a double with her. But that was a long time ago.'

'Saw her on August thirtieth, according to his calendar.'

'Well, maybe she started bugging him again.'

'Just business between them?'

'You should see her,' Chloe said, and smiled. '*Strictly* business, believe me.'

'Don Latham,' Carella said.

'Head of a company called Latham Records. The label is Black Power.'

'C.J.,' Carella said. 'Your husband saw him – or *her*,' he said, with a shrug, 'on the thirty-first of August, and again on September seventh, and he was supposed to have lunch with whoever it is today – I *guess* it was going to be lunch – at twelve noon. Mean anything to you?'

'No, you asked me that last night.'

'C.J.,' Carella said again.

'No, I'm sorry.'

'Okay, who's Jimmy Talbot?'

'Don't know him.'

'Davey... Kennemer, is it?'

'Kennemer, yes, he's a trumpet player.'

'And Arthur Spessard?'

'Another musician, I forget what he plays.'

'Okay, that's it,' Carella said, and closed the notebook. 'Tell me about George's brother,' he said abruptly.

'Santo? What do you want to know about him?'

'Is it true he ran away seven years ago?'

'Who told you that?'

'Ambrose Harding. Is it true?'

'Yes.'

'Ambrose said he may have gone back to Trinidad.'

'He didn't go to Trinidad. George went there looking for him, and he wasn't there.'

'Have any ideas where he might be?'

Chloe hesitated.

'Yes?' Carella said.

'George thought . . .'

'Yes, what?'

'That somebody killed his brother.'

'What made him think that?'

'The way it happened, the way he just disappeared from sight.'

'Did George mention any names? Anybody he suspected?'

'No. But he kept at it all the time. Wasn't a day went by he wasn't asking somebody or other about his brother.'

'Where'd he do the asking?'

'Everywhere.'

'In Diamondback?'

'In Diamondback yes, but not only there. He was involved in a whole big private investigation. Police wouldn't do nothing, so George went out on his own.'

'When you say his brother just disappeared, what do you mean?'

'After a job one night.'

'Tell me what happened.'

'I don't *know* what happened, exactly. Neither does anyone else, for that matter. It was after a job – they used to play in a band together, George and his brother.'

'Yes, I know that.'

'George and two other guys in the band were waiting in the van for Santo to come out. He'd gone to the men's room or something, I'm not sure. Anyway, he never *did* come out. George went back inside the place, searched it top to bottom, couldn't find him.'

'The other musicians who were there that night – would you know them?'

'I know their names, but I've never met them.'

'What are their names?'

'Freddie Bones and Vicente Barragan.'

'Bones? Is that his real name?'

'I think so.'

'How do you spell the other name?'

'I think it's B-A-R-R-A-G-A-N. It's a Spanish name, he's from Puerto Rico.'

'But you've never met either of them?'

'No, they were both before my time. I've only been married to George for four years.'

'How do you happen to know the names then?'

'Well, he mentioned them a lot. Because they were there the night his brother disappeared, you know. And he was always talking to them on the phone.'

'Recently?'

'No, not recently.'

'Four years,' Carella said. 'Then you never met George's brother, either.'

'Never.'

'Santo Chadderton, is it?'

'Santo Chadderton, yes.'

'Is this your first marriage?'

'Yes.'

'Was it George's?'

'No. He was married before.' She hesitated. 'To a white woman,' she said, and looked him straight in the eye.'

'Divorce her or what?'

'Divorced her, yes.'

'When?'

'Couple of months after we met. They were already separated when we met.'

'What's *her* name, would you know?'

'Irene Chadderton. That's if she's still using her married name.'

'What was her maiden name?'

'I don't know.'

'Does she live here in the city?'

'Used to, I don't know if she still does.'

'Would *she* have known Santo?'

'I suppose so.'

'Would she know anything about his disappearance?'

'Anybody who ever had anything to do with George knows about his brother's disappearance, believe me. It was like a goddam obsession with him. That's the *other* thing we argued about, okay? My dancing here, and him talking about his *brother* all the time! *Searching* for him all the time, checking *newspapers*, and *court* records, and *hospitals* and driving everybody *crazy*.'

'You told me you had a good marriage,' Carella said flatly.

'It was good as most,' Chloe answered, and then shrugged. The flap of the gown slid away from one of her breasts with the motion, exposing it almost completely. She made no effort to close the gown. She stared into Carella's eyes and said, 'I didn't kill him, Mr Carella,' and then turned to look at the wall clock again. 'I got to get back up there, my audience awaits,' she said breathlessly and smiled suddenly and radiantly.

'Don't forget this,' Carella said, handing her the envelope.

'Thank you,' she said. 'If you learn anything . . .'

'I have your number.'

'Yes,' she said, and nodded, and looked at him a moment longer and then turned to walk towards the bar. Carella put on his coat and hat – both still wet – and went to the register to pay his check. As he walked out of the place, he turned to look towards the bar again. Chloe was in the same position the other dancer had assumed less than forty-five minutes ago – back arched, elbows locked, legs widespread, furiously smiling and grinding at a customer sitting not a foot away from her crotch. As Carella pushed open the door to step into the rain, the customer slid a dollar bill into the waistband of her G-string.

6

It was almost 2.00 p.m. when he got back to the squadroom and began hitting the phone books. There were no listings for either Irene Chadderton or Frederick Bones in any of the city's five directories, but he found a listing for Vicente Manuel Barragan in the Calm's Point book. He dialled Directory Assistance for further information, and was told by the operator that she had nothing at all for an Irene Chadderton anywhere in the city, and whereas she *did* have a listing for a Frederick Bones, it was an unpublished one. Carella identified himself as a working detective and she said, 'This'll have to be a callback, sir.'

'Yes, I know that,' he said. 'I'm at the 87th Precinct, the number here is Frederick 7–8024.'

He hung up and waited. He knew the operator would first check out the number he had given her, to make certain he was indeed calling from a police station. She would then need permission from her supervisor before revealing Bones' unpublished number – even to a cop. The phone rang ten minutes later. Carella picked it up. The operator gave him a number in Isola, and when he requested the address she supplied that as well. He thanked her and walked over to where Meyer Meyer was telling a joke to Bert Kling, who sat in a swivel chair behind his desk, his feet up on the desk, listening with something akin to childlike anticipation. Kling was the youngest detective on the squad, a tall, blond strapping kid (they thought of him as a kid even though he was in his early thirties) with guileless hazel eyes and an open face more suited to a beet farmer in Grand Forks, North Dakota, than a detective here in the big bad city. Carella caught only the punchline as he approached Kling's desk – 'I say, old boy, are you trying to escape?'

Kling and Meyer burst out laughing simultaneously. Meyer stood beside the desk looking at Kling and laughing at his own joke, and Kling sat there in his chair, his feet on the floor now, laughing so hard Carella thought he would wet his pants. Both men laughed for what seemed a solid three minutes, though it was surely only thirty or forty seconds. Carella stood by waiting. When Meyer stopped laughing at last, he handed him the sheet of paper on which he had listed the names, addresses and phone numbers of Frederick Bones and Vicente Manuel Barragan.

'What we're looking for,' he said, 'is information on what happened the night Santo disappeared, seven years ago.'

'You think somebody really did him in?' Meyer asked.

'His brother thought so, that's for sure. Conducted a one-man investigation all over the city, even went back to Trinidad looking for him. If somebody really *did* knock off the kid...'

'And if George was getting close to who did it...'

'Right,' Carella said. 'So let's find out what happened back then, okay? Which one do you want?'

'They sound like a vaudeville team,' Meyer said. 'Barragan and Bones.'

'I'll flip you,' Carella said.

'Not with your coin,' Meyer said. 'If we flip, we use a neutral coin.'

'My coin *is* neutral,' Carella said.

'No, your coin is crooked. He has a crooked coin, kid.'

'I say, old boy, are you trying to escape?' Kling said, and began laughing again.

'Have you got a quarter?' Carella asked him.

Still laughing, Kling reached into his pocket. Carella accepted the coin, examined both sides of it, and handed it to Meyer for his approval.

'Okay,' Meyer said, 'heads or tails?'

'Heads,' Carella said.

Meyer flipped the coin. It hit the corner of Kling's desk, flew off it at an angle, struck the floor on its edge and went rolling across the room to collide with the wall behind the water cooler. Carella and Meyer both ran across the room. Squatting near the cooler, they examined the coin.

'It's tails,' Meyer said triumphantly.

'Okay, you get the vaudeville performer of your choice,' Carella said.

'Barragan's way the hell out in Calm's Point,' Meyer said. 'I'll take Bones.'

Some days you can't make a nickel.

Frederick Bones' address was indeed 687 Downes, which was in the heart (or perhaps the kidney) of Isola and only a fifteen-minute subway ride from the station house. Meyer drove the distance downtown in his beat-up old Chevy, his wife Sarah enjoying the rights to the family's second car, a used Mercedes-Benz. Meyer knew exactly what his father (rest his soul) would have said if he'd lived to see the car: 'Are you buying from the Germans already? What kind of Jew are you?' Meyer sometimes wondered.

He had no such doubts about what kind of Jew his father Max had been. His father Max had been a *comical* Jew. It was Max who'd decided to send his only son through life with a double-barrelled monicker – Meyer Meyer, very funny, Pop. 'Meyer Meyer, Jew on Fire,' the kids used to call him when he was growing up in a neighbourhood almost exclusively Gentile. He kept trying to think up clever taunts with which he might counter-attack. Somehow, 'Dominick Rizzo, Full of Shitzo,' did not do the trick, especially since it only caused Dominick to come after him with a baseball bat the very same day Meyer had his poetic inspiration, occasioning the taking of six stitches at the right side of Meyer's head in order to keep his ear from falling off. 'Patrick Cassidy, Kiss My Assidy' resulted in fifteen-year old, two-hundred pound Patrick chasing twelve-year old, one hundred and twenty-pound Meyer for eight blocks before he caught him, whereupon Patrick lowered his trousers, flashed a huge harvest moon, and ordered Meyer to kiss it unless he wanted a broken Hebe head. Meyer bit Patrick on the ass instead, an unprovoked and inconsiderate attack that contributed little towards relieving Judeo-Hibernian tensions. When Meyer got home later that afternoon he washed his mouth out with Listerine, but the taste of Patrick's Irish ass lingered and did not improve the taste of his mother's fine *knaydls*. At the dinner table that night, his comical father Max told a joke about an Italian sewer worker who complained about taking shit from a Jew.

It was not until Meyer got to be sixteen years old and five feet eleven and three-quarter inches tall that the kids in the neighbourhood stopped calling him names. He had begun lifting weights by then, and when he wasn't pumping iron, he was pumping gas at the local service station and wishing he would hurry up and gain the extra quarter of an inch that would make him a six-footer. He figured that once he got to be six feet tall and weighed a hundred and ninety pounds, he would grab Dominick and Patrick by the scruffs of their necks and bang their heads together. He was so busy measuring himself that he didn't notice the name-calling had stopped. Dominick Rizzo joined the Navy and got killed in the war. Patrick Cassidy became a cop. It was Patrick, in fact, who talked Meyer into quitting law school and becoming a cop himself. Patrick was now a Deputy-Inspector temporarily assigned to the DA's Office and investigating organized crime. Whenever he ran across Meyer, he asked him if he wanted to see the teeth marks that were still on his behind. Meyer always felt uncomfortable in his presence. But he did not feel guilty about having bought the Mercedes.

He parked the Chevy a block from Bones' apartment building – the closest spot he could find – and then walked through the pouring rain towards 687 Downes, a tidy-looking brownstone in a row of similarly tidy-looking buildings. In the lobby, he looked for a mailbox marked with Bones' name, found none, and rang the bell marked SUPER. A white man in his late fifties opened the inner lobby door. Meyer showed his shield and his identification card, and told the man he was looking for Frederick Bones.

'Freddie Bones, huh?' the super said. 'You just missed him.'

'By how long?' Meyer asked.

'By three months!' the super said, and burst out laughing. His teeth were tobacco stained, he was sporting a grizzled three-day-old beard on his cheeks and his chin. He cackled loudly in the hallway, and seemed amazed that Meyer was not sharing his amusement.

'Moved away, did he?' Meyer asked.

'Got *sent* away,' the super said, and burst out laughing again.

'Sent where,' Meyer asked.

'Castleview, upstate.'

'The prison?'

'The prison, right enough,' the super said.

'Shit,' Meyer said.

The neighbourhood in which Vicente Manuel Barragan lived had until as recently as five years ago been an Italian ghetto, but it was now almost exclusively Hispanic, and the neon signs that blistered the falling rain announced *BODEGA* and *CARNICERIA* and *JOYERIA* and *SASTRERIA*. 2557 Patterson Boulevard was a wide avenue with a tree-planted divider running up the middle of it. The trees had not yet begun to turn; the leaves hung limp and green in the downpour. Beneath the trees, patches of grass sprang up between the tightly spaced cobblestones that paved the divider. The avenue itself had once been paved with cobblestones, but it had been resurfaced with asphalt, and the blacktop glistened in the rain, reflecting the glow of the street lamps, already illuminated in defence against the three p.m. gloom. The traffic light on the corner turned from red to green, and the blacktop echoed the change, a shimmering green ball suddenly appearing in the road ahead. Carella found a space across the street from 2557, thanked his lucky stars, turned down the visor to which was rubber-banded a hand-lettered sign announcing POLICE OFFICER ON DUTY, and then got out of the car, remembering to close the window this time. In the pouring rain, he ran across the street to Barragan's building, raced up the front steps two at a time, threw open the glass-panelled entrance door, and stepped inside to a small foyer lined with brass mailboxes. A black plastic inset under one of the mailboxes told him that BARRAGAN was in Apartment 3C. He rang the bell, and then reached for the knob on the inner lobby door just as an answering buzz sounded.

The building was spotlessly clean. A blue and white-tiled inner lobby, walls newly painted a muted blue, light bulbs in all the wall sconces, not a trace of graffiti anywhere. The steps smelled of Lysol. He took them up to the third floor, and heard the sound of someone playing a woodwind instrument – clarinet or flute, he could not tell at first – as he came down the hallway to Apartment 3C. The music was coming from inside the apartment, a flute he guessed now. He rang the bell and the music stopped mid-passage.

'Who is it?' a man called.

'Police,' he answered.

'Police?' the man said. 'What the hell?'

Carella heard footsteps approaching the door. The door did not open. Instead, the peephole flap rattled back, and the man said from within, 'Let me see your badge, please.'

Carella flashed the tin.

'Okay,' the man said. The peephole flap fell back into place. Carella heard the lock click open. The door itself opened a moment later.

'Mr Barragan?'

'That's me,' the man said. He was a light-skinned Hispanic with a heavy black moustache under his aquiline nose, thick black hair styled to fall softly over his forehead and ears, dark brown eyes that studied Carella with curiosity now. 'What's the trouble?' he asked.

'No trouble,' Carella said. 'I'm investigating a homicide, and I thought you might be able to help me. All right if I come in?'

Barragan looked at him. 'Is this about Georgie?' he asked.

'Yes. You know he was killed then?'

'I read about it in the paper. Come on in,' Barragan said, and stepped aside to let Carella by. Beyond the entrance foyer, Carella could see an open arch leading into a kitchen, another arch leading to a living room. A music stand was set up in the centre of the living room, a straight-backed chair behind it. On the seat of the chair, Carella saw a flute – he'd been right about that.

'You want a beer or anything?' Barragan asked.

'Not allowed,' Carella said, 'but thanks.'

'Mind if I have one? I've been practising the past three hours, my throat's kinda dry.'

'No, go right ahead,' Carella said.

He waited in the foyer. In the kitchen, he saw Barragan opening first the refrigerator door, and then a can of beer. When he came back into the foyer again, he was carrying the beer can in one hand and a glass in the other. Together, they went into the living room and sat side by side on the couch. Through the large rain-streaked living-room windows, Carella could see in the distance the elevated Calm's Point Expressway, bustling with traffic that edged slowly through the heavy rain.

Barragan poured beer into his glass, took a deep swallow, said, 'Ahhh, good,' and then put the can on the floor, and began sipping more leisurely from the glass. 'What do you want to know?' he said.

'You played in a band years ago with George and...'

'Yes, I did,' Barragan said.

'... and his brother Santo, is that right?'

'Santo, yeah. He played bongos. We had Georgie on guitar, me on flute, Santo on bongos and a guy named Freddie Bones on the steel drum. That's his real name, Freddie Bones. Black guy from Jamaica. It wasn't such a bad combo. I heard worse,' Barragan said, and smiled. His teeth looked startlingly white under the thick black moustache.

'I want to know what happened seven years ago,' Carella said.

'When Santo split, do you mean?'

'*Did* he split? Or did something happen to him?'

'Who knows?' Barragan said, and shrugged. 'I'm assuming he split of his own accord. I mean, Georgie checked with the police later, and there was no kind of report about anything happening to Santo, so I figure he just *decided* to go, and he *went*.'

'Where?' Carella said.

'I don't know where. California? Mexico? Europe? Who knows where somebody goes when he decides to go?'

'Why'd he decide to go?'

'Same reason the band broke up later.'

'What was that?'

'Too much star-power. Too much Georgie Chadderton. I hate to speak bad about the dead, but the man was a pain in the ass, you dig? A full-time ego trip. Thought the rest of us were there just to make him look good. I mean, *shit*, man, I'm a fair flute player, and Freddie was terrific on that steel drum, he could make that thing sound like a fuckin orchestra. So Georgie takes all the solos. On a *guitar*, no less. Like, man, unless you're really outstanding on the guitar, all it's good for is laying down chords for instruments that can run the melody line. You find very few guitar players can do justice to a melody. So here's a band with a flute and a steel drum in it – now what are those two instruments *for*, huh, man? For *melody*, am I right? Well, Georgie had us playing riffs behind his half-ass guitar stuff. *Whang*, *whang*, *whang*, and behind him is me doing *tootle-ee-oo-doo* over and over, and Freddie hitting two-note chords on the steel drum. For the birds, man. We finally had enough of it.'

'When was this? When did the band break up?'

'A year after Santo split, I guess it was.'

'Tell me what happened that night.'

'That was a long time ago, man. I'm not sure I can remember it all.'

'As much as you can remember,' Carella said. 'First of all, when *was* it, exactly? Can you remember the date?'

'Sometime in September,' Barragan said. 'A Saturday night the first or second week in September, I'm not sure.'

'All right, go ahead.'

'It was raining, I remember that. The band used to have this VW van we travelled in, maroon and white, we used to take it everywhere we played. The gig that night . . .'

'Who owned the van?'

'We all did. We chipped in for it. When the band broke up, Freddie bought us out.'

'Sorry, go ahead.'

'Like I said, it was raining very hard that night. The gig was at the Hotel Palomar in Isola – downtown, you know the place? Near the Palomar Theatre? Very big hotel, very classy affair. We were the relief band, we were playing a lot of Latin shit in those days, rumbas, sambas, cha-chas, the whole bag. This was before Georgie got on his calypso trip. The other band – I forget the name of it – Archie Cooper? *Artie* Cooper? Something like that. Big band, ten or twelve pieces. This was a big fancy dress ball – costumes, you know? A benefit of some kind, I forget now what it was – multiple sclerosis or muscular dystrophy, one of the two. Georgie got us the relief gig through a guy playing second trumpet on the Cooper band – Archie was it? Arnie? Georgie'd done the horn man some favours a while back, and when the kid heard they needed a Latin band as relief, he thought of Georgie and gave him a ring. It was a good gig. We used to play some good gigs when we were together. Well, like I told you, I've heard worse bands.'

The rain lashed the living-room windows. Carella kept staring at the dissolving panes of glass, listening to Barragan as he told now about the rain on that night seven years ago, rain coming down in buckets as the musicians, the gig over, their instruments packed, ran for the parked VW van at two-thirty in the morning, Freddie Bones with a newspaper tented over his head, his steel drum hanging from a strap on his left shoulder and banging against his hip as he ran through the rain, Georgie cursing and complaining that his new guitar case would get wet, Barragan himself laughing and running, slipping and almost falling, his flute case tucked under his raincoat to protect it. He was the one who slid open the door of the van, he was the one who climbed in first, Georgie getting in behind the wheel and still complaining about the rain. Bones lit a cigarette. Georgie started the engine, and then wiped off the windshield with his gloved hand, and looked towards the revolving doors at the front of the hotel, where men and women were coming out under the canopy and looking for taxis. 'Where's Santo?' Georgie said, and the three of them looked at each other, and Barragan said, 'He was right behind me when we came out of the john,' and Georgie said, 'So where's he now?' and wiped the windshield again, and again looked towards the revolving doors. 'He'll be here in a minute,' Bones said, 'calm down, why don't you? You're always up there on the ceiling someplace.'

They waited another ten minutes, and then Georgie got out of the van and went back into the hotel to look for his brother. He himself was gone for ten minutes before Barragan and Bones decided to go inside to look for him. 'This fuckin hotel is swallowing up the whole Chadderton family tonight,' Bones said, and both men laughed and went through the revolving doors, and then upstairs to what was called the Stardust Ballroom, which wasn't the Grand Ballroom, but a smaller ballroom on the mezzanine floor of the hotel. There were still some guests around, laughing and talking, but most of them had split when the musicians began packing. Barragan and Bones went into the ballroom, and talked to a sax player on the Cooper band – *Harvey* Cooper, that was it! – and asked him if he'd seen Georgie around, and he said last he'd seen of Georgie was him going into the men's room down the hall. So they went down the hall to the men's room, Bones making a crack about maybe both Santo *and* Georgie having fallen in, and Barragan laughed, and they pushed open the door to the men's room, but Georgie wasn't in there, and neither was Santo. They found Georgie outside the hotel's side entrance, talking to the doorman there, asking him about Santo. The doorman hadn't seen anybody come out carrying a set of bongo drums. Georgie described his brother. The doorman hadn't seen anybody answering that description, either.

'What did he look like?' Carella asked.

'Santo? Good-looking kid, lighter-skinned than his brother, black hair, sort of amber-coloured eyes.'

'How tall?' Carella asked, writing.

'Five nine, five ten, around there.'

'Can you make a guess at his weight?'

'Sort of skinny kid. Well, not skinny. Slender, I guess you'd call it. Muscular, you know, but slender. Sinewy, I guess you'd say. Yeah.'

'How old was he then, do you know?'

'Seventeen. He was just a kid.'

'That would make him twenty-four now,' Carella said.

'If he's alive,' Barragan said.

Even driving as hard as he could through the torrential rain, Meyer did not get to Rawley, upstate, until a little after six p.m. He had phoned ahead first to verify that a man named Frederick Bones was indeed a prisoner at Castleview there, and then had phoned Sarah to tell her he wouldn't be home for dinner. Sarah sighed. Sarah was used to him not being home for dinner.

Castleview State Penitentiary was situated on a point of land jutting out into the River Harb, a natural peninsula dominated by the grey stone walls that crowded the land to its banks on all three sides. A concrete foundation some thirty feet high slanted into the water itself, creating the image of a fairy-tale castle surrounded by a moat. There were eight guard towers on the walls – one at each corner of the prison's narrow end, two spaced along each of the walls angling back towards the main gate, and another at each corner of the wall fronting the approach drive. The massive main gate was constructed of solid steel four inches thick. Meyer rang the bell alongside it, and a panel in the gate opened.

'Detective Meyer, 87th Precinct,' he said to the face behind the bars. 'I called earlier. I've got an appointment to talk with one of your inmates.'

'Let's see your ID,' the guard said.

Meyer showed him his shield and his lucite-encased ID card. The panel slammed shut. There was the sound of a bar being thrown back, and then the sound of heavy tumblers falling. The gate opened. Meyer found himself in a small entrance courtyard, walls on either side of him, a steel-barred inner gate directly ahead of him. The guard told him he'd picked a bad time for a visit; the men were at dinner. Which is where I should be, Meyer thought, but did not say. He asked instead if he could look at Bones' records while he waited for the dinner hour to end. The guard nodded curtly, picked up a phone hanging on the wall just inside the entrance door, spoke briefly to someone on the other end, and then went back to reading his girlie magazine. In several moments, a second guard approached the barred inner gate, unlocked it, slid it open, and asked, 'You the detective wants to see somebody's record?'

'That's me,' Meyer said.

'You picked a hell of a time to come up here,' the second guard said. 'We had a prisoner got stabbed in the yard yesterday.'

'Sorry,' Meyer said.

'No sorrier'n he is,' the guard said. 'Well, come on.'

He let Meyer into the yard, and then locked the gate behind him. The prison walls loomed enormously around them as they walked through the rain to a building on their left. In the guard towers, Meyer could see the muzzles of machine guns pointing down at the yard. He had lots of friends here, Meyer did – or rather business associates, so to speak. All part of the game he thought. The good guys and the bad guys. Sometimes, he wondered which were which. Take a cop like Andy Parker . . .

'In here,' the guard said. 'Records is down the hall. Who you interested in?'

'Man named Freddie Bones.'

'Don't know him,' the guard said, and shook his head. 'Is that his straight handle?'

'Yes.'

'Don't know him. Just down the hall there,' he said, pointing. 'Dinner's over at seven. You want to talk to this guy, you'll have to do it then. They get pissed off if they miss their television shows.'

'Who do I see after I'm through here?' Meyer asked.

'Assistant Warden's office is around the corner from Records. I don't know who's got the duty right now, just talk to whoever's there.'

'Thanks,' Meyer said.

'Got him with an icepick,' the guard said. 'Fourteen holes in his chest. Nice, huh?' he said, and left Meyer in the corridor.

The clerk in Records was reluctant to open the prison files without a written order authorizing him to do so. Meyer explained that he was investigating a homicide, and that it might be helpful for him to know something of Bones' background before actually talking to the man. The clerk still seemed unconvinced. He made a brief phone call to someone, and then hung up and said, 'It's okay. I guess.' He found Bones' folder in a battered file drawer that had seen far better days, and made Meyer comfortable at a small desk in one corner of the office. The folder was as brief as the clerk's phone call had been. This was Bones' first offence. He had been convicted for 'the unlawful sale of one-ounce or more of any narcotic' (the narcotic having been heroin in his case), an A–1 Felony which – under the terms of the state's stringent hard-drug laws – could have grossed him from fifteen years to life in prison. Plea bargaining, which was permitted only within the A–Felony class, had netted him ten. He could be paroled in three and a half, but that would be a lifetime parole; spit on the sidewalk or pass a traffic light, and he'd be right back behind bars again.

Meyer finished his homework and looked at his watch. It was a quarter past six. He carried the folder back to where the clerk was busily typing something no doubt important. The clerk did not look up. Meyer stood by his desk, the folder in his hand. The clerk kept typing. Meyer cleared his throat.

'You finished?' the clerk said.

'Yes, thank you,' Meyer said. 'Anyplace I can get a sandwich and something to drink?'

'You mean inside the walls?'

'Yes.'

'There's a swing room across the yard. Show the tin and they'll let you in.'

'Thanks,' Meyer said.

He left Records, stopped in at the Assistant Warden's office to tell him he was here and ready to talk to Bones, and made arrangements for him to be brought into the Visitors' Room at seven sharp. The guards' swing room across the yard was equipped with machines serving up sandwiches and soft drinks. Meyer bought himself an orange crush and a ham on rye. He wondered what his father would have said about the ham. The guards were talking about nothing but the inmate who'd had his chest ventilated the day before. Meyer guessed things were tough all over, inside *or* out.

At five minutes to seven, he went over to the Visitors' Room, and was admitted by a guard who asked him to take a seat on one side of the long table that ran the length of the room. At seven on the dot, a tall, extremely handsome black man in prison threads came into the room and took a seat opposite Meyer at the long table. They were separated by a sheet of clear plastic three inches thick; Meyer had heard someplace that the plastic was the same sort used in the gun turrets of bombers during World War II. There were telephones before both men on their separate sides of the table. Each karal was separated from the one on either side of it by sound-proof dividers that granted at least a modicum of privacy to visitors and inmates. A sign on the wall advised that visiting hours ended at 5.00 p.m. and asked that visits be limited to fifteen minutes. The room was empty now, save for Meyer and the man who sat opposite him. Meyer picked up his telephone.

'Mr Bones?' he said, feeling very much like a straight man in a musical show.

'What'd I do *this* time?' Bones asked into his phone. He smiled as he asked the question, and Meyer unconsciously returned the smile.

'Nothing that I know of,' he said. He took out a small leather case, allowed it to fall open over his shield, and held the shield up to the plastic divider. 'I'm Detective Meyer of the 87th Precinct in Isola. We're investigating a homicide, and I thought you might be able to give me some information.'

'Who got killed?' Bones asked. He was no longer smiling.

'George Chadderton,' Meyer said.

Bones merely nodded.

'You don't seem surprised,' Meyer said.

'I ain't surprised, no,' Bones said.

'How good is your memory?' Meyer asked.

'Fair.'

'Does it go back seven years?'

'It goes back thirty,' Bones said.

'I want to know what happened the night Santo disappeared.'

'Who says he disappeared?'

'Didn't he?'

'He split, that's all,' Bones said, and shrugged.

'And hasn't been heard from since.'

Bones shrugged again.

'What happened, do you remember?'

Bones began remembering. As far as Meyer could tell, he was remembering in great detail and with a maximum of accuracy. It was not until several hours later – when Meyer compared notes with Carella on the telephone – that he recognized Bones' story was not without its inconsistencies. In fact, there were only two congruent points between the story Barragan had told Carella and the one Bones told Meyer; both men agreed that George C. Chadderton was an egotistical prick, and both men agreed it had been raining on the night Santo Chadderton disappeared. As for the rest...

Bones remembered the job as having taken place at the Hotel Shalimar in downtown Isola, a hostelry every bit as palatial as the hotel Barragan remembered, but some ten blocks distant from it and on the *north* side of the city as opposed to the south. Meyer, listening to Bones, not yet knowing that Barragan had pinpointed the hotel as the *Palomar*, jotted into his notebook *Hotel Shalimar*, and then asked, 'When was this exactly, can you give me some idea?'

'October,' Bones said. 'Sometime the middle of October.'

Later that night, Meyer would learn that Barragan had recalled the date as 'Sometime in September, a Saturday night the first or second week in September.' For now, blissful in his ignorance, Meyer simply nodded and said, 'Yes, go on, I'm listening,' and indeed did listen very carefully to every word Bones uttered, and faithfully transcribed each of those words into his notebook, the better to point up later the frailties of eye witnesses even if they don't happen to be in a Japanese movie.

The job, according to Bones, was a wedding job. Two society families, he couldn't remember the names. But the groom had just got out of medical school, Dr Somebody – wait a minute, Bones would get it in a minute – Dr Coolidge, was it? He was sure the kid was a doctor, there were a lot of doctors at the wedding that night, *Cooper*, that was it. Dr Harvey Cooper! Everybody in tuxedos and long gowns, a real swanky affair with good-looking guys and gorgeous broads – especially one blonde who kept hanging around the bandstand all night long, giving Santo the eye. According to Bones, the blonde – who had not so much as put in a bit-part appearance in Barragan's story – was one of those tall, healthy-looking, full-breasted, long-legged women he always associated with California – man, the women out there were enough to drive a man out of his gourd, especially if the man happened to be a musician, which Bones happened to be. He could remember one time, this was after the Chadderton band broke up, he was doing a series of one-nighters on the Pacific Coast, from the Mexican border all the way up to . . .

Meyer said he hated to interrupt, but he wanted to get back to the city at a decent hour, and also he didn't want to cut in on Bones' television-viewing, which he understood . . .

'No, that's okay,' Bones said, 'television stinks anyway, all cops-and-robbers shit,' and went on to conclude his story about this woman he'd met in Pasadena, big tennis-playing California-type woman, long legs and great tits, pearly white teeth, took her to his room back at the motel, showed her how a black man aces a serve in there, yessir, showed her a few little tricks she hadn't picked up out there on the Coast.

'Well, that's fine,' Meyer said, 'but about Santo—'

'I'm only sayin,' Bones said, 'that there's a certain kind of woman can easily be classified as a *California* woman, do you dig?'

'I dig,' Meyer said.

'It's a *type*, man, you fathom me?'

'I fathom you,' Meyer said. 'You're saying this woman who was hanging around the bandstand that night was a California *type*, I get you. Blonde and tall and . . .'

'Big-titted.'

'Yes, and long-legged.'

'Right, and lots of white teeth. Cali*forn*ia, man. That's what that *is*, man, a California *type*. Do you understand me now?'

'Yes, I do,' Meyer said. 'So what happened with this woman? You wouldn't remember her name, would you?'

'Her name was Margaret Henderson, she was married to a man named Thomas Henderson, who happened to be chairman of the dance they were throwing at the tennis club out there, where Margaret had won the women's singles.'

'That's in Pasadena, you mean.'

'Yeah. Margaret Henderson. Big tall blonde lady with gorgeous gams and the biggest set of—'

'I meant the one here at the Shalimar.'

'No, not as big as Margaret's. Nice, you understand, full, very nice – but not like Margaret's.'

'I meant her name,' Meyer said.

'Oh. No, I wouldn't know her name. It was Santo who spent all the time with her.'

Bones went on to say that the way Santo had spent his time with the mysterious blonde lady who had no name was by dancing very close to her while the relief band (Bones seemed to think the *other* band was the relief band, whereas Barragan believed just the opposite) played these very slow tunes that could put a person to sleep. Didn't put Santo to sleep, though, not with this gorgeous California-type no-name lady in his arms dressed all in white, slinky white satin gown split almost to the thighs, suntanned tennis-player legs showing on both sides of the gown, gold bracelets on her arms, flashing those white teeth at him, long blonde hair falling to her naked shoulders, sweet California lady, mmm, sweet.

'Man, she had him in her spell from minute number one,' Bones said.

'What do you mean?' Meyer asked.

'Dragging him around the floor like he was hypnotized.'

'Uh-huh,' Meyer said, and looked up from his notebook. 'Did

71

he ever *leave* the ballroom with her? Where *was* this, anyway?'

'The Hotel Shalimar, I told you.'

'Yes, I know, but any particular ballroom?'

'The Moonglow Ballroom.'

'Did he ever leave with her? Did you see him leaving with her?'

'Once. Well, let me correct that, man. I didn't see him *leaving* with her, but I saw him *outside* with her.'

'Outside where?'

'In the hallway outside. I was going to the men's room, and I saw Santo and the blonde comin up the stairs.'

'From where?'

'From the floor downstairs, I guess,' Bones said, and shrugged.

'When you say he looked hypnotized...'

'That was just an expression.'

'You weren't suggesting...'

'Dope?' Bones said.

'Dope, yes'

'I don't think Santo was doing dope.'

'Not even a little pot now and then?'

'No,' Bones said, 'I don't think so. Not Santo. No, definitely not. He respected his body too much. Whenever we had a rehearsal – we used to rehearse in the basement of the First Episcopal in Diamondback – Santo used to go in the ladies' room and...'

'The ladies' room?'

'Yeah, cause there was a mirror in there, a full-length mirror. There were mirrors in the *men's* room, too, you understan, but they were over the sinks, and Santo wanted to see his gorgeous bod in full living colour, you dig?'

'Yes, mm, I dig,' Meyer said. 'So he went in the ladies' room, right?'

'Well, there was no danger of anybody walkin in on him. I mean, we were down there all alone, rehearsin. This was in the basement of the church, you fathom, man?'

'I fathom. What was he, a weight lifter or something?'

'How'd you guess? Wait a minute, you done some liftin yourself didn't you?'

'Once upon a time,' Meyer said.

'Did you used to go in the ladies' room and admire yourself?'

'No, not the ladies' room.'

'You look pretty good for a man your age,' Bones said. 'How old are you, anyway?'

Meyer was reluctant to tell Bones how old he really was because then he'd have to explain further that bald-headed men sometimes took on an appearance that belied their true youthfulness, sometimes in fact appeared stodgy and stuffy when their hearts were really in the highlands – and then he remembered that he had not taken off his Professor Higgins hat. It was still sitting there on top of his head, hiding his baldness and causing him to wonder what *else* there was about him that might prompt a casual observer to refer to him as 'a man your age'.

He decided to ignore Bones' question, decided also to sidestep any further discussion of those days when he was but a mere lad pumping iron in his bedroom, lest some inadvertent clue – like mentioning the emperor's name, for example, or making reference to the chariot races that week – would enable Bones to pinpoint his decrepitude more precisely. Instead, and solely because a *femme fatale* now seemed to have entered the picture in a very healthy, long-legged, full-breasted California-type way, and seemed to have cast a spell upon Santo the moment she slithered across the floor of the Moonglow Ballroom to perch herself upon his shoulder as he bonged his bongos, Meyer asked the question that – properly answered – might at least have brought up the curtain on the three-act drama known as *Santo's Disappearance* (to be retitled *Rashomon* as soon as Meyer compared notes with Carella) and the question was this:

'Tell me, Mr Bones, is it possible that Santo *left* the hotel with this woman? After the job, I mean? Is it possible he simply *left* with her?'

Anything was possible, of course, but the question – on the face of it – was patently absurd. If Bones had seen Santo leaving the hotel with the mysterious blonde (who would become even more mysterious later on when Carella revealed that Barragan hadn't once mentioned her), if indeed Bones had even the faintest suspicion that Santo and the blonde had vanished into the stormy night together, under the same umbrella perhaps, why wouldn't he have mentioned this to the late George C. Chadderton? And wouldn't this noble gentleman (a prick according to Barragan and Bones alike) then have limited his search to only those ladies of

California-type, long-legged, big-breasted persuasion? Of course. Even recognizing this, Meyer waited breathlessly for Bones' answer.

'Yes,' Bones said, 'I think that's exactly what happened.'

'Would you elaborate on that?' Meyer said.

'I think he split with her.'

'And then what?'

'I don't know what,' Bones said.

'When's the last time you saw him?' Meyer said.

'During the last set.'

'Then what?'

'He went down the hall with Vinnie.'

'Vinnie?'

'Vinnie Barragan.'

'By down the hall . . .'

'To take a leak,' Bones said.

'Then what?'

'Georgie and me packed up and went downstairs to wait for them.'

'Where'd you wait?'

'Under the canopy there. The hotel canopy.'

'Yeah, go ahead.'

'We saw Vinnie comin out of the elevator, so we started runnin for the van. Couple minutes later, Vinnie came over to the van, but there was no Santo with him. So we go back in the hotel lookin for him, but he's gone.'

'And you think he left with the blonde, is that it?'

'Isn't that what *you'da* done, man?'

'Well,' Meyer said, and let the word dangle. He frankly did not know *what* he might have done had a beautiful blonde in a slinky white gown come around casting spells on him, but he sure as hell knew what his wife Sarah would have done if ever she'd spotted him leaving the Hotel Shalimar or *any* hotel with such a blonde on his arm. Within minutes, the cops of Midtown North would have been investigating the strange and baffling death of a bald-headed detective whose skull had been crushed by a stale bagel. 'Did you mention this to George?' he said. 'That his brother might have left with the blonde?'

'Nope,' Bones said.

'How come?'

'Fuck him,' Bones said, summing up quite simply how he'd felt about the late George C. Chadderton.

'This blonde,' Meyer said, 'I wonder if you can describe her a bit more fully.'

'Gorgeous,' Bones said.

'How tall would you say she was?'

'Five ten at least,' Bones said.

'How old was she?'

'At first I'd have said her twenties, but I think she may have been older than that. Her early thirties, I'd say.'

'What makes you say that?'

'You can tell by the way a chick carries herself, you dig? This one was older. Maybe thirty, maybe even a little older than that. Healthy, you understand, all these California types are healthy as hell, man, they can fool you with all that healthiness, you can think they're twenty when they're really fifty.'

'But this woman looked to be in her early twenties, is that right?'

'No, she *carried* herself that way.'

'I don't understand,' Meyer said, puzzled. 'Did she *look* thirty, or did she . . . ?'

'Well, how would I know *how* she looked, man?'

Meyer blinked. 'What do you mean?' he said.

'She was wearing a mask,' Bones said.

'A mask?' Meyer said, and blinked again. 'At a wedding?'

'Oh,' Bones said. 'Yeah.' He blinked, too. 'Maybe I got something mixed up, huh?' he said.

Carella and Meyer, on the telephone together at eight-thirty that night, agreed that somebody – either Barragan or Bones – had sure as hell got something mixed up. It was Meyer's guess that *Bones* was the man with the faulty memory, and Carella agreed that perhaps the tall slinky blonde had indeed been a figment of the musician's imagination since she seemed to have gone completely unnoticed by Vicente Manuel Barragan, who was otherwise possessed of total recall when it came to anything that had happened that night seven years ago, dredging up even snatches of dialogue such as Bones' remark about the hotel swallowing up the whole Chadderton family. It seemed further odd to Carella that Bones' tennis-playing lady in Pasadena appeared to be an exact replica of the blonde who'd lured Santo first on to the dance floor where they'd danced cheek to cheek to the strains of the Harvey Cooper orchestra (amazing that Cooper was an orchestra leader in Barragan's story but the *groom* in Bones' story) and later went out into the night where together and respectively (if not respectfully) they had proceeded to exorcize *his* pubescent passion and *her* oncoming menopause, afterwards disappearing from the face of the earth forever. In Barragan's story, the band had been playing at a fancy dress ball, which seemed more likely than the wedding Bones remembered, especially since the blonde – if she existed at all – suddenly began wearing a mask when Bones thought about her a bit further. Barragan seemed certain that the affair had been a benefit for multiple sclerosis or muscular dystrophy. Was that where Bones had come up with the notion that Harvey Cooper was not only the groom but also someone who had recently been graduated from medical school? And was it the Stardust Ballroom or the Moonglow Ballroom? Or neither? Or all of the above?

'I think we'll have to do some further work on this in the morning,' Carella said judiciously. 'In the meantime they're waiting for me back at the table.'

'Who's they?' Meyer asked.

'Teddy. And Bert and his wife.'

'Some people get to eat in nice restaurants,' Meyer said, 'while other people eat in prisons upstate.'

'I'll talk to you in the morning,' Carella said.

'Yeah, good night,' Meyer said.

'Good night,' Carella said.

In bed with Teddy that night, holding her close in the dark, the rain lashing the window panes, Carella was aware all at once that she was not asleep, and he sat up and turned on the bedlamp and looked at her, puzzled.

'Teddy?' he said.

Her back was to him, she could not see his lips. He touched her shoulder and she rolled over to face him, and he was surprised to see that there were tears in her eyes.

'Hey,' he said, 'hey, honey... what...?'

She shook her head and rolled away from him again, closing herself into her pillow, closing him out – if she could not see him, she could not hear him; her eyes were her ears, her hands and her face were her voice. She lay sobbing into the pillow, and he put his hand on her shoulder again, gently, and she sniffed and turned towards him again.

'Want to talk?' he said.

She nodded.

'What's the matter?'

She shook her head.

'Did I do something?'

She shook her head again.

'What is it?'

She sat up, took a tissue from the box on the bedside table, blew her nose, and then put the tissue under her pillow. Carella waited. At last, her hands began to speak. He watched them. He knew the language, he had learned it well over the years, he could now speak it better than hesitantly with his own hands. As she spoke to him, the tears began rolling down her face again, and her hands fluttered and then stopped completely. She sniffed again, and reached for the crumpled tissue under her pillow.

'You're wrong,' he said.

She shook her head.

'I'm telling you you're wrong.'

She shook her head again.

'Honey, she likes you very much.'

Her hands began again. This time they spilled out a torrent of words and phrases, speaking to him so rapidly that he had to tell her to slow down, and even then continuing at a pace almost too fast for him to comprehend. He caught both her hands in his own, and said, 'Now come on, honey. If you want me to listen . . .' She nodded, and sniffed, and began speaking more slowly now, her fingers long and fluid, her dark eyes glistening with the tears that sat upon them as she told him again that she was certain Augusta Kling didn't like her, Augusta had said things and done things tonight—

'What things?'

Teddy's hands moved again. *The wine,* she said.

'The wine? What about the wine?'

When she toasted.

'I don't remember any toast.'

She made a toast.

'To what?'

To you and Bert.

'To the case, you mean. To solving the case.'

No, to you and Bert.

'Honey...'

She left me out. She drank only to you and Bert.

'Now why would she do a thing like that? She's one of the sweetest people...'

Teddy burst into tears again.

He put his arms around her and held her close. The rain beat steadily on the window panes. 'Honey,' he said, and she looked up into his face, and studied his mouth, and watched the words as they formed on his lips. 'Honey, Augusta likes you very much.' Teddy shook her head. 'Honey, she *said* so. Do you remember when you told the story about the kids ... about April falling in the lake at that PBA picinic? And Mark jumping in to rescue her when the water was only two feet deep? Do you remember telling...?'

Teddy nodded.

'And then you went to the ladies' room, do you remember?'

She nodded again.

'Well, the minute you were gone, Augusta told me how terrific you were.'

Teddy looked up at him.

'That's just what she said. She said, Jesus, Teddy's terrific, I wish I could tell a story like her.'

The tears were beginning to flow again.

She looked him dead in the eye. Her hands began to move.

Because I'm a deaf mute, she said.

'You're the most wonderful woman in the world,' he said, and kissed her, and held her close again. And then he kissed the tears from her face and from her eyes, and told her again how much he loved her, told her what he had told her that day years and years ago when he'd asked her to marry him for the twelfth time and had finally convinced her that she was so much *more* than any other woman when until that moment she had considered herself somehow less. He told her again now, he said, 'Jesus, I love you, Teddy, I love you to death,' and then they made love as they had when they were younger, much younger.

7

He knew she was on the island, he had heard the launch pulling into the dock more than an hour ago, but she had not yet come to see him, and he wondered about this, wondered if he'd done something to displease her. She had left the island shortly after she'd fed him on Friday night, and he had not been fed since. The clock on the wall – a new acquisition he'd had to beg for – read 9.15. He'd had no breakfast today, and no lunch, and he wondered now if she was going to forget about dinner, too. Sometimes, he cursed the clock. Without the clock, there had been an almost blissful sense of disorientation. Minutes faded into hours to become days and then weeks and months. And years. He had looked up at the clock when he'd heard the launch last night – 8.30 p.m., which meant that she'd be on the mainland by 9.00, that's how long the trip took, a half-hour. Figure close to two hours into the city, she'd have been in Isola by a little before 11.00.

He wondered where she went in the city, wondered about her life outside this room and off this island. He had seen her in the city only once, the night they'd met, and that had been seven years ago – she had let him keep a calendar before she allowed him to have the clock. He would try to count the days, but there were no windows in the room and he never knew when the sun had risen or when it was setting. In the first year, he miscalculated by a month. He thought it was Easter. By his reckoning, trying to keep time without a clock, marking off by guesswork the days on the calendar, he thought it was Easter already. She laughed and told him it was only February the twelfth, he'd been there only five months, was he growing tired of her so soon?

The room – his cage, he called it – was perhaps fifteen feet wide by twenty feet long, he had paced it off the first time she'd locked him in here. He had been on the island only a week then, and had told her he wanted to go back to the mainland, and she'd said sure, she just wanted to make a phone call, why didn't he mix himself a drink, relax a bit, she wouldn't be a minute. He trusted her then; this was after a week of fucking their brains out all over the house – her bedroom, the living-room floor, the kitchen with her bare ass on the countertop and her legs wrapped around his waist, the playroom, and *this* room, which had been a guest room before it became his cage and which – she told him – had been a psychiatrist's office before she bought the house. That explained the double doors.

The doors were massive, made of sturdy oak, one opening into the room with the knob on the left, the other opening out with the knob on the right. If you were inside the room you opened the first door, you found yourself smack up against the second door. This was for privacy. When the psychiatrist owned the house, he didn't want anyone to hear the rantings of the crazy people who paid him sixty dollars an hour to lie on his couch. Thick double doors. Piano hinges on each of the doors, you couldn't take out any pins and lift the doors off their hinges because there weren't any exposed pins to take out. Locks on both doors, the inside one and the outer one. No windows on any of the walls because this was a room that had been part of a big cinderblock rectangular-shaped basement with the furnace in one corner before the psychiatrist built some walls around the furnace and divided the remaining space into equal halves – the playroom next door where Santo had fucked her on the pool table the first week he was here, and this room here, his cage that had once been the psychiatrist's office, but was now a proper guest room with a wall unit opposite the bed, and a couch against one of the walls, and pictures on the walls, and the big double bed itself of course, and the private bathroom with a sink, a toilet and a tub.

'Sure,' she'd told him, 'you just relax, make yourself a drink. I have these phone calls to get off my mind, and then we'll hop in the boat and I'll take you back to the mainland, okay, sweetie?' Sure, sweetie. He'd gone to the bar that was part of the wall unit opposite the bed, and he'd mixed himself a scotch and soda, and then he'd sat on the couch listening to the stereo. This was seven years ago, the record collection was old even then, most of the tunes going back a long, long time. She hadn't replaced any of the records in the past seven years, he listened to the same stuff over and over again, the records worn and scratchy now, the way *he* was worn and scratchy, seven years, seven years in this room. But that night long ago, after they'd spent a week together out here on the island, beautiful that September, woman with her own private little island off Sands

Spit, man, he was impressed! Couldn't get enough of him, told him she was twenty-eight years old, but he saw a college graduation picture of her in the living room, and there was a date on the back of it, and he figured a person graduated college when they were twenty-two, right? Well, maybe younger if they were really smart, so okay give her the benefit of the doubt, say she graduated when she was twenty, nobody graduated college younger than twenty, which according to the date on the back of the graduation picture would've made her thirty-two years old and not what she claimed to be, not twenty-eight like she claimed. Which made her thirty-nine years old now, an old lady.

Where was his dinner, wasn't she gonna bring him no dinner tonight, was she going to starve him the way she did for two weeks that time he almost escaped? Would've made it, too, if it hadn't been for the dog. She knew he was scared of dogs, he'd told her so, pillow talk during their first week together, terrified of dogs, you know what I mean? When I was eight years old, I got bit by a dog on the roof. Goddamn fox terrier, guy had taken him up on the roof to do his business, fuckin mutt came at me and tore a piece out of my leg. I had to get rabies shots, you ever have rabies shots? Christ, the pain, I been scared of dogs ever since, I shit in my pants a dog even comes near me. He was over the wall and out when she let the dog loose – big German shepherd, came after him with his fangs bared, knocked him to the ground, he went tumbling over in the tall sea grass at the ocean's edge, clawing at the dog's big head, trying to keep those teeth away from him, the ocean pounding in, her voice coming in over the roar of the surf, 'No, Clarence, no,' some fucking name for a killer German shepherd, Clarence! Picked up the dog's leash in one hand, and told Santo to head back for the house like a nice little boy, saw where he'd picked the locks on both doors and locked him in the bathroom for the night, with the dog sitting outside the door. All night long, he could hear the dog growling. She starved Santo for the next two weeks, as punishment for having tried to escape, and when finally she fed him again, there was something in the food, it knocked him out completely. He didn't know how long he was out, but when he woke up there were new locks on both doors, deadbolt locks, he couldn't have picked them even if he was a pro. And from then on, the dog was always outside those big double doors, sitting in the hallway.

But that was later, that was – he kept losing track of time. The first time she'd locked him in here, yes, he was listening yes, to her records, and sipping at his scotch, just digging the sound and thinking he'd be back in the city again soon, playing another gig with Georgie and the guys, sipping, smiling, and then becoming aware of time all at once, looking at his wristwatch and realizing she'd been gone a good half-hour. Well, leave it to a woman, goes to make a few phone calls and takes forever. Smiling, he got off the couch and went to the door and twisted the knob the way he would have ordinarily, not suspecting a thing yet, and then discovering the door was locked, she had locked the door on him. He began yelling for her to come unlock the door, but if she heard him she didn't come do it. He doubted if she heard him, anyway, through those big double mothers. She didn't come back till the next morning, to bring him a tray of breakfast. She had a gun when she came into the room, he didn't know whether she'd had it in the house here all along, or whether she'd taken the boat over to the mainland to buy it. He wasn't familiar with guns, he couldn't tell one calibre of gun from another. But this didn't look like no dainty little gun a lady would keep in her handbag. This looked like a gun could blow a man's head off. She told him to back away from the door, and he said, 'Hey, come on, what is this?' and she wagged the gun at him and just said 'Back.' Then she put the breakfast tray on the floor and said, 'There's your food, eat it,' and went out, locking both doors behind her.

The breakfast was the first time she put anything in his food. He drank his orange juice, and then ate his cornflakes and drank his coffee, and he didn't know which of the things he ate or drank was doped, but *something* was because he passed out cold almost immediately afterwards, and when he woke up again – he didn't know how many hours later – he was naked on the bed, all his clothes gone, his wristwatch gone, his wrists tied together behind his back, his feet tied together at the ankles. He started yelling for her again. But again, he didn't know whether she could hear him through those double doors. Anyway, he was beginning to understand that she would come to him only when she wanted to. There was no sense yelling or screaming, there was no sense doing anything except trying to figure a way out.

He knew what the island looked like, she'd shown him around it during that first week when he was still a guest and not a prisoner, fucked her on the boat and on the beach, fucked her in the little pine forest that ran along the southern shore, fucked her day and night, never met a woman like her in his life, and told her so. But, you know, he missed the city, wanted to get back to the city – 'Are you getting tired of me?' she asked. 'No, no, just want to walk those streets again, you know, hear those sidewalks humming under my feet, huh, baby? I'm a city boy, born and raised there, my mom's from Venezuela and my pop's from Trinidad – haven't seen *him* since I was three and he took off with a girl used to waitress up in Diamondback – but me and my brother Georgie are one-hundred per cent American Yankee Doodle Dandy boys, yessir,' he said, and burst out laughing. 'Stay just another day,' she said.

That first week, she told him her daddy had bought the island for her when she was sixteen, a birthday present; you're the only sixteen-year-old girl in the world who has her own private island, daddy had told her. Santo pictured him as some kind of asshole rich guy with white duck pants and a double-breasted blue blazer, white yachting cap on his head, Here you are, darlin, here's your own private island – while people all over the world were digging in garbage cans for food. Built her a house when she got married, told his daughter she ought to have a little place where she could get away from it all, little seaside hideaway half an hour from the mainland, only it wasn't so little; there were four bedrooms in the place, not to mention the playroom in the basement and the guest room that used to be the psychiatrist's—

That was the first time he caught her lying. That was during the first week, he wasn't even her prisoner then, they were still, you know, making it day and night and promising undying love to each other. He caught the lie, and he said, Hey, how come if your daddy bought you this island when you were sixteen, and then he built this house for you when you were twenty-one and got married – then how come you told me you bought this house from a man who used to be a psychiatrist and who put those big double doors in downstairs so nobody could hear his patients yelling they're Napoleon, how come, huh?

So she admitted then that she hadn't bought the house from a psychiatrist at all, she had in fact been *married* to the psychiatrist who'd put in those big double doors downstairs so that his patients could feel free to divulge the deepest secrets of their labyrinthine pasts without being overheard by anyone. It still sounded very fishy to Santo, and he told her so. This was on the fourth day, he guessed it was. This was when they were still eating, drinking and making merry. She finally told him the truth the next day, or at least he *guessed* it was the truth, he couldn't really say for sure. They were walking on the beach. He was wearing an old sweater she'd loaned him, said it had belonged to her psychiatrist husband, who wasn't a psychiatrist at all – but of course he didn't know that until after she'd told him the truth. There were gulls circling a dead fish that had washed ashore, raising a terrible racket, white and grey against the clear September sky, their beaks a more intense yellow than the pale gold of the sunshine in which they floated. The ocean was very calm. Her voice was very calm, too.

She told him it was true that her father had bought the island for her when she was sixteen, and she told him it was further true that he'd built the house here for her and her husband when they got married. 'When I was twenty-one,' she said, 'I'm twenty-eight now,' which was another lie, but he didn't discover that one until he looked at the back of the graduation picture in the living room and saw the date. Anyway, the way she was telling it now, her husband left her after they'd been married only six months, just picked up and left her one day, and she'd had this, well, what you might call a nervous breakdown. Her father refused to have her committed to a hospital, so he arranged for private care in the house here on the island, which was when he had the double doors installed, both of them with locks on them. So that she wouldn't hurt herself. She became suicidal, you see. When her husband left her. She tried committing suicide several times. The double doors, securely locked, were for her own protection. A nurse sat outside them day and night. This was when she was still twenty-one and her husband left her.

Santo listened to all this and thought, Well, I hooked on to a real bedbug this time, but he expressed sympathy for all she'd been through, poor kid, and asked her how she was feeling now, and she said 'Can't you *tell* how I'm feeling? I'm feeling marvellous!' He supposed that was true, she certainly looked healthy and strong and she fucked like a jackrabbit, but he'd once known a mentally retarded girl in Diamondback who everybody on the block used to fuck, take her up on the roof and fuck her, and whereas she didn't have all her marbles when it came to arithmetic or spelling, she knew how to jazz a man clean out of his mind. Which might be the same with this girl, this *woman* really, said she was twenty-eight, but he knew she was thirty-two – she might be somebody who still ought to be kept behind locked doors except when she was fucking her brains out, which if she had her way she'd have done day and night through Christmas, except he told her he had to get back to the mainland.

Took him thirty seconds to realize he was a prisoner. If she hadn't told him that story about the breakdown and the locked double doors, he'd have maybe thought, Well, the woman's havin a little sport with me, she's got me locked in here, but she's gonna come down here in just a little while wearing only a black garter belt and mesh stockings and high-heeled patent leather pumps, and she's just gonna squirt whipped cream all over me and eat me up alive and beg my pardon for playin such a bad joke on me, makin me think I was a prisoner here. That's what he *might* have thought if she hadn't just two days earlier told him the story about going bonkers when her husband left right after they got married. She might have been lying about *that*, too, but he didn't think somebody lied about having a mental breakdown. No, this room he found himself in – this prison, this cage – used to be *her* prison, her cage with a nurse sitting outside it, maybe ready with a strait-jacket or a shot of something to knock her out, who the hell knew? And now *he* was the prisoner, and she was outside there, putting dope in his food whenever she wanted to, and coming to the room to pass the time of day with him, and showing him the big mother German shepherd the very day she bought him, which was three days after she locked him in – this was after she'd doped his food the first time, and he was lying bound hand and foot on the bed. The doors opened and she brought in the German Shepherd, fuckin thing looked like a *grizzly* bear he was that big. Santo backed away from him, and she smiled, the bitch, showing her even white teeth, tossing her long blonde hair. 'Don't be frightened, sweetie,' she said, 'Clarence is the gentlest human being on earth.' Clarence! And Clarence growled deep in his throat the way gentle human beings *never* do, man, he growled and those black lips of his or whatever you call them, that soft black flesh around the mouth drew back to show teeth that had to be six inches long, each and every one of them, the gentlest human being on earth looked like he was ready to tear a big fat hunk of meat out of Santo's leg or maybe leap for his throat and rip out his windpipe. And she smiled. She smiled, the bitch. 'Clarence is going to be on the island from now on,' she said. And later, after he tried to escape that first time and the dog came after him, later she told him that Clarence was going to be sitting outside his room from now on, just the way her nurse used to sit out there when she was having the trouble that time. 'If there's anything you need,' she said, smiling, 'you just ask Clarence.' Smiling.

At first, Santo thought he could hold out on her. Okay, you bitch, you want to keep me prisoner on this fuckin island with a fuckin German Shepherd roaming the grounds, okay, you know what you're gonna get from me? You're gonna get *this*, sister, that's what you're gonna get, you're gonna get nothin, zero, zilch, nada, bubkes, *that's* what! But when she came in to make love that first time – this was maybe two or three weeks after she bought the dog – she locked the doors behind her, both doors, and then hung the keys on Clarence's collar, and said, 'Sit, Clarence,' and the fuckin mutt sat just inside the door, and watched her as she walked to the bed. She was wearing a pale blue nightgown, nothing under it, he could see her body through the thin nylon, a beautiful body, it was her body that had attracted him to her in the first place, tall and slender, with good breasts and long legs, she came to the bed and sat on the edge of it and said 'Don't you want to make love, Santo?' and he told her he didn't want to make love, he wouldn't make love to anybody who kept him prisoner with a goddamn dog named Clarence ready to bite him, get the dog out of here, get out of here yourself, I don't want to make love to a bitch like you!

But . . . you know . . . it had been almost three weeks already, three weeks since he'd had *any* woman at all, three weeks since they'd been going at it day and night, and here she was now, crawling on to the bed beside him, and wriggling out of the gown, and then taking him in her hands and then in her mouth, and then suddenly moving away from him, rolling on to her back and throwing her legs wide the way she had that night in the kitchen, and suddenly he was on top of her and not caring whether he was her prisoner or her slave or whatever, only wanting her, wanting her, and hating himself for wanting her.

He dreamt constantly of escape. He held back a fork from his tray one time – she never let him have a knife, the bitch, his food was always cut for him when she brought it in – kept the fork and tried digging a hole in the bathroom wall, get out of this fuckin room into the basement, get around the dog somehow, but the fork broke on the cinder block, and when she found it missing later, she punished him again, there was always the punishment when he did something wrong, something she thought was wrong. Another time, he pretended he was sick, stuck his finger down his throat and vomited all over the floor, told her he thought he had appendicitis or something, figured if he could get her to call a doctor ... but no, she told him no doctor, she made him wipe up the vomit, he said he was going to die, she said 'No, you're not going to die.' Always dreaming of escape. Get out of here, get to the boat. Get free.

He heard a key turning in the inner door. He waited. The door opened. She stood there holding Clarence's leash in one hand. She smiled, led Clarence into the room, said, 'Sit, Clarence,' and then went out into the corridor for Santo's tray of food. She carried it to the coffee table in front of the couch, put it down, and – still smiling – said, 'Are you hungry, sweetie?'

He did not answer her. He sat immediately and began eating.

'Did you miss me?' she asked.

He still said nothing. He continued wolfing down the food. From across the room just inside the door, Clarence sat on his haunches and watched.

'I had some business to take care of in the city,' she said.

'I'm not interested,' he said.

'I thought you might be.'

'I'm not.'

She shrugged, went to the door, and took the dog's leash in her hand again.

'I'll be back later,' she said.

'You ever wonder what would happen if you should die?' he asked suddenly, looking up from the food on his tray. 'I'd starve to death in here, do you realize that?'

'Yes, I do,' she said. 'But don't worry, sweetie, we've got a good long life ahead of us.'

He said nothing.

'What shall I wear later?' she asked.

'I don't care what you wear,' he said.

'What's your favourite? I want to make you happy tonight.'

'You can make me happy by leaving me alone.'

'I don't believe that.

'Believe it, it's true.'

'Shall I wear the black wig?'

'I told you I don't care.'

'Finish your dinner,' she said. 'I'll surprise you, all right? I'll wear something you've never seen before.'

'If you want to surprise me, you'll come in later and tell me I'm a free man.'

'No. I can't do that.'

'Why not?'

'I need you, Santo.'

'I want to leave here.'

'Yes, I know that.'

'I'm going crazy here. If you keep me here any longer, I'll go out of my mind. I'll *die*, do you understand? I'll die in this room.'

'You won't die,' she said, and smiled again. 'Not unless I *want* you to die. Please remember that, Santo.' She looked up at the clock. 'I'll be back in an hour. Will you be ready for me in an hour?'

'No.'

'Be ready,' she said.

'I hate you,' he said softly.

'You love me,' she answered, and smiled again. She was leaving the room when she seemed to remember something. She turned, looked at him, and said, 'Oh, by the way – C.J. won't be visiting us any more.'

8

On Monday morning, September 18, while Meyer was on the phone checking with both the Muscular Dystrophy Association and the National Multiple Sclerosis Society in an attempt to determine whether either or both had sponsored a benefit ball early in September seven years ago, Carella took a call from a man named Henry Gombes at Ballistics.

'On these spent bullets found at the scene,' he said.

'This the Chadderton case?' Carella asked.

'Chadderton, Chadderton,' Gombes said, obviously consulting a sheet of paper in front of him, 'yes, Chadderton, Culver and South Eleventh, September fifteenth, that's right.'

'That's right,' Carella said.

'I'll send the report on later,' Gombes said, 'but meanwhile, do you want to take some of this stuff down?'

'Shoot,' Carella said.

'No ejected cartridge casings found at the scene, which indicates the weapon wasn't an automatic pistol. Five bullets were recovered, though, three of them badly deformed...'

'Those would've been the three that hit the victims,' Carella said.

'Two victims, were there?'

'Yes.'

'One still alive from what I understand.'

'That's right.'

'Did he say how many shots he'd heard?'

'He couldn't remember.'

'The reason I ask ... the fact that only five bullets were found at the scene doesn't necessarily indicate the revolver had only a five-shot capacity.'

'It was empty when the killer tried to finish him off,' Carella said.

'Is that right? Mmm. Well, in any case, the recovered bullets all measured .3585 inches in diameter, which tells us we're dealing with a .38-calibre Smith & Wesson cartridge. Your twist in inches was 18 3/4 to the right, and your groove diameter was .357, which would be the markings a .38 Smith & Wesson revolver would leave on a bullet, and which – when combined with the six lands we found – would seem to point pretty conclusively towards a .38 calibre Smith & Wesson revolver firing .38-calibre Smith & Wesson cartridges. You've got your Regulation Police Model 31 taking Smith & Wesson .38's, and you've got your Terrier Model 32, which also takes the Smith & Wesson .38's, and both guns have a five-shot capacity. Now your Chiefs Special and your Bodyguard

Model and also your Centennial take .38 S & W *Specials*, which have the same twist and groove as your regular .38, but your .38 Special has a different diameter than your .38, and the reading we got – as I told you – was .3585 which is the diameter of a .38 bullet and not a .38 *Special* bullet. Our micrometers here are calibrated to one one-thousandth of an inch, so I don't think we've made any mistakes about the calibre of this gun, it's a .38, all right, and given all the other factors, I'd say a Smith & Wesson .38, either the Regulation Police or the Terrier, both of which have five-shot capacities. Your Regulation Police – what do you carry, Carella ?'

'The Special.'

'Mm, well, your Regulation comes only with a four-inch barrel. Your Terrier comes with a two-inch barrel, and it's a lighter gun, seventeen ounces as opposed to eighteen for the Regulation. Are we dealing with a man or a woman here ?'

'We don't know yet.'

'Not that the ounce makes any difference, but the shorter barrel might. Easier to get in a handbag, do you see ?'

'Yes,' Carella said.

'So that's it,' Gombes said. 'A .38 calibre Smith & Wesson revolver, either the Regulation Police Model 33 or the Terrier Model 32. Hope I was able to help you,' he said, and hung up.

Meyer was still on the phone. Carella went down the hall to the Clerical Office and asked Miscolo to contact Communications and ask them to send out an inter-departmental flier to all precincts asking for any information bearing on a suspect .38 Smith & Wesson revolver, Regulation Police Model 33 or Terrier Model 32, used in a fatal shooting on the night of September 15. Miscolo said he would call Communications as soon as his coffee perked. Carella went back up the hall to the squadroom, where Meyer was just putting up the phone.

'Any luck ?' he asked.

'It wasn't Muscular Dystrophy, and it wasn't Multiple Sclerosis,' Meyer said. 'Maybe it *was* a wedding, after all. Maybe the groom *was* a Dr Harvey Cooper and maybe . . .'

'Let's try the AF of M,' Carella said. 'Find out if they've got a member named Harvey Cooper. If they do . . .'

'Yeah, but will their job records go back seven years ?'

'It's worth a try. If you get anything, move on it. I want to start visiting some of these people who were in Chadderton's appointment calendar.'

'How many names have you got there?'

'Ten or so. Let me see,' Carella said, and began counting the names he'd listed in his notebook. 'Eight that Chloe Chadderton could identify, two she didn't know, and two sets of initials – C.J. and C.C.'

'Have you called any of them yet?'

'I was about to do that now.'

'Want to split the list with me?'

'First see what you get at the AF of M.'

Cynthia Rogers Hargrove was wearing a quilted dressing gown over what appeared to be a granny nightgown with a laced Peter Pan collar. A pearl choker was around her neck. Mrs Hargrove was seventy-six years old if she was a day. She sat opposite Meyer Meyer at a damask-covered table in the dining alcove of her Hall Avenue apartment, the pouring rain streaking eastern windows that might otherwise have been streaming sunshine. Mrs Hargrove spoke with the sort of voice Meyer associated with only the very wealthy – it was not only in Britain that a person's vocal inflections gave away his class. Mrs Hargrove was Vassar out of Rosemary Hall out of private elementary school someplace in the city. Mrs Hargrove was sleek-lined sloops racing off Newport. Mrs Hargrove was afternoon tea in Palm Beach. Mrs Hargrove was breakfast at ten o'clock on a Monday morning when almost everyone else in the city had been up since seven and had consumed his first meal of the day before eight. In this land of the free and home of the brave, in this nation where all men were created equal, Mrs Hargrove was nonetheless living testament to the wag's adage that *some* men were created *more* equal than others. Meyer felt somewhat intimidated in her presence. Perhaps because he'd never eaten a toasted English muffin with genuine Scottish gooseberry jam on it. As he bit into it, he was certain the crunch could be heard clear uptown and crosstown in the very muster room of the Eight-Seven. Hastily, he sipped at his coffee, hoping to muffle the sounds of mastication.

'The Blondie Ball, we called it,' Mrs Hargrove said.

Meyer blinked at her, and then said, 'The Blondie Ball?'

'Yes. Do you know the comic strip characters? Blondie and Dagwood? Are they familar to you?'

'Yes, certainly,' Meyer said.

'That was our theme. The comic strip. More coffee?' she asked, and reached for the silver coffee pot just to the right of her plate. 'How did you happen to get to me?' she asked, pouring.

'I called the AF of M,' Meyer said, 'and they . . .'

'AF of M?'

'American Federation of Musicians.'

'Yes, surely,' Mrs Hargrove said.

'Yes,' Meyer said, 'and asked them if they could check their records . . . I discovered the leader has to file contracts with them, the band leader . . .'

'Oh yes, I would imagine,' Mrs Hargrove said.

'Yes,' Meyer said, 'and I asked them to check on a musician named Harvey Cooper . . .'

'Oh, yes.'

'The name means something to you?'

'Yes, he's the man I hired for the job.'

'Yes,' Meyer said, 'this was seven years ago, September the eleventh, to be exact, this is all information the union gave me. And they also supplied me with your name and address, which was on the contract you signed.'

'Yes, how simple really.'

'It took us a little while to get there,' Meyer said. 'Earlier, we were looking for something sponsored by either the Muscular Dystrophy Foundation or the National Multiple Sclerosis . . .'

'Oh no, nothing quite that grand,' Mrs Hargrove said. 'Do have another muffin, Mr Meyer. They shall go to waste otherwise.'

'But it *was* a charity ball, isn't that so?'

'Yes. But what one might call a *private* charity, rather than one of the national organizations, do you understand?'

'What was the charity?'

'We were trying to establish a scholarship fund for the local high school. So that deserving youngsters might go on to college. Most of the local residents, as you can appreciate, send their children to preparatory schools when they're of age. But the neighbourhood high school is really quite good, and we felt the youngsters there should be given the same opportunities the more privileged young-sters enjoy.'

'I see,' Meyer said. 'So the purpose of the ball was to raise money for this scholarship fund?'

'Yes.'

'How much did you hope to raise?'

'The estimated four-year tuition and living expenses for a student at a quality institution of higher learning is approximately twenty-five thousand dollars. We hoped to raise enough to send three students to college for the full four-year terms.'

'Then you hoped to raise seventy-five thousand dollars?'

'Yes.'

'And how much did you actually raise?'

'Twenty thousand more than that. The ball was quite successful. I imagine the Blondie theme had a lot to do with it.'

'What does that mean actually?' Meyer asked. 'The Blondie theme?'

'Well, it was a fancy dress ball, you understand. The women all had to come as Blondie and the men had to come as Dagwood. Some of them brought their dogs, of course, posing as Daisy, the dog in the strip. I tried to discourage that, I made it clear in the pre-ball announcements that animals were not encouraged, hoping of course they would understand we didn't want a *plethora* of Daisys. But some people missed the point, however bluntly I'd worded it. We had three hundred and eighty Blondies, an equal number of Dagwoods, and at least a dozen Daisys.'

'Dogs running around, do you mean?'

'Yes. Well, not precisely running around. We were prepared for such an occasion, you see. We had contacted an organization that supplies dog-walkers...'

'Dog-walkers?'

'Yes. College students, usually, who'll take dogs for their ritual walks during the *day*, for example, in a situation where both people in a marriage are working people, or at *night* should anyone simply not desire the responsibility of walking an animal – a position I find quite understandable, by the way. I loathe dogs, don't you?'

'Well, I wouldn't say I...'

'Positively loathsome,' Mrs Hargrove said. 'Then again, *all* animals are. Why people would want to keep pets is beyond my imagination. Filthy little things, all of them. In any event, we had this cadre of trained dog-walkers on hand to re-deliver, so to speak, any wayward pup whence it had come. Only two of the patrons objected. One of them had a dachshund that was supposed to represent Daisy, can you visualize that, and the other had a Pekingese. We put them in separate cloakrooms – the dogs, not the patrons – and solved the problem that way. But really, can you imagine what bedlam we'd have had if everyone were allowed to bring a dog? Some people have no sense at all when it comes to animals. None whatsoever. Loathsome beasts, all of them.'

'When you say you had three hundred and eighty Blondies . . .'

'Yes, we sold that many admission tickets. Two hundred and fifty dollars a couple. Three hundred and eighty women masquerading as Blondie and three hundred and eighty men with their hair sticking up in front, the way Dagwood's sticks up – the poor man has a cowlick at the front of his head – and wearing bow ties. Blondie and Dagwood.'

'What was the purpose of that, Mrs Hargrove?'

'The purpose? Oh, it was just a gimmick, Mr Meyer. But it earned us ninety-five thousand dollars in admissions, which wasn't bad. And the Cadillac we gave as first prize for the best impersonation was donated by a local dealer.'

'Was there a contest or something for the best costume?'

'Well, not merely the costume. Dagwood and Blondie, after all, are not that distinctively dressed in the comic strip. In fact, I think it was the very simplicity of the theme that accounted for its success, don't you see? The women, after all, could wear whatever they chose, so long as they were blonde in the bargain. And the men only needed a bow tie and a little hair pomade. But it was for the overall *impression* that the prize was awarded. The way a couple walked and moved, the *re*presentation, the im*per*sonation of Blondie and Dagwood. They were all masked, you understand . . .'

'Masked, yes.'

'Yes. So there was absolutely no question of favouritism on the part of the judges. They could judge only by . . . oh, intangibles. Whether a couple actually created the *image* of the comic strip characters come to life.'

'I see. If I understand this correctly then, *all* of the women were wearing blonde wigs.'

'Well, not all of them.'

'You said ...'

'Yes, but some of them were natural blondes.'

'Oh yes, of course.'

'Or if not natural blondes, at least accepting a little assistance from a beautician. *Those* women, of course, did not *need* wigs.'

'Of course not.'

'But you're correct in assuming that the overall impression was of a ballroom *full* of three hundred and eighty blondes, yes.'

'Yes,' Meyer said.

'Yes.'

'All of them masked,' Meyer said.

'Yes. Which is where I think the fun came in, don't you? Can you picture a room full of masked blonde women? Doesn't it sound a great deal of fun?'

'Yes,' Meyer said, 'it does. Mrs Hargrove, the musicians' union told me the affair was held at the Hotel Palomar ...'

'Yes, downtown, directly opposite the Palomar Theatre.'

'Which ballroom, ma'am, can you remember?'

'Yes, the Stardust Ballroom.'

'Is that a large ballroom?'

'Not so large as their *Grand* Ballroom, but we didn't want a room so enormous that the people would rattle around in it. We rather cherished the notion, you see, of all those masked blondes and masked men in polka-dot ties dancing cheek to cheek and buttock to buttock in a more intimate ballroom. That's why we chose the Stardust Ballroom. That was the fun of it, you see, that was the point.'

'Did you have any opportunity to talk with any of the musicians that night, Mrs Hargrove?'

'Only Mr Cooper. Mr Cooper handled all the arrangements for me, my contract was with Mr Cooper, he supplied both bands. They were quite good actually. The other band played Latin-type music, do you know?' she said, and lifted both hands and snapped her fingers.

'But aside from Mr Cooper, you didn't talk to any of the musicians in either band?'

'No sir, I did not.'

'Then the name George Chadderton would mean nothing to you.'

'Nothing whatsoever.'

'Or Santo Chadderton?'

'Nothing,' Mrs Hargrove said.

All the way uptown, Meyer kept thinking of an expression Mrs Hargrove had used: a plethora of Daisys. Take the last word out of the proper-name category and basket it, so to speak, as a common noun in the plural, and you end up with 'A Plethora of Daisies', which – it seemed to Meyer – was an uncommonly good title for a novel. He had begun noticing of late how many lousy novels had very good titles, and was beginning to suspect that a good title was enough to sell even the most meretricious book. He could see the title A Plethora of Daisies adorning the jacket of a hardcover novel. He could see it in perhaps less refined type on the cover of a paperback book, *A Plethora of Daisies*, he could see it in lights on a movie marquee: A PLETHORA OF DAISIES. He really liked that damn title.

When he got back to the squadroom, he told Carella all about his meeting with Mrs Hargrove, and Carella told him all about his visits with two of the people on his list of names – Buster Greerson and Lester Hanley – both of whom had shared strictly business, and somewhat casual, relationships with Chadderton. One of them expressed surprise that he was dead; the other had read about it in the papers. Carella and Meyer both agreed it was a damn shame there'd been so many blondes in attendance – natural, bleached or bewigged – that night seven years ago, since all they knew about the woman who'd spent a goodly amount of time with Santo was that she was a tall willowy California-type blonde. This was the first time the word 'willowy' had put in an appearance; it was Meyer who used the adjective, perhaps because he'd been thinking novelistically ever since leaving Mrs Hargrove.

'I got a list of all the guests from her,' he said, 'and I ...'

'The Blondie Ball,' Carella said, shaking his head.

'Yeah, the Blondie Ball. Not the ones who bought tickets at the door, but everybody else. I thought I might check the Palomar, just to see if anybody on the guest list also happened to take a room there that night.'

'You can check it,' Carella said, 'but I think it'll be a waste of time. We've got ourselves a plenitude of blondes . . .'

'Not to mention a plethora of daisies,' Meyer said.

'And we don't even know which of them were *real* blondes. So even if one of the guests did check into a room with Santo, how's the hotel register going to indicate that fact? All we'll know is that somebody who was at the ball happened to stay at the hotel that night. What we *won't* know . . .'

That was when the telephone rang.

It was a Detective Alex Leopold of Midtown South calling to say he'd caught their flier on the suspect .38, and thought there might be a connection between their case and the one he was handling – a hooker shot to death on the sidewalk late Friday night, with a weapon Ballistics said had been a .38 Smith & Wesson.

Alex Leopold was a dyspeptic little man (little for a police detective; actually, he was five feet ten inches tall) who immediately told Carella and Meyer that he wished he was still back at the Eleventh Precinct in Calm's Point. In the Eleventh, you didn't get hookers killed on a Friday night. In the Eleventh, which was the precinct enclosing exclusive Calm's Point Heights (Cee Pee Aitch, as it was known affectionately to any foot patrolman lucky enough to claim the area as his beat), the most vigorous crime reported in a month of Sundays would have been the burglarizing of a famous novelist's apartment, or the kidnapping of a prize pootch from the town house of a suburban artist who used the Cee Pee Aitch address as a *pied à terre* in the city. Cee Pee Aitch still had gaslit lamp posts in its quaint old cobblestoned streets. Cee Pee Aitch did not have hookers in its quaint old cobblestoned streets; in the Eleventh, Alex Leopold would have been surprised indeed to have found a dead one on his doorstep.

The hooker found dead this past Friday night (well, really 4.12 a.m. on Saturday *morning*, but dark in the streets, and night in the streets, and whereas the DD report was dated 9/16, Leopold thought of it as 9/15 in his mind) hadn't exactly been found on his doorstep, but close enough for comfort nonetheless, the Midtown South station house being on Jefferson and Purdy, three blocks from where Clara Jean Hawkins was left bleeding on the sidewalk with a fatal bullet-hole tunnel drilled through her chest and her heart, another hole in her larynx, and yet another in her face, just to the right of her nose. Leopold had taken the squeal at 4.15 a.m., three minutes after a citizen called on the 911 emergency number to report somebody bleeding on the sidewalk. By the time he got to the scene, Forbes and Phelps from Homicide were already standing there in the rain, bitching. In all the years Leopold had worked out of the Eleventh, he had never handled a homicide. He had worked there for twenty-two years. He made the mistake of mentioning this to either Phelps or Forbes, he couldn't tell them apart and didn't care to, and they immediately categorized him as a sissy cop from a silk-stocking precinct, which wasn't far from the truth, but which irked the shit out of him at 4.15 a.m. on a rainy Friday night/Saturday morning with a black girl full of holes lying dead on the sidewalk.

The only identification in her handbag was a social security card with her name on it: Clara Jean Hawkins. No driver's licence, no credit cards, no electric or telephone company bills, just the social security card. At the scene, Forbes or Phelps, or perhaps both, suggested that perhaps the girl was a hooker – what with it being four o'clock in the morning and all – but Leopold put this notion aside, accustomed as he was to the high level of crime in the Eleventh. He routinely did what had to be done, and then went back to the office to consult the city's telephone directories. There were seventy-eight listings for Hawkins in the Isola directory alone. Determined to call each and every one of them – it was by then ten past five in the morning, when most decent citizens were asleep – he began dialling and struck paydirt at 5.27 a.m. when a sleepy-voiced woman named Dorothy Hawkins said Yes, she knew Clara Jean Hawkins, Clara Jean was her daughter.

Now, at a quarter past noon, some fifty-five hours after Leopold had located the girl's mother, he gave his report to Carella and Meyer. 'Turned out she hasn't been living at home for the past few months now,' he said. 'Her mother says she was a hooker, lived in a pad run by a pimp named Joey Peace. I never heard of him, I'm from the Eleventh.'

'I never heard of him, either,' Meyer said.

'Just goes to show,' Leopold said, and wagged his head philosophically.

'Did you try to get a line on him from the IS?' Carella asked.

'No record. Not under the Peace alias, anyway. That's got to be an alias, don't you think? Joey Peace? That can't be the man's kosher handle.'

'Did you try the phone book?' Carella asked.

'Yeah, no Peace. The dead girl's mother doesn't know who he is, she only heard her daughter mention the name. Doesn't know who any of the other girls are, either, the three others who are supposed to be living in the apartment with her daughter and this Peace character. So where do I go from here? I've got a positive make on the girl, and I know what she did for a living – according to her mother, anyway. But that's all I know so far, and all I'm likely to know unless *your* case can throw some light on *mine*.'

'Few possibilities we ought to check out first,' Carella said.

'Like what?' Leopold asked.

'Well,' Carella said, 'I think we ought to drop in on the various hot-bed hotels in the Midtown South area, find out if anyone recognizes the girl's name or her picture, see if we can't get a line on her pimp that way. Under ordinary circumstances, we wouldn't get any cooperation. But this is a homicide, they may be willing to tell us what they know. Next, I think we ought to check out the massage parlours. Same questions – do you know anybody named Clara Jean Hawkins, do you know anybody named Joey Peace, tell them right out the girl is dead and we're trying to find her killer, hint it might be some psycho sex-fiend customer, scare them a little. Next, it wouldn't hurt to chat up some of the active pimps in the Eleventh, I'm sure there's a file on them in your office – I'm surprised, in fact, that you haven't got at least a *card* on this Joey Peace. Anyway, let's find out who's working the precinct, and chat them up, no threats of arrest, nothing like that, just a nice kerbside heart-to-heart, all we want to know is who's Clara Jean Hawkins, and who's this guy Joey Peace. We might hit paydirt, who knows? So okay? First the hotels and massage parlours, and then the pimps themselves. Meanwhile, we'll put out a flier on Joey Peace, just an info request to all precincts, one of them might have something on him in their Lousy File. I'm really glad you called, Leopold. We'd about come to a dead end.'

'Yeah,' Leopold said. There was a dazed expression on his face. He wasn't quite sure *he* was so glad he'd called.

9

There is nothing cops like better than continuity, even if it takes a couple of corpses to provide it. Before Alex Leopold raised his baffled head, Carella and Meyer were looking for a connection between the dead George Chadderton and his missing brother Santo. Now, thanks to a few .38 calibre Smith & Wesson slugs, they were looking for a connection between a dead calypso singer and a dead hooker, both of them black, and both of them from Diamondback, both of them possibly killed with the same weapon. Now that the preliminary connection had been made, Carella asked Ballistics to compare the bullets that had slain Clara Jean Hawkins with the bullets that had slain George Chadderton in an attempt to pinpoint positively whether or not the weapon had been used in both murders. He asked for a rush on the comparison tests, and Gombes promised he'd get back to him by four that afternoon, saying he would ordinarily have tackled the job sooner except that they'd just got what seemed like a breakthrough in a sniper case that had been baffling the Three-Six for months, and he had to get to that first. He called back at ten minutes to five. He called to report that the same gun, most likely a .38 Smith & Wesson, either the Regulation Police or the Terrier, had very definitely been used in both murders. He asked Carella if there was anything else he could do for him at the moment. Carella told him no, and thanked him, and then hung up and sat staring at the phone for several moments.

He had by that time spent most of the afternoon with Leopold and Meyer, doing all the legwork he'd earlier suggested. They had together hit all of Midtown South's hot-bed hotels and massage parlours, and had talked to most of the pimps in the precinct's Lousy File, but they still had not come up with a make on Joey Peace. Sighing, Carella picked up the phone again and called first Danny Gimp and then Fats Donner, both valued police informers, to ask if they knew a hooker named Clara Jean Hawkins or a pimp named Joey Peace. Fats Donner, who was rather more sexually orientated than Danny Gimp, laughed when he heard the pimp's name, and then asked if it was spelled P-I-E-C-E, which he thought might be a singularly good name for a pimp. He had nonetheless never heard of a gentleman of leisure who called himself by such a monicker. Neither had Danny Gimp. Both men promised to go on the earie, but each expressed doubt that he'd come up with anything. 'Very often,' Fats said in his most unctuously oily pale blubbery way, 'a pimp will use a nickname known only to the girls in his own stable. This is protection against other pimps, not to mention the law.' Carella thanked him for invaluable insight into the world's oldest profession, and then hung up.

He was feeling testy and irritable. According to George Chadderton's appointment calendar, the singer had seen Clara Jean Hawkins a total of four times before each of them was killed, and was scheduled for another meeting with her on the day after the murders. The first two calendar entries had called her 'Hawkins', and the remaining three had called her 'C.J.' It was possible that these androgynous jottings, considering the lady's occupation, were designed to throw Chloe Chadderton off the track. But if the singer had been enjoying the dead girl's professional services, why would he have risked listing his appointments with her at *all*? If their relationship had been purely sexual, would he for Christ's sake have put it in writing? Frowning, Carella went to where Meyer was typing up his report on the visit to Mrs Hargrove.

'I think it's time we had a meeting on this damn case,' he said.

It *was*, in fact, time to put on the old thinking caps, time to become deductive detectives, time to become reasoning *raissoneurs*, time to look into that old crystal ball and dope this thing out. So they got together in a police ritual as old as time, hoping to snowball the case – throw in ideas and suppositions, shoot down some theories, elaborate on others. The men involved in the crap game were Carella and Meyer, the detectives officially assigned to the Chadderton case; Lieutenant Peter Byrnes, who was in command of the squad and had every right to know what his men were up to; Detective Cotton Hawes, whose puritanical upbringing often succeeded in bringing back to stark Bostonian reality any theory that was veering too far from magnetic north; and Detective Bert Kling, whose boyish good looks masked a mind as innocent as a baby's backside.

'He's got to be new on the job,' Meyer said.

'No arrests yet,' Carella said.

'Which is why there's nothing on him down at IS,' Kling said.

'Or in the various Lousy Files around town,' Carella said.

'And which is why he's only got four chicks in his stable,' Hawes said, totally unaware that he'd mixed a metaphor. He sat perched on the edge of Meyer's desk, the rain-soaked windows tracing a slithering pattern across his face, lending to it a somewhat frightening look. The look was strengthened by the fact that Hawes had a white streak running through his red hair, just above the left temple, a memento from a knife-wielding building superintendent away back then when Hawes was but a neophyte cop who never mixed his metaphors.

'Nothing in the phone book, huh?' Kling asked.

'Nothing.'

'Okay,' Byrnes said, somewhat brusquely, 'so far you're handling Leopold's case brilliantly. You're tracking down the pimp the girl worked for, wonderful, you'll probably find him one of these days, and maybe you'll learn he didn't like the way she was doing her nails or combing her hair, so maybe he put a couple of .38 slugs in her last Friday night, great. If you're right, you've solved Leopold's case and he'll get a promotion to Detective/First, great. Meanwhile, what are you doing to find *Chadderton's* killer?'

Byrnes delivered this somewhat lengthy (for Byrnes) speech in a tone of voice entirely devoid of sarcasm. His blue eyes were without the slightest trace of malicious amusement, his mouth betrayed neither smirk nor snarl, his words were in fact as mild as the balmy zephyrs of spring, which warm breezes all the detectives gathered around Meyer's desk would have preferred to the blustery rain outside the squadroom this very moment. But they all knew Byrnes pretty well, they had all over the years grown accustomed to his flat delivery and his no-nonsense appearance, the iron-grey hair and the blue eyes that followed you like tracer bullets in the night. They heard each word fall soddenly now like the raindrops outside, *ploppity-plop-plip* on to Meyer's desk top and on to the worn green linoleum around the desk, *ploppity-plip-plop* all over their case like a big puppy pissing on paper under the kitchen sink.

'Well, what we thought . . .' Carella said.

'Mm, what did you think?' Byrnes asked, again without sarcasm, but somehow his words kept dampening things.

'We thought the connection between the girl and the pimp . . .'

'Mm-huh?'

'Is ... uh ... Chadderton wrote a song about a hooker.'

'He did, huh?' Byrnes said.

'Yes, sir,' Carella said. 'In which he exhorts her ...'

'Exhorts?' Byrnes said.

'Yes, sir. Exhorts, right?' Carella said to Hawes.

'Sure, exhorts.'

'Exhorts her to quit being a whore, you know.'

'Uh-huh,' Byrnes said.

'So what we thought ...' Meyer said.

'What we thought,' Carella said, 'is that *if* this Joey Peace is the one who killed the *girl*, then since it's the same *gun* and all, since Ballistics has nailed it as the same *gun*, then maybe he *also* killed George Chadderton because Chadderton was trying to convince the girl to get out of the life and all.'

'Where does it say that?' Byrnes asked.

'That Chadderton was trying to convince the Hawkins girl to get out of the life.'

'That's just a supposition,' Carella said.

'Ah,' Byrnes said.

'But he *did* write a song about a hooker,' Hawes said.

'Where does it say the song's about this particular hooker?' Byrnes said.

'Well ... I don't know,' Hawes said. 'Steve, *is* it about this particular hooker?'

'Not according to Harding.'

'Who's Harding?' Kling asked.

'Chadderton's business manager. He says Chadderton's songs weren't about anybody in particular.'

'Then he *wasn't* writing about the Hawkins girl,' Byrnes said.

'Well, I ... guess not,' Carella said.

'Then where's the connection?'

'I don't know yet. But, Pete, they were killed with the same damn pistol. Now *that's* connection enough, isn't it?'

'It's connection enough,' Byrnes said, 'yes. And it'll be very nice if when you find this Joey Peace, you also find a Smith & Wesson .38 Police Special ...'

'No, either a Regulation or a Terrier,' Carella said.

'What*ever*,' Byrnes said. 'It'll be very nice if you find the murder weapon tucked in his socks or his undershorts, and it'll be very nice if he admits he killed the girl and also killed Chadderton in the bargain because Chadderton wrote a song about somebody who could've been the Hawkins girl, so yes, it'll be very nice if Joey Peace is your man. But, gentlemen, I can tell you after too many damn years in this lousy business that nothing is ever as easy as it seems it might be, nothing ever is. And if it stops raining this very goddam minute, I for one will be very goddam surprised.'

It did not stop raining that very goddam minute.

The only thing that ended that minute was the meeting. Hawes and Kling went home, Byrnes went back into his office, and Meyer went back to his desk to finish typing up his report. Carella phoned Midtown South and asked to speak to Detective Leopold, intending to report to him on the positive finding from Ballistics. He was advised by a detective named Peter Sherman that Leopold had left for the day. Carella hung up, checked his personal phone listings for the name 'Palacios, Francisco', and dialled the number.

Francisco Palacios owned and operated a store that sold medicinal herbs, dream books, religious statues, numbers books, tarot cards, and the like. Gaucho Palacios and Cowboy Palacios ran a store *behind* the other store, and *this* one offered for sale such medically approved 'marital aids' as dildoes, French ticklers, open-crotch panties, vibrators (eight-inch and ten-inch), leather executioner's masks, chastity belts, whips with leather thongs, and ben-wa balls in both plastic and gold plate. The sale of these items was not illegal in this city; the Gaucho and the Cowboy were breaking no laws, this was not why the ran their store *behind* the store owned and operated by Francisco. Instead, they did so out of a sense of responsibility to the Puerto Rican community. They did not, for example, want an old lady in a black shawl to wander into their shop and faint dead away at the sight of the playing-cards featuring men, women, police dogs and midgets in fifty-two marital-aid positions, fifty-*four* if you counted the jokers. Both the Gaucho and the Cowboy had community pride to match that of Francisco himself. Francisco, the Gaucho and the Cowboy were, in fact, all one and the same person, and they were collectively a police informer.

'Palacios,' a voice said.

'Cowboy, this is Steve Carella, I need some help.'

'Name it,' the Gaucho said.

'I'm looking for a pimp named Joey Peace. Ever hear of him?'

'Not offhand. Is he from here in El Infierno?'

'Don't know anything about him but his name. Supposed to have had four hookers in his stable, one of them murdered this past Friday night.'

'What's her name?'

'Clara Jean Hawkins.'

'White, black?'

'Black.'

'Okay, let me check around. You gonna be there tomorrow?'

'I'll be here,' Carella said.

'I'll call you.'

'Thanks,' Carella said, and hung up. It was still raining. He walked to where Meyer was busily typing at his own desk, and told him he was heading uptown to Diamondback to talk to the dead girl's mother – did Meyer want to come along? Considering the tone of Carella's voice, Meyer thought it might be best to accept the invitation graciously.

Dorothy Hawkins was a light-complexioned black woman in her early fifties, Carella guessed, her body sinewy rather than slender, her face gaunt rather than finely chiselled; even Meyer, with his newfound novelistic turn of mind, might have chosen those more severe descriptive adjectives to define the woman who opened the door for them and let them into her Pettit Lane apartment. The time was 6.30 p.m. Mrs Hawkins explained that she had just got home from work. She worked assembling transistor radios in a factory out on Bethtown. A shot glass of whisky sat on the kitchen table before her; she explained that it was bourbon and asked the detectives if they would care for some.

'Take the chill off this mis'able rainy weather,' she said.

When the detectives declined, she drank the whisky neat and in a single swallow, and then went to the cabinet, took down the half-full bottle and poured herself another shot. The detectives sat opposite her at the kitchen table. A wall clock threw minutes into the room. There were no cooking smells in the apartment; Carella wondered if Mrs Hawkins planned to drink her dinner. Outside, lighting tinted the slanting rain, transmogrifying the window pane trickles into nests of disturbed green snakes.

'Mrs Hawkins,' Carella said, 'my partner and I are investigating a case we feel is linked to your daughter's death, and we'd like to ask you some questions about it. If you feel you'd like to answer them, we'd be most appreciative.'

'Yes, anythin,' she said.

'First off,' he said, 'do you know anyone named George Chadderton?'

'No,' she said.

'We have reason to believe that he knew your daughter. Did she ever mention him in your presence?'

'I don't recall hearin his name, no.'

'Nor Santo Chadderton, is that right?' Meyer asked.

'Nor him neither,' Mrs Hawkins said.

'Ma'am,' Carella said, 'you told Detective Leopold that your daughter was a prostitute ...'

'Yes, that's true.'

'How did you know that for a fact?'

'Clara Jean told me.'

'When did she tell you this?'

'Two, three weeks ago.'

'Until that time, did you have any idea she was ...'

'I had an idea, but I wasn't sure. She kept tellin me she was workin nights some hotel downtown. Doin some kind of clerkin work downtown.'

'Did she mention any hotel by name?' Carella asked at once.

'She did, but I forget it now.'

'Downtown where?'

'I don't remember. I ain't too familiar the other parts of the city 'cept Diamondback here.'

'When did she stop living here, Mrs Hawkins?' Meyer asked.

'Oh, got to be six months at least. Told me she needed t'live closer to the job, the hotel where she was clerkin nights. Said it was dangerous takin the subway uptown here after she finished work, three, four o'clock in the mornin. I could unnerstan that, it seemed reasonable to me.'

'And you didn't suspect anything at the time?'

'No, she was always a good girl, never had no trouble with her. Never hung aroun the street gangs like some of the other girls this neighbourhood, never messed with dope. She was a good girl, Clara Jean.'

'You're sure about the dope, are you?' Meyer said.

'Positive. You go ask the doctor done the autopsy. You ask him did he find any dope inside my little girl, did he find any marks on her arms or legs, you just ask him. I used to watch her like a hawk, search her arms an legs every afternoon when she come home from school, every night when she come home from a date. If I'da seed so much as a pin prick, I'da broke her head.'

'Where'd she go to school, Mrs Hawkins?'

'Right here in Diamondback. Edward Victor High.'

'Did she graduate?'

'Last January.'

'Then what?'

'She took a month off, said she wanted a li'l rest before she started lookin for work. In March, she got a job waitressin here in Diamondback, but she wasn't makin much money at it, so she left that in April musta been, and took the job clerkin at the hotel downtown – leastwise that's what she tole me. Moved out of here in May. How many months is that?'

'Five, ma'am.'

'I thought it was six. I tole you *six* before, didn't I?'

'Yes, ma'am.'

'Well, it's five then.' She shook her head. 'Seems longer.'

'Where was she waitressing?' Meyer asked.

'Caribou Corner, here in Diamondback. That's a steak joint, I don't know why they give it such a godawful name. A caribou's some kind of big *moose* or somethin, ain't it?'

'I think so,' Meyer said.

'Name like that don't make *me* want to eat no steak, I can tell you that.'

'Caribou Corner,' Carella said. 'C.C.'

'Pardon?' Mrs Hawkins said.

'Right, that's what it meant,' Meyer said. 'Clara Jean at Caribou Corner.'

'Mrs Hawkins,' Carella said, 'are you *certain* your daughter never mentioned anyone named George Chadderton?'

'I'm positive.'

'When she moved out, did she take everything she owned with her? All her personal possessions? Diaries, address books . . .'

'Didn't keep no diary. But she took all her other things with her, yes. You mean where she kept her phone numbers an all?'

'Yes.'

'Took 'em with her.'

'Did she leave *anything* of hers here?'

'Well, some nightgowns an a few bras and panties, like that. So if she come up to spend a day an she needed somethin to sleep in, or a fresh change of underthings, they'd be handy.'

'Did she come here often?'

'Ever now and then.'

'When did you last see her alive?'

'Thursday.'

'She was here this past Thursday?'

'Well, past two months, she been comin home ever Thursday.'

'Why's that?'

'Just to see her mama, I guess,' Mrs Hawkins said, and suddenly avoided Carella's eyes.

'Mm-huh,' he said. 'This is something new, though, huh? The Thursday visits?'

'Well, past couple of months.'

'You say she moved out in May . . .'

'Yes, May.'

'And this is September.'

'That's right.'

'So if she started visiting you on Thursdays a couple of months ago . . .'

'That's right, Thursdays.'

'That'd mean she started visiting you in July, is that right?'

'I s'pose,' Mrs Hawkins said.

'Had she come to see you at all in May and June?'

'No, that's when she just moved out, you know.'

'But in July she started coming up here every Thursday.'

'Yes,' Mrs Hawkins said. Her eyes still would not meet his. She rose suddenly, went to the cabinet, took down the bottle of bourbon and poured herself another shot. She drained the glass at once, and poured it full again. Silently, the detectives watched her.

'Mrs Hawkins,' Carella said, 'have you got any idea why your daughter suddenly started coming up here every Thursday?'

'I tole you. To see her mama,' Mrs Hawkins said, and lifted the shot glass again.

'What time did she usually get here?'

'Oh, in the mornin sometime.'

'What time in the morning?'

'Oh, sometime before noon. I'd be at work, you see, but I'd usually call on my lunch hour, and she'd be here.'

'Sleeping?'

'What?'

'When you called, would she be sleeping?'

'No, no, wide awake.'

'Did she ever mention having worked the night before?'

'Well, I never asked her. When she first started comin, I thought she was workin for that hotel, you see. Wednesday night was when she got paid, she tole me, and Thursday was when she come uptown to see her mama.'

'With her paycheque?'

'Well, no, it was cash.'

'How much cash?'

'Well . . . two hundred dollars ever Thursday.'

'And you never suspected that this money might be coming from prostitution?'

'No, I never did. Clara Jean was a good girl.'

'But finally she told you.'

'Yes.'

'Just two or three weeks ago.'

'Yes.'

'What'd she tell you?'

'That she was prostitutin herself, and that the man takin care of her an three other girls was somebody named Joey Peace.'

'Confessed all this to you, huh?'

'Yes.'

'How come?'

'We was feelin close that day. I had taken sick and didn't go to work, and when Clara Jean come to see me, she made me some soup an we sat in the bedroom watchin television together. Just before she went to the . . .' Mrs Hawkins cut herself short.

'Yes?' Carella said.

'Down to the grocery,' Mrs Hawkins said, 'she tole me what she'd been doin these past months, the prostitutin herself, you know.'

'Did she say anything about that two hundred dollars every week?'

'Well, no, she didn't.'

'She didn't mention, for example, that this might be money she was keeping from Joey Peace?'

'No, she never said nothin about that.'

'Because you know, I guess, that most pimps demand *all* of a girl's earnings,' Carella said.

'I woulda guessed that.'

'Yet your daughter came around with two hundred dollars in cash every Thursday.'

'Yes. Well, yes, she did,' Mrs Hawkins said, and lifted the shot glass again.

'Did she take it with her when she left?'

'Well, I . . . I just never asked her what she done with it.'

'Then how'd you know she had it with her each week?'

'She showed it to me one time.'

'Showed you two hundred dollars in cash?'

'That's right, yes.'

'Just the one time?'

'Well . . . I guess more than one time.'

'How *many* times, Mrs Hawkins?'

'Well, I guess . . . I s'pose ever time she come here.'

'*Every* time? *Every* Thursday?'

'Yes.'

'Showed you two hundred dollars in cash every Thursday?'

'Yes.'

'Why?'

'I . . . I don't unnerstan what you mean.'

'Why did she show you two hundred dollars in cash every Thursday?'

'Well, she didn't exactly *show* it to me.'

'Then what *did* she do?'

'Just tole me she had it, that's all.'

'Why?'

'So I'd know that ... so I'd ... so in case anythin happened to her ...'

'Did she think something was about to happen to her?' Meyer asked at once.

'No, no.'

'Then why'd she want you to know about the money?'

'Well, just in case, that's all,' Mrs Hawkins said, and reached again for the bourbon bottle.

'Hold off on the sauce a minute,' Carella said. 'What was your daughter doing with that two hundred bucks a week?'

'I don't know,' Mrs Hawkins said, and shrugged.

'Was she hiding it here from her pimp?' Meyer asked.

'No,' Mrs Hawkins said, and shook her head.

'Then where was she keeping it?' Carella asked.

Mrs Hawkins did not answer.

'If not here, where?' Meyer said.

'A bank?' Carella said.

'What bank?' Meyer said.

'Where?' Carella said.

'A bank, yes,' Mrs Hawkins said.

'Which one?'

'The State National. On Culver and Hughes.'

'A savings account?' Carella asked.

'Yes.'

'Where's the passbook?'

'I don't know. Clara Jean kept it in her pocketbook, she always had it in her pocketbook when she come up here.'

'No, she didn't keep it in her pocketbook,' Meyer said. 'It wasn't in her pocketbook the night she was killed.'

'Well then maybe it's in that apartment she lived in with the other girls.'

'No, if she was hiding the money from her pimp, she wouldn't have kept the passbook in that apartment.'

'So where is it, Mrs Hawkins?'

'Well, I just got no idea.'

'Mrs Hawkins, is it *here*? Is the passbook here in this apartment?'

'Not to my knowledge. Not unless Clara Jean left it here without tellin me about it.'

'Mrs Hawkins,' Carella said, 'I think it's here in this apartment, and I think you *know* it's here, I think you know *exactly* where it is, and I think you ought to go get it for us because it might...'

'Why?' Mrs Hawkins said, suddenly and angrily, 'so you can go to the bank and take out all the money?'

'How could we possibly do that?' Carella asked.

'If you got the passbook, you could take out all the money.'

'Is that what *you* plan to do?' Meyer asked.

'What *I* plan to do is *my* business, not *yours*. I know the police, don't think I don't know the police. Firemen, too, we don't call them The Forty Thieves for nothin in this neighbourhood. I had a fire in my apartment on St Sebastian once, they stole ever'thin wasn't nailed to the floor. So don't tell me about the police an the firemen. You done that autopsy on her 'thout checkin with me, didn't you? Her own mother, nobody ast was it all right to cut her up that way.'

'An autopsy is mandatory in a homicide,' Carella said.

'Ain't nobody ast me was it all right,' Mrs Hawkins said.

'Ma'am, they were trying to ...'

'I *know* what they was tryin to do, don't you think I know about bullets an all? But they shoulda ast. Was I a white woman livin on Hall Avenue, they'da ast in a minute. So you think I'm gonna turn over a bank account got twenty-six hundred dollars in it? So somebody can go draw out all the money, and that's the last I'll see or hear of it? I know the police, don't think I don't know how you operate, all of you. Take me six months to earn that kinda money after taxes.'

'Mrs Hawkins,' Meyer said, 'the passbook is worthless to us. And possibly to you as well.'

'Worth twenty-six hundred dollars, that passbook.'

'Not unless it's a joint account,' Meyer said.

'Or a trust account,' Carella said.

'I don't know what neither of those mean.'

'Whose name is on the passbook?' Carella asked.

'Clara Jean's.'

'Then, ma'am, the bank simply will not honour any signature but hers without letters testamentary or letters of administration.'

'Clara Jean's dead.' Mrs Hawkins said, 'Ain't no way she can sign her name no more.'

'That's true. Which means the bank'll hold that money until a court determines what's to be done with it.'

'What you *think's* gonna be done with it? They was only me an Clara Jean in the family, I'm all who's left now, they'll give the money to me, that's what.'

'I'm sure they will. But in the meantime, no one can touch it, Mrs Hawkins. Not you, not us, not anybody.' Carella paused. 'May we see the passbook? All we need is the account number.'

'Why? So you can get the bank to pay over the money to you?'

'Mrs Hawkins, you surely can't believe that any bank in this city would turn over money in a personal savings account ...'

'I don't know *what* to believe no more,' Mrs Hawkins said, and suddenly began weeping.

'Where's the passbook?' Carella asked.

'In the ... there's a vase on top of the television set in my bedroom. It's in the vase. I figured nobody'd search in the vase,' she said, drying her eyes and suddenly looking across the kitchen table to Carella. 'Don't steal the money,' she said. 'If you got ways of stealing it from me, please don't. That's my daughter's blood in that account. That's the money was gonna buy her out of the life.'

'What do you mean?' Carella said.

'The record album,' Mrs Hawkins said. 'That's the money was gonna get that album made.'

'What album?' Meyer said.

'The idea she had for an album.'

'Yes, *what* album?'

'About all her experiences in the life.'

'In The Life,' Carella said, and looked at Meyer. 'There it is. There's the connection. Who was going to do this album, Mrs Hawkins? Did she say?'

'No, she only tole me she needed three thousand dollars for it. Said she was gonna get rich from it, take us both out of Diamondback, maybe move to California. So ... please don't steal that money from me. If ... if a court's got to decide, like you say, then let them decide. I was thinkin, you see, of maybe goin west, like Clara Jean wanted for us, but if you steal that money from me ...'

And suddenly she was weeping again.

*

They did not take the passbook when they left Dorothy Hawkins' apartment because, frankly, they weren't sure of their right to do so, and they didn't want any later static about misappropriation, especially this month when fourteen cops at the Two-One in Majesta had been arrested by departmental shooflies for selling narcotics previously appropriated from sundry arrested addicts and pushers. Carella and Meyer were too experienced to go begging for trouble, not when they knew that all they needed was the passbook number and a court order asking the bank to release to them a duplicate statement on the account from the day of initial deposit to the present date.

Early Tuesday morning, in a teeming rain that was causing all the city's forecasters to crack jokes about arks, they drove downtown to High Street, and requested and obtained an order from a municipal judge. At ten minutes to eleven that same Tuesday morning, September 19, the manager of the State National Bank on Culver Avenue and Hughes Street in Diamondback read the order and promptly asked his secretary to have a duplicate statement prepared for 'these gentlemen from the Police Department'. Carella and Meyer felt vaguely flattered. The photocopy was made within minutes; they left the bank at precisely 11.01, and went to sit in Carella's automobile, where together they looked over the figures. The day was not only wet, it had turned unseasonably cold as well. The engine was running, the heater was on, the windshield fogged over as the men read the statement.

Clara Jean Hawkins had opened the account on June 22, with a deposit of two hundred dollars. There had since been twelve regular weekly deposits of two hundred dollars, up to and including the last one made on September 14, just before her death. Thirteen deposits in all, for a balance of twenty-six hundred dollars. A glance at Carella's pocket calendar showed that the dates of deposit were all Thursdays, corroborating Mrs Hawkins' statement that her daughter visited every week on that day. That was all they learned from Clara Jean Hawkins' savings account.

It seemed like a hell of a long way to have to come for very little.

10

Just as Meyer had felt *A Plethora of Daisies* would have been a magnificent title for a novel about, for example, a man who is stabbed through the heart with the stem of a frozen daisy, the murder weapon thereafter melting in the eighty-degree heat, if only something like that hadn't been done in Dick Tracy when Meyer was just a kid being chased around the goddamn neighbourhood by friendly goyim, he now felt similarly – and in agreement with Mrs Hawkins – that Caribou Corner was perhaps the worst name ever devised for a restaurant, and especially for a steak joint. In trying to think up names that were potentially worse when it came to attracting customers to an eatery, he could think only of The Hairy Buffalo. The hero of *A Plethora of Daisies* would take his girlfriend to a steak joint called The Hairy Buffalo. Somebody there would shoot at him from behind a purple curtain. The hero's name would be either Matthew, John, Peter, Andrew, Thomas, Jude, Phillip, Bartholomew, Simon or James the Greater or Less since most good guys in fiction were named after the twelve apostles, the exception being anybody named Judas Iscariot who – five would get you ten – turned out to be a bad guy, and who had already been replaced by Matthias, anyway. Sometimes, good guys were named after Paul or Barnabas, alternate apostles. Sometimes they were named after other biblical chaps like Mark, Luke or Timothy. Bad guys were generally called Frank, Randy, Jug, Billy-Boy or Baldy. Nice wishy-washy guys were called Larry, Eugene, Richie and Sammy (but not Sam). Shlemiels were called Morris, Irving, Percy, Toby and – come to think of it – Meyer, thank you, Pop.

The man who owned Caribou Corner was called Bruce Fowles.

The name Bruce – in fiction and according to Meyer's research – had only two connotations. Bruce was either a fag, or Bruce was a hairy-chested macho villain working *against* the stereotype of the pantywaist. Bruce Fowles, in real life, was a white man in his late thirties, perhaps five feet nine inches tall and weighing a hundred and sixty, with sandy-coloured hair going slightly bald at the back of the head (Meyer noticed this at once). He was wearing blue jeans and a purple tee shirt imprinted with the head of a shaggy elk, or moose, or something at any rate with a great pair of antlers spreading over pectorals and clavicles and threatening to grow wild around Bruce Fowles' throat. He came out of the restaurant kitchen drying his hands on a dish towel. If Meyer were naming him, he'd have called him Jack. Bruce Fowles looked like a Jack. He extended his hand, and took Meyer's hand in a good Jack Fowles grip, never mind this Bruce crap.

'Hello,' he said, 'I'm Bruce Fowles. My waitress says you're from the police. What's the violation this time?'

'No violation that I know of,' Meyer said, smiling. 'I'm here to ask some questions about a girl who worked for you back in March, according to our information.'

'Would that be Clara Jean Hawkins?' Fowles asked.

'You remember her then?'

'Read about her in the newspaper the other day. Damn shame, She was a nice girl.'

'How long did she work here, Mr Fowles?'

'Look, we don't have to stand here, do we? Would you like a cup of coffee? Louise,' he called, gesturing to a waitress, 'bring us two coffees, will you please? Sit down,' he said. 'I'm sorry, I didn't get your name.'

'Detective Meyer,' Meyer said, and reached into his pocket for identification.

'I don't have to see your badge,' Fowles said. 'If ever anybody looked like a cop, it's you.'

'Me?' Meyer said. 'Really?' He had always thought he looked somewhat like an insurance agent, especially since he'd bought the Professor Higgins hat. The hat was on his head now, soggy and shapeless from the rain outside. Both men sat at a table near the swinging door leading to the kitchen. The time was twenty minutes to twelve, a little early for the lunch hour.

'Cops have a distinctive cop look,' Fowles said. '*Restaurateurs*, as it happens, also have a *restaurateur* look. It is my firm belief that people either choose their occupations because of the way they look, or else they evolve into what they look like *because* of the occupation they've chosen. Tell me the truth, if you saw me walking along on the street, wouldn't you know immediately that

I owned a restaurant? I mean, you wouldn't arrest me for a pusher, would you?'

'No, I wouldn't,' Meyer said, and smiled.

'Similarly, I didn't have to know you were a cop to spot you as one. Even if Louise hadn't told me there was a cop outside to see me, I'd have known what you were the minute I came through that door. Where's the coffee, by the way? Service in this place is terrible,' he said, smiling, and signalling to the waitress again. When she came to the table, he said, 'Louise, I know we have to send across the street for the coffee, but do you think we might have two cups before midnight?'

'What?' she said.

'The coffee,' Fowles said with infinite patience. 'The coffee I asked you to get us. Two coffees, please. Detective Meyer here just came in out of that typhoon, and he's drenched to the skin, and he would like a cup of coffee. I wouldn't particularly like one, but since I'm the alleged boss here, I think it might be nice if I were offered one just for the hell of it. What do you think, Louise?'

'What?' Louise said.

'Coffees, two coffees,' Fowles said, and shooed her away with his hands. 'Louise'll be a waitress till the day she dies,' he said to Meyer. 'She'll be seventy-eight and doddering around here with a bewildered expression on her face, blinking her eyes, a trifle slack-jawed, lotsa muscle but no brains,' Fowles said, and tapped his temple with his forefinger.

'How about Clara Jean Hawkins?' Meyer said.

'A different breed of cat,' Fowles said. 'I knew she'd leave one day, and it didn't surprise me when she did. Waitressing is usually a stop-gap job for most girls. At least waitressing in a place like *this*, which is a combination between a cafeteria, a greasy spoon, and a local hangout. I thought of calling it The Ptomaine Ptent, with a P in front of the tent, decorate it like a circus tent, put things on the menu like elephant steak and tiger piss. If anybody asked for an elephant steak we'd explain it had to be for at least a party of twelve because we'd have to kill the whole elephant -- what do you think of that name, The Ptomaine Ptent?'

'I like it only a little better than Caribou Corner.'

'Awful, right? There's something perverse in me, I know it.

Maybe it's the fact that I started this place with my wife's money. Maybe I want it to fail, do you think that's a possibility?'

'*Is* it failing?'

'Hell, no, it's a roaring success.' He glanced at his watch. 'You're here early. If you came in at twelve-thirty, we'd have to seat you in the men's room. And dinnertime is a madhouse. Listen, I shouldn't kick,' Fowles said, and rapped his knuckles on the wooden table.

'Tell me more about Clara Jean Hawkins.'

'To begin with, smart. That attracts me in a woman, doesn't it you? Brains?'

'Yes, it does,' Meyer said.

'Speaking of geniuses, where's Louise?' Fowles said, and turned towards the swinging door and bellowed at the top of his lungs, 'Louise, if you don't bring that coffee in three seconds flat, I'm going to have you arrested for loitering!'

The swinging door flew open at once. Louise, looking harried and flushed, came out of the kitchen carrying a tray upon which were two cups of coffee. Meyer could well imagine her trying to serve tables at the height of the lunch or dinner hours. He wondered why Fowles kept her on.

'Thank you, Louise,' Fowles said, and moved the sugar bowl closer to Meyer's side of the table. 'Sugar?' he asked. 'Cream? Thank you, Louise, you can go back in the kitchen and bite your nails now, go on, thank you very much.' Louise pushed her way huffily through the swinging doors. 'Total idiot,' Fowles said. 'She's my niece. My wife's brother's daughter. A *trombenik*, do you understand Yiddish? You're Jewish, aren't you?'

'Yes,' Meyer said.

'So am I, my maiden name is Feinstein, I changed it to Fowles when I went into show biz. The Bruce is genuine, my mother's brilliant idea, she used to be in love with Bruce Cabot when he played Magua in *Last of the Mohicans*. Two hundred years before I'm born, right, but she remembers old Bruce Cabot, and she names me Bruce Feinstein, terrific, huh? I did some television work four or five years ago, never really made it, decided to open a restaurant instead. Anyway, that's when I became Bruce Fowles, when I landed the part of Dr Andrew Malloy on *Time and the City*. You are doubtless familiar with *Time and the City*?

118

No? You mean the police force doesn't spend its time in the day room watching soap operas on television?'

'Swing room,' Meyer said.

'I thought it was day room. We did an episode – *some* episode, it lasted six months – where some cops were quarantined inside the station house, one of them had the plague or some damn thing and the writers called it the day room.'

'Swing room,' Meyer said.

'I take your word for it. Where were we?'

'We were talking about smart girls like Clara Jean Hawkins.'

'Right. She lasted here longer than I thought she would. Smart, young, and pretty besides. Clean for this shitty neighbourhood. By which I mean no fooling around with dope. We get enough pushers in here during the lunch hour to supply the entire city of Istanbul for two weeks in August.'

'How about pimps?' Meyer asked.

'We get our share. This is Diamondback, you know. Would that I were operating a place downtown, but I'm not.'

'Know anybody named Joey Peace?'

'No, who is he?'

'A pimp,' Meyer hesitated. 'Clara Jean Hawkins' pimp.'

'You're kidding me,' Fowles said. 'Is *that* how she ended up?'

'Yes,' Meyer said.

'I can't believe it. Clara Jean? Never in a million years. Hooking? Clara Jean?'

'Hooking,' Meyer said. 'Clara Jean.'

'How the hell did she ever get into that?' Fowles said, shaking his head.

'I was hoping *you* could tell *me*,' Meyer said. 'Ever see her in deep conversation with anyone who might've been discussing career opportunities?'

'No, never. She was cheerful and friendly with everybody, but I didn't see any pimps sounding her. You know how they come on, they usually look for drifters, do you know what I mean, lost souls. Clara Jean had a look of confidence about her. I can't *believe* she ended up this way. I honestly cannot *believe* this.'

'Are you sure about the dope angle?' Meyer asked.

'Why? Was she a user when she died?'

'Not according to the autopsy.'

119

'Not according to me, either. One hundred per cent clean.'

'Any of the dealers make noises around her?'

'When don't they? If a nun came in here saying her beads, they'd sound her about a free fix. That's their business, isn't it? Without addicts, there are no dealers. Sure, they came on about junk joy ...'

'Junk ...?'

'Joy,' Fowles supplied. 'Shit City – but she wasn't buying, she saw clear through them. Look, Mr Meyer, she was born and raised in this sewer called Diamondback. If a girl gets to be nineteen and she isn't pregnant, or hooking or supporting a habit – or sometimes all three – it's a fuckin miracle. Okay. Clara Jean was her own person, not quite free, how the fuck *can* you be in Diamondback? Not quite twenty-one, and *never* going to be white – but with a good head on her shoulders and a hell of a lot going for her. So how does she end up a hooker bleeding out her life on a sidewalk at four o'clock in the morning? Isn't that what the newspaper said. Four a.m.?'

'That's what it said.'

'I should've realized right then. I mean, what kind of woman is out on the street alone at four in the morning?'

'Maybe she wasn't alone,' Meyer said: 'Maybe whoever killed her was a client. Or even her pimp.'

'Joey Peace, is that what you said his name was?'

'Joey Peace.'

'Changed from what? Joseph Pincus?'

'That's possible,' Meyer said. 'Lots of pimps ...'

'I went to school with a kid named Joseph Pincus,' Fowles said idly. 'Joey Peace, huh?' He shook his head. 'It just doesn't ring a bell. I know most of the customers who come in here, and that name just isn't familiar to me.'

'Okay, let's get off that for a minute, maybe you'll remember something later on. You said Clara Jean didn't have much to do with your seamier customers ...'

'Just a smile and a nice word or two, right.'

'Ever get a man named George Chadderton in here?'

'Chadderton, Chadderton. No, I don't think so. White or black?'

'Black.'

120

'Chadderton. The name sounds familiar, but . . .'

'He was a calypso singer.'

'*Was*?'

'Was. He got killed Friday night, six hours before Clara Jean bought it with the same pistol.'

'Maybe I read about it,' Fowles said. 'I don't think I know the name from the restaurant here.'

'He was supposed to meet Clara Jean here at twelve last Saturday. That would've been the sixteenth.'

'No, I can't help you there.'

'Okay, how about while she was working here? Did she have any boyfriends? Anybody ever pick her up after work? Anybody call her on the phone?'

'No, not that I know of.'

'Have you got any waiters here?'

'Just waitresses.'

'Busboys?'

'Four.'

'How about the kitchen? Any male help?'

'Yeah, my cooks and my dishwashers.'

'Was she friendly with any of them?'

'Yes, she was a friendly person by nature.'

'Was she *dating* any of them, is what I mean.'

'I don't think so. I'd have noticed something like that. I'm in the place day in and day out, either in the kitchen or at the cash register. I'd have noticed something like that, don't you think?'

'Anybody named Joey work here?' Meyer asked suddenly.

'Joey? No. I've got a Johnny washing dishes, and I once had a busboy named José – well, I suppose that's a Joey, huh?'

'When was this?'

'José worked here . . . let me see . . . in the spring sometime.'

'March, would it have been?'

'March, April, something like that.'

'When Clara Jean worked here?'

'Well . . . yeah, come to think of it.'

'When did he quit the job?'

'Well . . . about the same time she did, as a matter of fact.'

'Uh-uh,' Meyer said. 'José *what*?'

'La Paz,' Fowles said.

Some ten blocks from where Meyer Meyer was discovering that 'Peace' was the English equivalent of the Spanish word '*Paz*', Steve Carella was discovering that Ambrose Harding was a very frightened man. He had come there only to ask Chadderton's business manager whether or not he knew anything about an album the singer may have discussed with Clara Jean Hawkins. Instead, Harding immediately showed Carella a corsage that had arrived not ten minutes earlier. There had been a knock on the door, and when Harding opened it – he did not take off the night chain – there was the box sitting outside in the hall. It was not the sort of box a corsage normally came in. Not a white, rectangular box with green paper inside it and a florist's name imprinted on the top surface. Not that kind of a box at all.

Looking at it, Carella thought it resembled some sort of gift box from one of the city's larger department stores. In fact, the box looked instantly recognizable to him, though he couldn't yet pinpoint the name of the department store. The box was perhaps five inches long by three inches wide by four inches deep. It was imprinted with an overall fleur-de-lis design in blue against a green field. The corsage inside the box was a pink orchid.

'Why does it scare you?' Carella asked.

'Because first of all,' Harding said, 'who the fuck would want to send me an orchid?'

He was sitting in an easy chair in his own living room, the window behind him lashed now with rain that seemed determined to set the city afloat. The time was only a little past noon, but the sky outside looked more like the five p.m. sky of a winter's day. The pink orchid sat on the coffee table in front of him, inside the box with the blue and green fleur-de-lis design. It looked innocuous enough. Carella could not understand why it seemed to terrify Harding.

'Any number of people might want to send you flowers,' Carella said. 'You were hurt, after all, they knew you were in the hospital . . .'

'*Flowers*, yeah,' Harding said, 'a *bouquet* of *flowers*. But not a corsage. I'm a *man*, why would anyone want to send me a corsage?'

'Well, maybe . . . well, I don't know,' Carella said. 'Maybe the florist made a mistake.'

'Which is another thing,' Harding said. 'If somebody's gone to all the trouble of buying me a corsage – an *orchid* no less – how come it's delivered by somebody who vanishes before I can open the door? How come it isn't in a florist's box? How come there's no card with it, how come the corsage just arrives like that, knock, knock on the door, who is it? and no answer, and there's the box sitting outside the door. How come, is what I'd like to know.'

'Well ... what do you *think* it is?' Carella asked.

'A warning,' Harding said.

'How do you read a warning into ... a ... well ... a ... a corsage?'

'There's a pin stuck in it,' Harding said. 'Maybe somebody's tryin to tell me I'm gonna get somethin stuck in *me*, too, man. Maybe somebody's tryin to tell me I'm gonna end up like Georgie did.'

'I can understand how you might feel that way ...'

'You're damn right, considerin somebody tried to empty a *pistol* in my head ...'

'But a flower,' Carella said, 'a corsage ...' and let the sentence trail, and shrugged.

'You take that thing with you,' Harding said.

'What for?'

'Give it to your lab people. See if it's poisoned or anything.'

'I'll do that, sure,' Carella said, 'but I really don't think ...'

'Somebody tried damn hard to kill me, Mr Carella,' Harding said. 'And missed out. Cause the gun was empty. Okay. Maybe that same party is sendin me flowers before the funeral, Mr Carella, you understand me? I'm scared. I'm out of the hospital now, where I ain't protected no more by nurses and doctors and people all around me. I'm home now, all by my little lonesome, and all at once I get a pink orchid left outside my door, and I can tell you it scares the shit out of me.'

'Let me talk to the lieutenant,' Carella said. 'Maybe we can get a man up here.'

'I'd appreciate that,' Harding said. 'And have somebody look at that flower.'

'I will,' Carella said. 'Meanwhile, there are some questions I want to ask you.'

'Go ahead,' Harding said.

'Do you know anyone named Clara Jean Hawkins?'

'No. Who is she?'

'Someone who knew George Chadderton. Did you know all of his business associates?'

'I did.'

'But not Clara Jean Hawkins.'

'Is she a business associate?'

'Apparently she was talking to George about doing some kind of album.'

'Is she in the record business?'

'No, she was a hooker.'

'A hooker? And she was talking to George about doing an album?'

'George never mentioned it to you?'

'Never. What kind of an album?'

'Based on her experiences as a prostitute,' Carella said.

'I can just see that in the top forty, can't you?' Harding said and shook his head.

'The girl seemed convinced the album would be made.'

'By who?'

'By someone who was going to charge her three thousand dollars for the privilege.'

'Ah,' Harding said, and nodded. 'Vanity recording.'

'What's that?' Carella asked.

'It's where a company charges you anywhere from two to three hundred dollars for what they call a test pressing, or some such bullshit. After that, they ...'

'A *test* pressing, did you say?'

'Yeah. If the company's so-called *judges* like what they hear, they'll recommend a major pressing.'

'For more money?'

'No, no, all included in the fee. There's still plenty of profit, believe me. The *major* pressing is usually an album, okay? Eight or nine songs on each side of it, all by suckers like yourself. That's eighteen songs at two, sometimes three hundred bucks a throw, that comes to four, five thousand dollars. So they'll press fifteen hundred albums – which in a legit operation might cost you twenty-five hundred bucks – and they'll give ten each to the eighteen "songwriters" on the album, and the rest they'll send to disc jockeys who'll throw them in the garbage, or to record stores around the country who won't even open the package. A racket, pure and simple. This was supposed to be an album, huh?'

'Yes.'

'And George was involved in it? I can't believe George would've got himself involved in a vanity operation. Lots of these houses supply the suckers with lyricists or composers free of charge, all part of the hype. But George? Are you sure about this?'

'He met with the girl four times in the past month. The words "In The Life" were doodled in his notebook. It's our guess they planned to use that as the title.'

'Well, I don't know what to tell you. He never mentioned it to me. I know he was itchin for bigger money than he'd been gettin lately, be a way for him to get Chloe to quit that job of hers. So maybe he got this girl involved with some vanity label, and maybe ... I just don't know. If George was gettin a kickback, it might *still* have been worth the company's while. Stead of havin to scrounge around for eighteen *separate* suckers, they'd have *one* sucker puttin up a full three grand, give George some of that, still make a profit. Yeah, maybe. I just can't say for sure.'

Carella took out his notebook, and opened it at the page of names he had copied from Chadderton's appointment calendar. 'I've got two names here that Chloe couldn't identify,' he said. 'Would either of them be connected with vanity labels?'

'Let me hear them,' Harding said.

'Jimmy Talbot?'

'Nope, he's a bass player. Damn good one, too.'

'Harry Caine.'

'You got it, mister. Owns a label called Hurricane. He's a crook if *ever* there was one.'

'Thanks,' Carella said, and closed the notebook.

'Don't forget to talk to your lieutenant about sendin a man up here.'

'I won't,' Carella said.

'And get that flower tested,' Harding said.

The round-the-clock on Ambrose Harding's apartment did not go into effect until 3.45 p.m. that afternoon. The reasons for the almost four-hour delay were many, and all of them authentic. To begin with, Carella did not go directly back to the office but instead went all the way downtown to Crescent Oval, where the offices of Hurricane Records were located. Crescent Oval was in that section of the city known as The Quarter, and number 17 Crescent Oval was a three-storey brownstone set between a sandal-maker's shop and a store selling health foods. A brass escutcheon to the right of the doorbell carried only the engraved legend 'Hurricane Records'. Carella rang the bell and waited. An answering buzz sounded within seconds. He opened the door, and moved into a panelled ground-floor landing, a flight of stairs angling upward dead ahead, a narrow corridor on the right of the steps, a door almost immediately to his right. On the door, another brass escutcheon engraved with the words 'Hurricane Records'. No bell. Carella knocked on the door, and a woman's voice said, 'Come in.'

The door opened on to an informal reception room painted in varying shades of purple, all of them muted, complementary, and rather soothing to the eye. The girl sitting behind a white formica-topped desk was eighteen or nineteen, he supposed, a good-looking black girl wearing a plum-coloured suit that further complemented the colouring of the walls and the carpet. She smiled warmly and said, 'May I help you, sir?'

'I'm a police officer,' Carella said, and immediately showed his shield.

'Oh,' the girl said, and smiled. 'And here I thought you were a rock singer.'

'Is Mr Caine in?' Carella asked.

'Let me check,' she said, and picked up the phone receiver.

She punched a button in the base of the instrument, waited, and then said, 'A police officer to see you, Mr Caine.' She listened, laughed, said, 'I don't think so,' listened again, and then said, 'I'll send him right in.'

'What'd he say that was funny?' Carella asked.

'He wanted to know if you were tagging his car. He found a space up the block, but it's alternate side of the street parking, and today is the *other* side of the street. But it's raining and he didn't want to go shlepping all the way over to the garage on Chauncey. I told him I didn't think you were tagging the car. You're not, are you?'

'I'm not,' Carella said.

'Okay, friend, pass,' the girl said, and smiled and indicated a door just beyond her desk. 'Make a right when you're inside,' she said. 'It's the second door in the corridor.'

Harry Caine was perhaps twenty-three years old, a dark-skinned black man wearing pearl grey trousers and a pink shirt, the sleeves rolled up over narrow wrists and slender forearms. He rose and extended his hand as Carella came into the room. Carella estimated his height at about five eleven. Thin, with narrow hips and shoulders, he could easily have passed for a teenage boy. The rock and roll album sleeves that decorated the walls all around his desk enlarged the initial impression – Carella might have been in some kid's room someplace; all that was missing was the blare of a stereo.

'I'm sorry,' Caine said, 'my secretary didn't tell me your name. I'm Harry Caine.'

'Detective Carella,' he said, and took Caine's hand.

'I'm illegally parked,' Caine said, and smiled. 'I know it.'

'I'm here about another matter.'

'Phew!' Caine said, and wiped his hand across his brow in exaggerated relief. His eyes, Carella noticed for the first time, were almost yellow. Extraordinary eyes. He had never seen anyone with eyes like that in his life. 'Sit down, please,' Caine said. 'Would you like some coffee?'

'No, thank you,' Carella said.

'What can I do for you?'

'You had lunch with George Chadderton last Thursday,' Carella said.

'Yes?' Caine said.

'Yes, at one p.m.'

'Yes?'

'Did you?'

'I did,' Caine said.

'What'd you talk about?'

'Why do you want to know?' Caine said, looking extremely puzzled.

Carella looked back at him. 'Don't you know he's dead?' he asked.

'Dead? No. George?'

'He was killed Friday night.'

'I've been out of town, I just got home last night. I didn't know, I'm sorry.' He hesitated. 'What happened to him?'

'Someone shot him.'

'Who?'

'We don't know yet.'

'Well, I'm ... I'm shocked,' Caine said. 'I can't say I feel any real grief – George wasn't the sort of person one felt much affection for. But I respected him as an artist and – I'm genuinely shocked.'

'How long had you known him, Mr Caine?'

'Oh, six months, I would say. We've talked record possibilities on and off for the past six months.'

'Is that what you talked about this past Thursday?'

'Yes, as a matter of fact. George called me last week sometime, said he had an album idea he wanted to discuss. Well,' Caine said, and smiled, 'George *always* had an album idea to discuss. The problem, of course, was that he wanted to do *calypso*, which is about as vital to the record industry as buggy whips are to transportation.'

'Was this in *fact* another calypso album he wanted to discuss?'

'Yes. But with a twist.'

'What was the twist?'

'Well, to begin with ...' Caine hesitated. 'I'm not sure I should mention this. I wouldn't want you to think Hurricane Records is a vanity label. It isn't.'

'Uh-huh,' Carella said.

'Although from time to time, in order to help launch the careers of individuals who might not otherwise be granted a forum ...'

'Uh-huh ...'

'We *will* charge a fee. But only in order to defray the cost of recording, packaging and distribution.'

'I see,' Carella said.

'But even in those circumstances, we pay royalties the same as Motown or RCA or Arista or any other label you might care to mention.'

'It's just every now and then ...'

'Yes, every so often ...'

'That you'll accept a fee.'

'Yes, to reduce our risk.'

'It's our understanding that C. J. Hawkins ... does that name mean anything to you?'

'Yes, that's the girl George and I discussed.'

'Was ready to put up three thousand dollars ...'

'Yes.'

'To have an album made by your company.'

'Yes.'

'Was George Chadderton supposed to get any of that money?'

'Yes.'

'How much?'

'A thousand.'

'And Hurricane Records was to get the remaining two thousand, is that it?'

'Yes.'

'Isn't that low? It's my understanding that most companies charging fees will get somewhere between two and three hundred dollars a song.'

'That's right,' Caine said.

'What does Hurricane charge per song?'

'Two-fifty.'

'And how many songs do you normally put on an LP?'

'Eight or nine on each side.'

'Which would come to, oh, four thousand dollars an album, isn't that right?'

'More or less.'

'But Hurricane was willing to do C.J.'s for two thousand.'

'*Three* thousand altogether.'

'*Your* share was only two. Eighteen songs for two thousand bucks. How come?'

'Well,' Caine said, 'not eighteen.'

'Ah,' Carella said. 'How many?'

'This was to be more like a demo album. As opposed to an album for distribution to disc jockeys and retail outlets.'

'How many songs on it?'

'We planned to press only one side.'

'Nine songs?'

'Eight.'

'For a three thousand dollar fee.'

'Hurricane's share was only two.'

'Why were you giving a thousand to Chadderton? Because he brought the girl to you?'

'No, he was getting paid for writing the songs and recording them.'

'What kind of songs?'

'Well, calypso, of course. That's what George wrote and performed. Calypso.'

'Which would suddenly become *vital* to the record industry, huh?' Carella said.

Caine smiled. 'Not vital perhaps, but worth a shot. Miss Hawkins had a great deal of information George was prepared to put into the songs.'

'Were they going to collaborate on them, is that it?'

'That part of it hadn't been worked out yet. I think it was George's intention only to pick her brain. Apparently, she had hundreds of stories to tell. She'd only been in the life since April, from what I understand, but apparently one learns very quickly in the streets.'

'Too bad she didn't learn a little more quickly *off* the streets,' Carella said.

'I'm sorry,' Caine said. 'I don't know what you mean.'

'I mean you were charging her three thousand bucks to record eight songs, which on my block comes to three hundred and seventy-five bucks a song, or a hundred and twenty-five more than you *usually* charge.'

'George was getting a thousand of that.'

'I see. You were getting only your *usual* fee, right?'

'If you care to look at it that way.'

'How would *you* care to look at it, Mr Caine? Together, you were leading that kid straight down the garden.'

'She wasn't a virgin,' Caine said, smiling.

'No,' Carella answered, 'but usually *she* charged for the screwing.'

The smile dropped from Caine's face. 'I'm sure you've got a million things to do,' he said. 'I don't want to keep you.'

'Nice meeting you, Mr Caine,' Carella said, and walked out of the office. He stopped at the desk in the reception room, and asked the girl there what kind of car Mr Caine drove. The girl gave him the year, make and colour, and then said, 'Uh-oh, did I do something wrong just then?' Carella assured her she had not.

Outside in the pouring rain, he searched the street from end to end till he found the car answering the girl's description. From a phone booth on the corner, he called Communications and asked for a computer check on the licence plate. Within minutes, he learned that the car was registered to a Mr Harry Caine who lived in Riverhead, and that it had not been reported stolen. For the next ten minutes, Carella walked in the rain looking for the beat cop. When he found him, he identified himself and then led him back to where Caine's car was illegally parked on the wrong side of the street.

'Ticket it,' he said.

The patrolman stared at him. The rain was drumming on Carella's uncovered head, the rain had soaked through his coat and his shoes and his trouser legs; altogether he looked like a drowned rat. The patrolman kept staring at him. At last he shrugged and said, 'Sure,' and began writing out the summons. The time he scrawled into the righthand corner was 1.45 p.m.

Carella did not get back to the office until two-thirty that afternoon, at which time the lieutenant had a reporter from the city's morning paper in with him, wanting to know not about the relatively obscure calypso singer found dead in the 87th Precinct this past Friday night, nor even about the more obscure hooker found dead in Midtown South six hours later, but instead about a rash of jewellery-store robberies which seemed to have leaped the dividing line that separated the scuzzy Eight-Seven from its posh neighbouring precinct to the west. The reporter was asking Lieutenant Byrnes whether he felt the robbers who'd held up a store on Hall Avenue just west of Monastery Road, were the same thieves who'd been raising havoc in the Eight-Seven for, lo, these many months. Byrnes refused to admit to any damn reporter on earth that any damn thieves were raising havoc in his damn precinct, and besides, he didn't consider six jewellery-store holdups to be havoc, nor did he even consider them to be a rash. In any event, he was occupied with the reporter until a quarter to three, at which time Carella gained access to his office, carrying with him a box with a green and blue fleur-de-lis design. A handkerchief tented over his hand, Carella lifted the lid from the box.

Drily, Byrnes said, 'You have to stop bringing me flowers. The men are beginning to talk.'

'Left outside Harding's apartment a little while ago,' Carella said. 'He thinks it means something.'

'Mm,' Byrnes said.

'Whether it does or not isn't important,' Carella said. 'He's damn scared, and I think he may have a point. Whoever tried to blow him away . . .'

'May try it again,' Byrnes said, and nodded.

'Can we spare a patrolman up there?'

'For how long?'

'At least till we pick up Joey Peace.'

'Have you talked to Meyer yet?'

'Yes, and he told me it's José La Paz. I've already called the Gaucho to let him know.'

'How long do you think it'll be before we flush him out?'

'I've got no idea, Pete. It could be ten minutes, it could be ten days.'

'How long do you want the cover on Harding?'

'Can you let me have a week? Round the clock?'

'I'll check it with the captain.'

'Would you, Pete? I want to get this down to the lab. Sam promised me a report by tomorrow morning if I can get it to him right away.' Both men looked at their watches. Byrnes was picking up the phone receiver as Carella left the office.

Captain Frick enjoyed being in command of the entire Eight-Seven, including those plainclothes cops who inhabited the ruckus room on the second floor of the station house. There were a hundred and eighty-six patrolmen assigned to the Eight-Seven and, together with the sixteen detectives upstairs, the small army under Frick's command constituted a formidable bulwark against the forces of evil in this city. Byrnes was now asking that three men in the uniformed ranks be taken from active duty elsewhere to be placed outside the door of a black business manager (not that his blackness mattered) on a round-the-clock basis, one man for every eight hours, three men each and every day of the week for the next week. Frick did not want to take this responsibility upon himself. Frick felt that three men fewer against the forces of evil were three men more on the side of the forces of evil. He told Byrnes he would get back to him, and at exactly one minute past three, he placed a call to the Chief of Field Services in Headquarters downtown on High Street, and asked if he might feel free to release three patrolmen each day for the next week for a round-the-clock on a black business manager whose client had been a homicide victim this past Friday night up here. The COFS wanted to know what the business manager's *blackness* had to do with a goddam thing on God's green earth, and Frick said, at once, 'Nothing, sir, it has nothing whatever to do with anything whatever,' and the COFS granted permission to assign the three men on a round-the-clock. It was by then 3.09 p.m., and it was still raining.

Frick knew, from his years of duty on the streets before he made desk sergeant and then lieutenant and then captain, that the eight-to-four tour of duty ended at 3.45 p.m., when the relieving patrolmen stood roll call in the muster room, after which the preceding shift was supposed to be relieved on post. He further knew that any smart criminal in this city should have planned the commission of his crimes for the fifteen minutes preceding 8.00 a.m., 4.00 p.m., and 12.00 midnight, since it was then that an overlap took place between those patrolmen who were returning prematurely to the station house, and those patrolmen who were standing roll call prior to going out on the street to 'relieve on post' – a tour of duty is a long eight hours, and one can perhaps forgive a bit of eagerness on the part of men who've been pounding a beat. Anyway, Frick knew it would be senseless to assign an off-going patrolman to the first watch on Harding's apartment, so he called down to the desk and asked that the sergeant assign a man from the four-to-midnight to the first segment of a round-the-clock that would continue through the next week at least, or certainly until further notice.

The first patrolman assigned to Harding's apartment was a rookie named Conrad Lehmann. He was also the *last* patrolman assigned there, since when he got there he found the door ajar and a black man lying dead on the kitchen floor with two neatly spaced bullet holes in his face.

11

Carella could not get used to thinking of Sam Grossman as *Captain* Sam Grossman, not after he'd been *Lieutenant* Sam Grossman for such a long time. High in a window in a tower to the east – or rather on the Police Laboratory-floor of the new towerlike glass, steel and stone Headquarters Building downtown on High Street – Grossman half-sat upon, half-leaned against a long white table bearing a row of black microscopes. He was wearing a white laboratory smock over a grey suit, and his eyeglasses reflected grey rain oozing along the window panes, grey sky stretching across a dull horizon, black pencil-line bridges sketched from the island to the distant grey reaches of the city. The effect was starkly modern, almost monochromatic – the whites, blacks and greys broken only by the cool blue and green of the fleur-de-lis box and the hot pink of the orchid on the lab counter.

'Which do you want first?' Grossman asked. 'The box or the flower?' There was in his voice a gentleness in direct contradiction to the coldness of the scientific knowledge he was expected to dispense. Listening to Grossman talk about the results of his various lab tests was rather like hearing a drawling New England turnip farmer explaining that contrary to Galilean or Newtonian concepts, time and space should be viewed as relative to moving systems or frames of reference.

'Let's start with the box,' Carella said.

'I take it you don't recognize the design.'

'I know it, but I don't know it.'

'B. Renaud on Hall Avenue.'

'Right, that's it.'

'Their standard gift box. They change the colour scheme every now and then, but the fleur-de-lis pattern is always the same. You might check them on when they last changed colours.'

'I'll do that. Anything else I should know?'

'Not a latent print on it, not a trace of anything but dust in it.'

'Anything special about the dust?'

'Not this time. Sorry, Steve.'

'How about the flower?'

'Well, it's an orchid, as I'm sure you surmised.'

'Yes, I guessed that,' Carella said, smiling.

'Variety common to the North Temperate Zone,' Grossman said, 'characterized by the pinkish flower and the slipper-shaped lip. You can buy it at any florist in the city. Just go in and ask for *Calypso bulbosa.*'

'You're kidding,' Carella said.

'Am I?' Grossman said, surprised.

'*Calypso bulbosa*? *Calypso*?'

'That's the name. Why? What's the matter?'

Carella shook his head. I'm sure Harding didn't know the name of that damn flower, but it scared hell out of him anyway. *Calypso bulbosa*. The killer was saying "See the pretty flower – it means death." And Harding knew it instinctively.' He shook his head again.

'Meanings within meanings,' Grossman said.

'Wheels within wheels,' Carella said.

'Turning,' Grossman said.

The person Carella spoke to at B. Renaud was a woman named Betty Ungar. Her telephone voice was precise but pleasant, rather like the voice of a robot who'd been lubricated with treacle.

'Yes,' she said, 'the fleur-de-lis pattern is ours exclusively. It is featured in all our newspaper and television advertisements, it is on our charge cards and our shopping bags, and of course it's on all of our gift boxes.'

'I understand the colours change every so often.'

'Every Christmas, yes,' Miss Ungar said.

'The box I have here on my desk,' Carella said, 'has a blue fleur-de-lis pattern on a green field. I wonder if you . . .'

'Oh, my,' Miss Ungar said.

'Is that a problem for you?'

'Blue and green. Oh my, that's considerably before my time, I'm afraid.'

'Are you saying the box is an old one?'

'I've been here for six years,' Miss Ungar said, 'and I can remember every colour variation we've used – the red on pink last Christmas, for example, the black on white the Christmas before, the brown on beige the Christmas before that . . .'

'Uh-huh,' Carella said. 'But this blue on green ...'

'Before my time.'

'Longer ago than six years, is that it?' Carella said.

'Yes.'

'Could you tell me exactly how long ago?'

'Well ... is this awfully important to you?'

'It might be,' Carella said. 'There's no way of telling if a piece of new information is important, you see, until it suddenly becomes important.'

'Um,' Miss Ungar said, managing to convey in that monosyllabic grunt a sincere lack of conviction concerning the urgency of Carella's mission, and a further suspicion of his homespun philosophy about the relative importance of clues and the theory of spontaneous celebrity. 'Hold on, would you, please?' she said.

Carella held on. While he held on, the store piped recorded music into the telephone. Carella listened to the music and wondered why Americans felt it necessary to fill every silence with sound of one kind or another – canned rock, canned shlock, canned shmaltz, canned pap, it was impossible to step into a taxi or an elevator or even a funeral home in America without speakers blaring, oozing or dripping sound of one kind or another. Whatever happened to silent grassy hilltops? It seemed he could remember once going to his aunt's farm in the state across the river, and sitting on a grassy hilltop where the world sloped away in utter silence at his feet. Occupied with such pastoral thoughts, a canned shlock-shmaltz arrangement of 'Sunrise, Sunset' massaging his right ear, Carella almost fell asleep. Miss Ungar's vaguely mechanical voice jarred him back to his senses.

'Mr Coppola?' she said.

'Carella,' he said.

'Um,' she said, this time managing to convey doubt that Carella knew his own name. 'I've checked with someone who's been here longer than I,' she said, 'and actually the blue on green was used the Christmas before I began my employment.'

'That would have made it Christmas seven years ago.'

'Yes,' Miss Ungar said. 'If I began work here six years ago, and if the blue on green was used the Christmas before I began work, why then yes, that would have been seven years ago.'

Carella had the feeling he'd just been called an idiot. He

thanked Miss Ungar for her time, and hung up. Seven years ago, he thought. He stared at the box; all theories of police work to the contrary, the new piece of information refused to become suddenly important.

The team of laboratory technicians who went over Ambrose Harding's apartment was not necessarily looking for clues that would connect his murder to those of George Chadderton and Clara Jean Hawkins. The recovered bullets – one of them found embedded in the window sill over the sink, the other one dug out of Harding's skull by the assistant medical examiner performing the autopsy – would tell the Ballistics Section whether or not the same pistol had been used in all three killings, and that would be connection enough. They were, instead, looking for *any* clue at all, anything that might move the case off the dime and into the realm of meaningful speculation.

There was already, and even before Ballistics came through with its report on the bullets, a sense of continuity bordering on serialization; one more murder and the network would surely renew for another season. In a city like this one, a single murder was nothing to attract a crowd; you could get your single garden-variety murder any day of the week, so ho-hum, what else was new? Two murders committed with the same weapon, however, or even two murders committed in the same part of the city within a relatively short period of time, or two murder *victims* who vaguely resembled each other in age, occupation or hair colouring were enough to cause one or another of the city's more creative journalists to speculate idly and out loud whether or not yet another demented assassin was loose on the streets while the police sat with their thumbs up their asses. But *three* murders? *Three* murders within the space of *five* days? Three murders which had in all probability been committed with the same weapon? Three murders of three blacks, one of them a denizen of, if not the underworld, then at least the soft white underbelly of the underworld, that night-time world of whispered invitations and promises discreetly fulfilled.

There was nothing that stimulated the public's imagination more than the murder of a prostitute. It provided the morally righteous with a sense of extreme gratification, the guilty party

137

punished if not by the hand of God, then at least by the hand of someone who understood the dangers prostitution posed in a society where men walked around with their flies open. For many others – those men and women who had at one time or another flirted with the notion either of *using* the services of a prostitute or *providing* the services of a prostitute (a common female fantasy) – the murder was proof, if any was needed, that in this city there indeed existed a large army of women ready and indeed willing to service anyone regardless of race, creed, colour, gender or persuasion. That the service in question was sometimes fraught with danger was a fact indisputably supported by the murder. The wages of sin is death, brother – but Jesus, it sounded exciting nonetheless. And for those who had in *fact* dallied hither and yon, here or there in this or that shoddy hotel room, or in X-rated motels across the river where one could watch a porn flick while simultaneously performing in one's own private real-life movie on a water bed, or in any of the massage parlours that lined the city's thoroughfares, north, south, east and west, for those, in short, who had stepped over the line dividing simple sex for fun and enjoyment (your place or mine, baby?) from sex for profit, sex as sin, sex as the longest-running business in the history of the race (your race or mine, baby?) for those simple folk as well, there was fascination in the murder of a prostitute because they wondered (a) whether a john like themselves had killed her, or (b) whether one of those ferocious-looking pimps with their wide-brimmed pimp hats had killed her, or (c) whether the girl who'd been killed was somebody who'd maybe given them great head just the night before – they all looked the same after a while. So yes, there were all sorts of exciting possibilities to consider when a prostitute got killed. Kill your average calypso singer, kill your average calypso singer's business manager, and nobody got too terribly excited, even if there *was* continuity to the murders. But kill a hooker? Blonde wig on the sidewalk, for Christ's sake! Skirt up around her ass! A bullet in her heart and two more in her head! Now *that* was unusual and interesting.

So was sand.

What the technicians found in Ambrose Harding's apartment was sand.

'Sand,' Grossman told Carella on the phone.

'What do you mean, sand?'

'Sand, Steve.'

'Like on a beach?'

'Yes, like on a beach.'

'I'm very happy to hear that,' Carella said, 'especially since there *are* no beaches in Diamondback.'

'There are a few beaches in Riverhead, though,' Grossman said.

'Yes, and lots of beaches out on Sands Spit.'

'And even *more* beaches on the Iodine Islands.'

'How much sand did your guys find up there?' Carella asked.

'Not enough to make a beach.'

'Enough to pave a sidewalk?'

'A minuscule amount, Steve. The vacuum picked it up. It seemed unusual enough to report, however. Sand in a Diamondback apartment? I'd say that was unusual.'

'And interesting,' Carella said.

'Unusual *and* interesting, yes.'

'Sand,' Carella said.

A look at the map of this city showed five distinct sections, some of which were separated by waterways and joined like Siamese twins by bridges at hip or shoulder, others with common borders that nonetheless defined political and geographical entities, one an island unto itself, entirely surrounded by water and – in the minds and hearts of its inhabitants – entirely surrounded by enemies as well. This was not a city as paranoid as Naples, which holds the undisputed record for that disease, but it was a fairly suspecting city nonetheless, a city that felt every *other* city on the face of the earth was rooting for its fiscal downfall only because it happened to be the foremost city in the world. The damn trouble with such a crazy paranoid supposition was that it happened to be true. This was not only *a* city, this was *the* city. The way Carella looked at it, if you had to ask what a city was, then you didn't live in one, or you only thought you lived in one. This city was the goddamnedest city in the world, and Carella shared with every one of its citizens – world-traveller or apartment-recluse – the certain knowledge that there was no place like it anywhere else. It was, quite simply, the one and onliest place to be.

Looking at a map of it, searching for sand in and around it,

Carella studied the long finger of land that was not truly a part of the city but that nonetheless, and despite the fact that it belonged to the neighbouring county, was righteously considered a backyard playground by anyone who lived in the city proper. Elsinore County, so-named by an English colonist well-versed in the works of his most illustrious countryman, consisted of some eight communities on the eastern seaboard, all of them buffered from erosion and occasional hurricane force winds by Sands Spit which – and with all due understanding of the city's chauvinist attitude – *did* possess some of the most beautiful beaches in the world. Sands Spit ran pristinely north and south, forming a natural seawall that was protection for the mainland but not for itself or for the several smaller islands clustered around it like pilot fish around a shark. These were called the Iodines.

There were six Iodine Islands in all, two of them privately owned, a third set aside as a state park open to the public, the remaining three rather larger than their sisters and developed more or less garishly with high-rise condominiums and hotels, their fearless occupants apparently willing to brave the hurricanes that infrequently – but often enough – ravaged Sands Spit, the clustering Iodines, and sometimes the city itself. The Iodines had been peculiarly named, but then again almost everything in and around this city had been peculiarly named. It was a well-known fact, for example, that there were no rivers with their heads (or even their tails) in that section of the city called Riverhead. There *was* a brook there, but it was called Five Mile Pond, and it was neither five miles long nor five wide, nor was it five miles from any distinctive landmark or geographical feature, but it was nonetheless a brook called Five Mile Pond in a section called Riverhead where there were no rivers. In fact, and this was rarely appreciated by those citizens of Riverhead who were constantly asking, 'Hey, how come there ain't no rivers in Riverhead?' the place had originally been called Ryerhurt's Farms after the Dutch patroon who'd owned vast acreage away back then, and eventually came to be known simply as Ryerhurt, which in 1919 was changed to Riverhead because race memory seemed vaguely to recall that Ryerhurt was a Dutchman, and during and immediately following World War I a Dutchman meant a *German* and not somebody who'd come to America from his native Rotterdam. It was a peculiar city.

The Iodine Islands had not a trace of iodine on them – neither saltpetre beds nor seaweed ash nor oil-well salt brine – and happily so since the discovery there of that halogen might have led to pillage and rape from all sorts of companies engaged in manufacturing pharmaceuticals, dyes, or photographic supplies. As it was, the Iodines were virtually virginal. No one was quite positive how they had been named; they had certainly never been privately owned by a Dutchman named Iodine, nor even an Englishman named Iodine, which was probably a more likely possibility since there *was* historical evidence, written and physical, of a British fort having once occupied a key position on the largest of the islands, facing the ocean approach to the then quite wealthy Elsinore County farmlands crouching behind Sands Spit. The smallest of the islands was once owned by a robber baron who'd taken his new bride there in the year 1904. It had since changed hands a dozen times. The other privately owned island had but a single house on it. The house was grey and weathered. Sitting starkly on the horizon, it resembled nothing so much as a prison.

He heard the motor launch coming back, that was one of the few sounds that penetrated the double doors, the high whining roar of the double engines, the changing sounds as she manoeuvred it in to the dock. She drove that thing the way normal people drove a car or rode a bike, she was really terrific at it. That first day she took him out here, this was after they'd spent the night at the hotel, she drove him way the hell out on Sands Spit someplace, he'd only been there to go to the beach before then, terrific beach at Smithy's Cove, used to go there with his brother and with Irene, he wondered how his brother was, wondered whether he and Irene had any kids now, wondered if—

Drove him out there, she had a Jaguar, terrific little white car, he wondered what she drove now. Left the car at the dock, had herself this Chris-Craft tied up there at the dock, looked too damn big for a woman to handle, even a woman like her who drove that car like she was in a race on some French track, terrific, she was exciting as hell then, back then. Same boat, it must've been. He caught a glimpse of it when he almost escaped that time, almost made it, almost escaped. He never thought of escaping any more. All he thought of was dying.

She'd left him enough food this time, he wasn't worried about starving to death, not this time. She'd come in before she left for the city, told him she had something to take care of, little errand to run, that strange smile on her face. Had a little box in her hands, asked him if he remembered the box. Expected him to remember every damn thing, every little gift she ever gave him. Told him the cologne had come in that box, didn't he remember the cologne? Her first Christmas gift to him, seven years ago? He told her Yeah, he remembered the cologne, but he didn't remember the fuckin cologne at all. Brought him enough food to last a whole damn week, though; he wondered how long she planned on being gone this time, but he didn't ask her. She had a habit, when you asked her for something, she made you pay for it later. Simplest thing. Like the clock. Just asking her for the clock. Things she made him do before she gave him the fuckin clock. Things she made him do even after he got the clock. He'd learned not to ask her anything any more. Just kept quiet most of the time. Did whatever she wanted. Anything she wanted. Knew she could drug his food whenever she felt like it, had to eat whatever she brought him or else starve to death. Knew she could knock him unconscious for days, if she felt like it, and then do whatever she wanted with him when he was unconscious. The time she did that with the ... with the needles. He trembled even now, just thinking of the needles. Woke up with all those needles in him. Fiercest pain he'd ever known in his life, a dozen needles, he'd ... he'd seen the needles and almost fainted just seeing them. She told him the needles were punishment. That night, she drugged him again. There was a period there when he was drugged more often than he was conscious. When he came to the next day, she'd taken all the needles out. Told him he'd heal in a while, and when he was better she expected him to perform again. That was a word she used a lot. Perform. As if he was still a musician, playing for her amusement, performing the way he'd performed that night long ago, dancing with her when the other band was playing, close up against her, smooth white gown, naked flesh above, held her close, held her very close, the pain of the needles in his cock.

He heard the lock turning on the inner door. He could never hear the lock on the outside door, the wood was too thick, he only heard the inside lock, and then the door opened, as it was opening now, and she stood there with the dog's leash in one hand, smiling.

'Good evening,' she said.

'Hello,' he said.

The dog looked at him. He began to shake every time he saw the dog. She told him once that if he misbehaved again, if he did anything to displease her, she would drug him and then let the dog do something to him while he was unconscious. She did not say what she would let the dog do. He . . . he kept remembering the needles. He kept thinking she might have the dog bite him while he was unconscious. Have the dog hurt him, wake up later to find himself chewed . . . chewed to pieces or something. The dog frightened him. But she frightened him more than the dog did.

'Miss me?' she asked.

He did not answer.

'I see you haven't finished your food,' she said.

'There was a lot of it.'

'Yes, but I knew I'd be gone overnight. That's why I left you enough food. Would you have preferred less?'

'No, no, it's just . . .'

'Then why didn't you eat what I left you?'

'I'll eat it all now, if you like.'

'Yes, I think I'd like that. I'd like you to eat all your food. I go to all the trouble of making sure you're properly fed . . .'

'If you let me go, you wouldn't have to feed me any more.'

'No,' she said, 'I'm not letting you go.'

'Why do you want me here?'

'I enjoy you here. Eat your food. You said you were going to eat all your food.'

He went to the couch, sat, and began picking at the food on his tray. He was not hungry, he had really eaten enough. But she was watching him.

'Would you like to know why I've been going to the city so often?' she asked.

He watched her warily. Too often, she set traps for him, and he was sorry later.

'Would you like to know?' she asked again.

'If you'd like to tell me,' he said cautiously, and poked his fork at the food.

'To protect you,' she said.

'Protect me how?'

'To save your life,' she said.

'Sure,' he said, 'to save my life.'

'Eat your food, Santo.'

'I'm eating it.'

'Or don't you like what I prepared for you?'

'I like it fine.'

'You don't seem to like it.'

'I'll eat it. I said I'll eat it, and I will.'

'Now,' she said. 'While I'm here.'

'All right, while you're here.'

'I don't want you flushing it down the toilet, the way you did with the liver that time.'

'I don't like liver.'

'Yes, but I didn't *know* that when I prepared ...'

'You knew it. I told you I didn't like liver. You made it on purpose. You made it because ...'

'If I did, then it was because you displeased me somehow.'

'I always seem to displease you somehow.'

'No, that isn't true. You please me enormously. Why would I keep you here if you didn't please me?'

'To torture me, that's why.'

'Have I ever tortured you?'

'Yes.'

'That's a lie, Santo.'

'The needles ...'

'That was punishment. And you were asleep, remember.'

'They were in me when I woke up!'

'Yes, to strengthen you.'

'How did you expect them to ...?'

'I don't like to talk about sex,' she said.

'You're a fuckin sex fiend, but you don't like to talk about it.'

'I certainly don't like to talk about what was becoming your inability to ...'

'My inability, *shit*! You beat me, you torture me, you drug me, and then you expect me to get a hard-on every time you walk in the room.'

'Yes,' she said, and smiled. 'That *is* what I expect, that's true. Eat your food, Santo.'

'I don't want any more,' he said, and pushed the tray away from him. 'I'm full.'

'All right,' she said.

Her voice was oddly mild, it frightened him. He watched her. She was standing just inside the door, one hand in the dog's leash. She was dressed in black from head to toe, black slacks, a black silk blouse, black boots.

'I'll give it to the dog instead, would that please you, Santo? Giving your food to Clarence?'

'If I'm not hungry . . .'

'Tomorrow I'll prepare food for the dog instead. I'll prepare *your* food for Clarence, would you like that, Santo?'

'Look, I really enjoyed what I ate, I really did. But I'm not hungry any more, you can't expect me to . . .'

'Yes, I can, Santo. I *can* expect you to.'

She dropped the dog's leash and walked to the coffee table. She picked up the tray, carried it back to the door, and put it down before the dog. He sniffed at the tray but did not touch the food until she said, 'All right, Clarence,' and then he began eating.

'He's better trained than you are,' she said.

'I'm not an animal,' Santo said.

'I should let you die,' she said. 'Instead of going to all this trouble.'

'What trouble?'

'In the city,' she said vaguely. 'Here. All this trouble trying to save you.' She watched the dog eating. 'How do you feel about C.J. not coming here any more?' she asked.

'I like C.J.,' he said.

'Oh, *yes*, how you like C.J.,' she said, and chuckled.

'Why isn't she coming any more?'

'Perhaps she doesn't want to.'

'I thought . . .'

'Yes, she *seemed* to be enjoying herself, didn't she? But perhaps she was getting a bit tired of your behaviour. Not everyone has my patience, you know.'

'*My* behaviour? You were the one who . . .'

'Anyway, I don't want to talk about sex. You know I hate talking about sex. I thought I could trust C.J. Are you finished?' she asked the dog. 'Are you finished, darling?'

'What do you mean? Why *can't* you trust her?'

'She was very young, *too* young, in fact. Young people don't seem to realize ...'

'*Was* young? What do you mean *was* young?'

'I'm going to explain something to you, Santo. Come here, come undress me.'

'No, I don't want to. Not now.'

'Yes, now. Do as I say.'

'I just finished eating, I don't feel like—'

'No, *you* didn't finish eating, *Clarence* finished eating for you, didn't you, darling? And I'm sure you don't want to annoy Clarence further by not doing what I'm asking you to do. I would hate to have Clarence ...'

'All right,' he said. 'All *right*, goddamnit!'

'Especially since you seem *very* sensitive about scars and bruises on your *glorious* body.'

'Yes, very sensitive.'

'Even when they're for your own good.'

'Yes, my own good, sure.'

'Unbutton my blouse,' she said. 'Yes, your own good.'

'The cigarette burns ...'

'Slowly, Santo. Button by button. Yes, that's it.'

'Were for my own good.'

'Yes, to teach you to quit smoking. Do you like me without a bra, Santo?'

'I *enjoyed* smoking.'

'Yes, but cigarettes were bad for you. Do you like my breasts, Santo? Kiss my breasts. Kiss my nipples.'

'Burned me all over my body.'

'Yes.'

'Drugged me, and then ...'

'Isn't it better that you've quit smoking? Let's not talk about things that *had* to be done to make you a better person, Santo. You're a better person since you stopped smoking. You're healthier, you're ...'

'You didn't have to burn me with those fuckin cigarettes! I'm your prisoner here, all you had to do ...'

'No, no.'

'... was quit *bringing* me cigarettes, that's all you had to do!

Look at these scars all over me! You burned me all over my body!
All over me.'

'No, not all over you,' she said, and smiled. 'Finish undressing
me, Santo. I want you very badly.'

'When *don't* you want me?'

'Hush, now. Carry me to the bed.'

'Fuckin sex fiend,' he said.

'Don't say that.'

'It's what you are. A fuckin female rapist.'

'No,' she whispered, 'no, I'm not, really. I want you to do what
C.J. loved to do.'

'C.J. loves to do *nothing*. She's a whore who gets paid for
whatever she does.'

'Yes, she was nothing but a whore. She didn't understand,
Santo. If she'd understood, she wouldn't have told.'

'Told? Told what?'

'In the beginning, no one knew. Not even the man who changed
the locks on the doors. I told him I wanted to lock my dog in
here. I told him I had a vicious dog.'

'You *do* have a vicious dog.'

'Gently, Santo, you *do* enjoy it, don't you? Tell me you enjoy it.'

'What'd she tell? What'd C.J. tell?'

'About us, I'm sure. Her *experiences*, she said. Can you imagine?
Told me in the boat going back last Thursday. A whore's experiences. Mmm, yes, Santo, that's very good. I'm not even sure about
the man who changed the locks, any more. Do you think he sus-
pects? Do you think he'll tell the way she did? I just don't know,
Santo, oh God, that's delicious. I don't want anyone else to know
about you ever again. I'm not going to make that mistake again.'

'Who'd C.J. tell?'

'Someone who isn't going to bother us any more.'

'Who?'

'Do it to me, Santo, *do* it.'

'Who?'

'Yes, that's it, yes. Oh Jesus, yes.'

12

By Thursday morning, everything in the squadroom was sticky
and soggy. DD report forms clung moistly to each other and to
the carbon paper that was supposed to be separating the triplicate
copies. File cards pulled from the drawers grew limp within
minutes of exposure to the dampness. Forearms stuck to desktops,
erasers refused to erase properly, clothing seemed possessed of
spongelike qualities – and still the rains came. They came in
varying degrees, either as torrential downpours or relentless
drizzles, but they came unabated; the city had not seen a patch of
blue sky for the past eight days.

When the call from Gaucho Palacios came at 10.00 a.m. that
morning, Meyer was in the middle of a joke about rain. His
audience was Bert Kling and Richard Genero. Genero had no
sense of humour, although Genero's mother thought he was a very
comical fellow. The funniest joke Genero ever heard in his life was
the one about the monkey humping a football. Every time Genero
told that joke, he cracked up. He did not think many other jokes
were funny, but he listened to them politely, and always laughed
politely when they were finished. Then he instantly forgot them.
Whenever he went to his mother's house, which was every Sunday,
he pinched her on the cheek and comically said to her, 'You're
getting to be a little fatty-boo, ain't you, Mama?', which his
mother found uproariously funny. Genero's mother loved him a lot.
She called him Richie. Everybody on the squad called him Genero,
which was odd, since otherwise they all called each other by their
first names. Even the lieutenant was either Pete or Loot, but certainly never Byrnes. Genero, however, was Genero. He listened
now as Meyer came roaring down the pike towards the punch line.

'Yeah,' Carella said into the phone, 'what've you got, Cowboy?'

'Maybe a line on this Joey La Paz. You still interested?'

'I'm still interested.'

'This may be nothin',' the Gaucho said, 'or it may be choice
meat. Here's what happened. This little girl come in the shop
maybe half an hour ago, looking over the goodies, and we start
talkin and it turns out she's in Joey's stable.'

'Where is he? Does she know?'

'Well, that's what I ain't got yet. This is like a funny thing going on here. Joey's moved underground cause he's afraid you guys are gonna pin that hooker kill on him. But this girl here – the one right here in my shop this minute – is scared to death *she's* gonna be the next one. She won't go back to the apartment . . .'

'Did she tell you where it is?'

'No. Anyway, Joey ain't there now. I told you, he dug himself a hole and pulled it in after him.'

'Here in the city?'

'The girl don't know.'

'Can you hold her there for me?'

'I can only sell her so much underwear,' the Gaucho said.

'I'll be there in five minutes. Keep her in the shop,' Carella said.

At his own desk, Meyer said, 'And here I thought it was raining!' and burst out laughing. Kling slapped the top of the desk, and shouted, 'Thought it was raining!'

Genero blinked, and then laughed politely.

The girl in the back room of the Gaucho's shop seemed surrounded by the tools of a trade far too sophisticated for her years. A slight, rather pretty redhead with a dusting of freckles on her cheeks and her nose, she looked like a thirteen-year-old who'd been called into the principal's office for a minor infraction. Her clothing – her costume, to be more accurate – exaggerated the notion that here was a child just entering puberty. She wore a white cotton blouse and a grey flannel skirt with knee-length white socks and patent leather Mary Jane shoes. Small-breasted and thin-wristed, narrow-waisted and slender-ankled, she appeared violated – nay, *desecrated* – just standing there in front of the Gaucho's walled display of leather anklets, penis extenders, aphrodisiacs, inflatable life-sized female dolls, condoms in every colour of the rainbow, books on how to hypnotize and otherwise win women, and one product imaginatively named Suc-u-lator. Batting her big blue eyes, the girl seemed lost in an erotic jungle not of her own making; but suddenly, Little Orphan Annie opened her mouth and a coven of lizards and toads came crawling up out of the sewer.

'Why the fuck did you send for a cop?' she asked Gaucho.

149

'I was worried about you,' Gaucho lied.

'What's your name?' Carella asked her.

'Fuck off, mister,' she said. 'What've you got me for? Buying a pair of sexy panties? Don't your wife wear sexy panties?'

'I haven't *got* you for anything,' Carella said. 'The Cowboy tells me you're scared somebody's about to . . .'

'I'm not scared of nothing. The Cowboy's wrong.'

'You told me . . .'

'You're wrong, Cowboy. You want to wrap this stuff, I'll pay for it and be on my way.'

'Where's Joey La Paz?' Carella asked.

'I don't know anybody named Joey La Paz.'

'You work for him, don't you?'

'I work for the five-and-ten.'

'Which one?'

'On Twelfth and Rutgers. Go check.'

'Where do you work nights?'

'I work days. At the five-and-ten on Twelfth and Rutgers.'

'I'll check,' Carella said, and took his pad from his inside jacket pocket. 'What's your name?'

'I don't have to give you my name. I didn't do anything, I don't have to give you a fuckin thing.'

'Miss, I'm investigating a pair of homicides, and I haven't got time for any bullshit, okay? Now what's your name? You're so eager for me to go checking on you, I'll start checking, okay?'

'Yeah, you go check, smart guy. My name's Nancy Elliott.'

'Where do you live, Nancy?'

The girl hesitated.

'I said where do you live? What's your address?'

Again, she hesitated.

'What do you say?' Carella said.

'I don't have to give you my address.'

'That's right, you don't. Here's what we'll do, Miss *Elliott*, if that's your real name . . .'

'That's my real name.'

'Fine, here's what we'll do. I've got reason to believe you have information concerning a person we're seeking in a homicide investigation. That's Joey La Paz, whose name I mentioned just a little while ago, in case you've already forgotten it. Now, Miss

Elliott, here's what we'll do if you refuse to answer my questions. What we'll do is have you subpoenaed to appear before the Grand Jury, and *they*'ll ask you the same questions I'm asking you, but with a difference. If you refuse to answer *them*, that's contempt. And if you *lie* to them, that's perjury. So what do you say? We can play the game my way or we can play it yours. Makes no difference at all to me.'

Nancy was silent.

'Okay,' Carella said, 'I guess you want ...'

'I don't know where he is,' she said.

'But you *do* know him.'

'I know him.'

'Want to tell me what your relationship is?'

'You *know* what it is, let's just cut the crap, okay?'

'Fine. Did you also know Clara Jean Hawkins?'

'Yes, I knew her.'

'When did you last see her alive?'

'The morning of the day she caught it.'

'Last Friday morning?'

Nancy nodded.

'Where?'

'The apartment.'

'Where's that?'

'Joey'll kill me,' she said.

'Where's the apartment?'

'On Laramie and German.'

'But you say he's not there now?'

'No, he split on Sunday, soon as he heard about C.J.'

'Why'd he split?'

'He's afraid you'll hang it on him.'

'Did he tell you that?'

'He didn't tell us nothing. He just split. I'm guessing, is all.'

'Who do you mean by us?'

'Me and the other girls.'

'How many of you?'

'Four, when C.J. was alive. Three of us now.' She shrugged. 'That's if Joey ever comes back.'

'Do you think he will?'

'If he didn't kill C.J.'

'Do you think he killed her?'

Nancy shrugged.

'The Cowboy told me you're scared of him. Is it because you think he killed her?'

'I don't know what he did.'

'Then why are you scared of him?'

She shrugged again.

'You *do* think he killed her, don't you?'

'I think he had *reason* to kill her.'

'What reason?'

'The moonlighting.'

'What do you mean?'

'She was cheating on him.'

'To the tune of two hundred bucks a week, am I right?' Carella said.

'I don't know how much her little party was bringin in each week.'

'What kind of party? Did she tell you?'

'Some kind of beach party,' Nancy said, and shrugged.

'Every week?'

'Every Wednesday. She went out there in the morning.'

'Out where?'

'The beach someplace.'

'Which beach?'

'Out on Sands Spit someplace.'

'*Which* beach there?'

'I don't know.'

'How'd she get there?'

'Took a train. And then whoever it was picked her up with a car.'

'Out there on Sands Spit?'

'Yeah, out there at the beach someplace.'

'And you think Joey found out about this? If he killed her, then it was because he found out.'

'Well, *I* didn't tell him, and C.J. sure as shit wouldn't have.'

'Then who did?'

'Maybe Sarah.'

'Who's Sarah?'

'One of the other girls. Sarah Wyatt. She's new, she still digs him a lot. Maybe she's the one told him.'

'Did C.J. mention it to her?'

'C.J. had a big mouth,' Nancy said, nodding.

'How about the other girl? The third one?'

'Lakie?'

'Is that her name?'

'That's her trade name, she's from up around the Great Lakes someplace, Joey tagged her with Lakie.'

'Did she know about C.J.'s moonlighting?'

'I don't think so. They didn't get along much. Lakie's kind of snooty, thinks she's got a golden snatch, you know what I mean? C.J. didn't go for that.'

'But she told the rest of you.'

'Well, yeah.'

'Why do you suppose she got so careless?'

'Maybe she was ready to cut out, and just didn't give a shit any more.'

'Shouldn't she have recognized the danger of ...?'

'She should have. Joey's a mean son of a bitch.'

'Does he own a gun?'

'Yes.'

'You've seen it?'

'Yes.'

'What kind of gun?'

'I don't know guns. He's got a permit for it.'

'A *permit*? How'd he swing that?'

'His cousin owns a jewellery store up in Diamondback. Joey got him to say he worked for him delivering diamonds and shit. So he got the permit.'

'What's the cousin's name?'

'I don't know. Some spic name, like Joey's.'

'Where in Diamondback?'

'The jewellery store? I don't know.'

'Does the cousin live up there?'

'I think so. He's married and has a hundred kids like all the other fuckin spics in this city.'

The Gaucho cleared his throat.

'Not you, Cowboy,' Nancy said. 'You're different.'

The Gaucho seemed unconvinced.

'Will you be going back to that apartment downtown?' Carella asked.

'I don't know, I'm sort of scared to. But like ... where *else* would I go?'

'If Joey shows up there, pick up the phone and call this number,' Carella said, writing.

'Sure, and he'll break my arm,' Nancy said.

'Suit yourself,' Carella said, and handed her the card on which he'd written the precinct's phone number. 'If he killed C.J., though ...'

'Sure,' Nancy said, nibbling at the inside of her mouth, 'What's a broken arm by comparison, right?'

A call to Pistol Permits revealed that José Luis La Paz had indeed been issued a Carry Permit on the third day of May, which was about the time he'd gone into business procuring young ladies for gentlemen of good taste. The licence application stated as his reason for needing a pistol the fact that he delivered precious gems as part of his job with Corrosco Jewellers at 1727 Cabot Street. The proprietor of the shop, who had signed his name to the confirming affidavit, was Eugene Corrosco. Carella thanked the man at Pistol Permits, looked up Corrosco Jewellers in the Isola yellow pages, and immediately dialled the store. A man speaking with a heavy Spanish accent told Carella that Eugene Corrosco was away on vacation. Carella asked when Mr Corrosco would be back, but the man didn't know. Carella thanked him, looked up *Corrosco, Eugene* in the white pages, and got a woman who said she was Mrs Corrosco. She didn't know where her husband was, or when he would be back. Belatedly, she asked who was calling.

'This is Marty Rosen,' Carella said. 'I talked to him last week about some very nice sapphires, he said to give him a call.'

'Well, Mr Rosen, he ain't here,' the woman said.

'And you don't know when he'll be back, huh?' Carella said.

'No, I don't know.'

'Cause I'll be going back to Chicago, you know, on Friday.'

'I'm sorry,' the woman said.

'Yeah, thanks anyway,' Carella said, and hung up.

He opened the top drawer of his desk, and pulled out the police map that divided the city into precincts. 1727 Cabot Street was smack in the middle of the Eight-Three, uptown in Diamondback.

The Eight-Three meant only one thing: Fat Ollie Weeks.

Stubby hand extended, shirt collar open, tie pulled down, sleeves rolled up over massive forearms, Fat Ollie Weeks came waddling across the squadroom of the 83rd Precinct to greet Carella and Meyer where they stood just outside the slatted rail divider. Both men were wearing sodden raincoats. Meyer was wearing his Professor Higgins hat, but Carella was hatless and even the short run from the car to the station house had left his hair looking like a tangle of brown seaweed.

'Hey, you guys, Jeez,' Ollie said, and gripped Carella's hand, 'I ain't seen you guys in a dog's age, ever since Kling had his bride stole right out from under him! Jeez, how the hell are you, I been meaning to call you. You brought ole Kosher Salami with you, huh?' he said, gripping Meyer's hand, 'how's old Oscar-Mayer Kosher Salami doin, huh?' he said, and burst out laughing.

Meyer took off the Professor Higgins hat, and shook the rain from it.

'What brings you guys up here to the Eight-Three, have a seat, willyez. Jeez, it's great to see you,' Ollie said. 'Hey, Gonzalez,' he shouted to the clerical office, 'bring some coffee out here, will you, hold the Spanish Fly,' and burst out laughing again, and said, 'He's Puerto Rican, I'm always kiddin him about puttin Spanish Fly in the coffee, you know what I mean? So, Jeez, how you doin down there in the Eight-Seven? I been meaning to call you guys, I swear to God, I really do enjoy workin with you guys.'

'We're up here looking for a pimp named Joey La Paz,' Carella said. 'Do you know him?'

'No, it don't ring a bell,' Ollie said. He shook his head. 'No.'

'Joey Peace?'

'No.'

'How about Eugene Corrosco?'

'Oh sure, I know Gene, but he ain't a pimp. Gene owns a jewellery store on Cabot. Just between you, me, and the lamp post, Gene does a little bit of fencing on the side, you dig? I'm waiting

155

to bust his spic ass the minute I hear he's also settin up burglaries, the way some of these guys do, you know? Sell you a diamond tiara for your wife, put a burglar on it, have him break in and steal the thing back, fence it next week across the river someplace. Very neat,' Ollie said. 'So far, Gene's just a smalltime fence, hardly worth a bust. I'm layin in the bushes so I can send him away for a long one. What's *your* beef with him?'

'No beef. We're trying to find La Paz. They're cousins.'

'This on the hooker got killed in Midtown South?'

'Yes,' Carella said.

'Figures. You're lookin for a pimp, got to be a hooker involved, right?' he said, and tapped his temple with his forefinger, and smiled at Meyer, and said, '*Tochis*, Meyer.'

Meyer did not smile back. Meyer did not like Ollie. Meyer did not know *anyone* who liked Ollie. Ollie was not only fat, which in the United States of America automatically made him a villain, he was also bigoted. And he smelled. His breath smelled. His body smelled. He was a vast uncharted garbage dump. He was also a good cop. By certain standards.

'So Gene's store is right around the corner,' Ollie said. 'What's the problem?'

'Away on vacation it seems,' Carella said.

'Vacation, bullshit,' Ollie said. 'Come on, let's go find that little asshole.'

The Puerto Rican section of Diamondback had been named by its inhabitants, who – perhaps in reaction to a city that seemed determined to grind them into the dust – had lost in the christening process the fine sense of humour that had caused them to name the biggest slum in Puerto Rico 'La Perla'. Following the same satiric tack, they might have named their Stateside ghetto 'El Paradiso'. Instead, they chose to call a spade a spade. The place was El Infierno, and the tenement smells here were Hispanic in origin, which meant that mixed in with the headier non-denominational stinks of cohabitation and waste were the more exotic aromas of *sancochado, ajiaco de papas, frijoles negros, arroz con salchicha* and *cabrito criollo*.

'Makes you hungry just walkin inside one of these fuckin buildings,' Ollie said. 'There's a Spanish joint around the corner, you guys want to get a bite to eat later. The prices are very reasonable, if you take my meaning, yes indeed, oh yes,' he said, winking and falling into his world famous W. C. Fields imitation. 'What this is here,' he said, returning to his normal speaking voice which was pitched somewhere between a grunt and a growl, a sort of whisky-seared rumble that came up from his huge barrel chest and rattled across the gravel pit of his throat to emerge from his thick lips with a stench of brimstone and bile accompanying it – Meyer wondered when Ollie had last brushed his teeth. Guy Fawkes Day? Which was not celebrated in the United States of America. 'What this is here,' Ollie said, 'is the place where Gene Corrosco keeps the shit he fences, yes indeed m'friends, doesn't know ole Ollie knows about it, he's gonna be in for some surprise, the little spic asshole. It's on the third floor here, get ready with the heat, m'friends, in case Corrosco decides his little stash is worth protecting.'

They were on the third floor already, following Ollie down the corridor towards the two apartments at the end of it. 'It's 3A, the one on the right,' Ollie said, 'let me give a listen first, huh?' He put his ear to the door as soon as they were outside the apartment, listening the way any good cop would listen before knocking on a door or kicking it in. His pistol was in his right hand, his left ear was to the door, he was breathing heavily after the climb to the third floor and his breath stank to high heaven. 'Two of them, from what I can tell,' he whispered. 'I'll bust the door down, you fan out behind me.'

'Ollie,' Carella said, 'we haven't got a warrant, I think . . .'

'Fuck the warrant,' Ollie said, 'this is Diamondback.' He moved away from the door, across the corridor, and then sprinted towards it with all the agility of a dainty hippo, hitting the lock with his shoulder instead of going for a kick at it; Meyer guessed Ollie would have had trouble bringing up his knee. The door splintered away from the jamb, nuts and bolts flying as Ollie followed it into the room, left shoulder still low after hitting the lock, swinging around now to bring his right hand, the gun hand, into position. Carella and Meyer were just behind him.

The room resembled nothing so much as a miniature warehouse. Ranged across the floor, virtually wall to wall, were a wide variety of brand-name television sets, radios, toasters, cameras, projectors, typewriters, micro-wave ovens, hair dryers, bicycles, skis, stereo turntables, amplifiers, tuners and speakers, and a partridge in a pear tree. Along one of the walls was a pipe coat rack upon which was hanging an assortment of coats fashioned of mink, sable, red fox, raccoon, lynx, opossum, silver fox, ocelot, Persian lamb and four colly birds. Two men were standing alongside a long table upon which was arrayed a glitter of bracelets, necklaces, brooches, tiaras, watches, pendants, earrings, silver flatware, silver goblets, silver pitchers, silver serving trays and five golden rings. Into the room, like twelve lords a'leaping, came graceful Fat Ollie followed by fumbling Steve Carella who was worried about illegal entry, and cautious Meyer Meyer who was afraid his hat would fall off, and he'd trip on it in front of these two hoods who were running a bargain basement up here in Diamondback.

'Well, well,' Ollie said, 'ain't this interesting! Just freeze it, Gene, my friends are very trigger-happy.'

Eugene Corrosco had turned away from the table the moment the door shattered inwards. He was a short man with a pock-marked complexion and a thick black Zapata moustache. He was almost as bald as Meyer, but not quite. His friend was a blond white man. The blond looked first at the cops and then at Corrosco; his eyes seemed to be accusing Corrosco of having withheld vital information, like for example the possibility that cops might come breaking in here. He seemed about to burst into tears.

'Hello, Detective Weeks,' Corrosco said. He had a very high voice, and he was grinning sheepishly, as if he'd just been caught with a girl on the roof rather than a roomful of stolen goods.

'Little tag sale, Gene?' Ollie said.

'No, no, just some stuff here,' Corrosco said.

'Oh yes,' Ollie said in his W. C. Fields voice, '*lotsa* stuff here, yes indeed.'

'Yeah,' Corrosco said, still grinning.

'You and your pal running a little hot-goods drop, Gene?' Ollie asked.

'No, no,' Corrosco said, 'Just some stuff here, that's all.'

'*Whose* stuff, Gene?'

'My mother's,' Corrosco said.

'Your mother's?' Ollie said, genuinely surprised. 'Well, well. Your mother's.'

'Yeah,' Corrosco said. 'She keeps it in storage here.'

'Likes television, your mother,' Ollie said.

'Yeah, she does.'

'Fourteen sets, I count.'

'Yeah, fourteen,' Corrosco said. 'She had fourteen rooms.'

'Watched television in all the rooms, huh?'

'Yeah, all the rooms,' Corrosco said.

'The toilet, too?'

'Huh?'

'Did she watch television in the toilet?'

'No, not the toilet,' Corrosco said.

'What'd she do in the toilet?' Ollie asked. 'Did she take pictures in the toilet?'

'Huh?'

'Lots of cameras here. Did your mother take pictures in the toilet?'

'Oh, yeah, in the toilet,' Corrosco said, grinning.

'Corrosco,' Ollie said, 'I am going to bust you for receiving stolen goods.'

'Gee, Detective Weeks,' Corrosco said.

'Unless . . .'

'How much?' Corrosco said at once.

'Did you hear *that*?' Ollie said, turning with a shocked expression to where Carella and Meyer stood just inside the open door, their pistols in their hands. 'Did you *hear* what this man just *said*?'

'I didn't say nothing,' Corrosco said.

'Me neither,' the blond said.

'I certainly hope you weren't attempting a bribe,' Ollie said.

'No, no,' Corrosco said at once. 'No, sir. Not me.'

'Me neither,' the blond said, shaking his head.

'I'll tell you what,' Ollie said.

'What?' Corrosco said at once.

'There's somebody we're looking for.'

'Who?' Corrosco said, again at once.

'Man named Joey La Paz.'

'Never heard of him,' Corrosco said.

'You never heard of your own cousin?'

'He's my cousin?' Corrosco said. 'No, he can't be my cousin. If I never heard of him, how could he be my cousin?'

'Gene,' Ollie said, 'I'm sorry to have to do this to you because Criminal Possession of Stolen Property can be either a Class-A misdemeanour, or a Class-E or Class-D felony, depending on the value of the property. That means you can gross either a year, four years or seven years in jail, depending. That's a lot of time, Gene. But what can I tell you? The law is the law and I wouldn't be doin my duty if I allowed this wilful transgression . . .'

'La Paz, did you say?'

'Joey La Paz,' Ollie said, nodding.

'Oh, yeah. I thought you said Lopez.'

'No, La Paz.'

'Yeah, that's right. Sure.'

'Sure what?'

'Sure, he's my cousin.'

'Where is he, Gene?'

'How should I know?' Corrosco said. 'Do you know where *your* cousin is?'

'No, but then again I ain't the one who's got cop trouble in a roomful of stolen goods.' He took a step closer to Corrosco. Corrosco backed away against the table. Ollie wrapped his fist into Corrosco's shirt, put his face very close to Corrosco's and then, in a hissing little whisper, said, 'Listen to me, spic. I want your cousin. If I don't get your cousin, I get you. If you're lucky, you'll get a spic judge who'll let you off easy. Take your choice, Gene. You or your cousin.'

'What do you want him for?' Corrosco asked.

'You ain't readin me, are you?' Ollie said, and sighed, and let go of his shirt. 'Okay,' he said, 'get your hat. You, too, Blondie.'

'I just came by to say hello,' the blond man said.

'You can say hello to the judge.'

'I mean it. Tell him, Gene. Tell him I just came by to say hello.'

'Shut up,' Corrosco said. 'My cousin's in an apartment on Saint Sab's and Booker.'

'What's the address?' Ollie said, taking out his pad.

'629 Saint Sab.'

'Name on the mailbox?'

'Amy Wyatt.'

'Who's that? One of his hookers?'

'No, her mother.'

'*Whose* mother?'

'Sarah Wyatt's.'

'Girl in his stable?'

'Yeah, but recent.'

'Okay, Gene, thanks a lot. Now get your hat.'

'Get my *hat*?' Corrosco said. 'What *for*? You told me ...'

'That was before you got cute with me. Get your fuckin *hat*!'

'That ain't fair,' Corrosco said, pouting.

'Who says it has to be?' Ollie asked.

La Paz came off the bed with a pistol in his hand, swinging it at the door the moment the lock imploded into the room. He was wearing only dark narrow trousers, no shirt, no shoes or socks. His skin was a creamy tan, and he kept himself in good shape, muscles rippling across his chest and up the length of his arm as he levelled the pistol at Ollie's broad chest.

'Just pull the trigger, shithead,' Ollie said.

La Paz hesitated.

'Go on, pull it,' Ollie said. 'My two friends here'll shoot you fulla holes and stuff you down the toilet like the piece of shit you are. Pull the fuckin trigger, go *on*!'

Carella waited with bated breath, half-hoping La Paz would respond positively to Ollie's dare. Instead, he lowered the gun.

'Good boy,' Ollie said. 'Throw it on the floor.'

La Paz threw it on the floor.

'Up. On your feet. Grab paint,' Ollie said. He shoved La Paz against the wall, and then tossed him, between the legs and down the sides of his trousers. 'Okay,' he said. 'Turn around. Who else is in this shithole?'

'Nobody,' La Paz said.

'Where's Amy Wyatt?'

'She works. She ain't here.'

'All alone, huh?'

'Yeah.'

'I hope you don't fall down and hurt yourself or nothing,' Ollie said. 'Be nobody here but us to call an ambulance, huh? These gentlemen here want to ask you some questions. I hope you co-operate with them, Joey, cause I don't like trouble in my precinct, okay?'

'How'd you get to me?'

'We got ways, m'boy,' Ollie said in his W. C. Fields voice. He picked up the pistol, looked at it, and then said to Carella, 'You ain't chasin a .32 Colt, are you?'

'No,' Carella said.

'Too bad,' Ollie said, and tucked the pistol into his waistband. He turned back to La Paz. 'Answer the man's questions,' he said.

'Sure,' La Paz said. 'What do you want to know?'

'Tell me about Clara Jean Hawkins,' Carella said.

'I knew it,' La Paz said.

'What'd you know?'

'That this was gonna be about her.'

'What the fuck'd you *think* it was gonna be about, you dumb fuck?' Ollie said. 'Girl gets killed, what d'you *think* these guys are lookin for, a fuckin dumb *procurin* bust? This is *homicide*, you dumb shit, you better answer these guys straight.'

'I didn't kill her,' La Paz said.

'Nobody ever killed anybody,' Ollie said. 'The world is full of victims, but nobody ever victimized them. Go on, Steve, ask him what you gotta ask.'

'What do you know about a weekly beach party out on Sands Spit someplace?' Carella said.

'A *what*?'

'You heard the man, you deaf or something?' Ollie said.

'A beach party?' La Paz said, and shook his head. 'I don't know what you mean.'

'He means did you send some of your girls partying out at the *beach* is what he means, you dumb fuck,' Ollie said.

'Is that what you mean?' La Paz asked.

'You tell me,' Carella said.

'I don't know anything about any beach parties out on Sands Spit.'

'Wednesday night beach parties,' Carella said.

'No, I don't know anything about them.'

'Do you know where Clara Jean Hawkins went every Wednesday night?'

162

'Yeah, to see her mother. Her mother's sick, she used to go see her every Wednesday night, stayed over till Thursday.'

'You didn't mind that?'

'Middle of the week's sort of slow anyway,' La Paz said, and shrugged.

'What time would she get back on Thursday?'

'Time enough. She'd be out on the street maybe ten, eleven o'clock at night. I had no complaints about her visiting her mother, if that's what you're trying to establish here.'

'I'm not trying to establish anything,' Carella said, 'just cool it.'

'Just cool it, you punk,' Ollie said, 'he ain't trying to establish anything.'

'He's saying I didn't like her going to see her mother . . .'

'That ain't establishing anything,' Ollie said. 'Just answer the man's fuckin questions and keep your mouth shut. Go ahead, Steve.'

'Have any harsh words with her lately?'

'No, we got along fine.'

'Same as you got along with the other girls?'

'Same.'

'Same as Sarah Wyatt?'

'Sarah's different.'

'How so?'

'We got a thing going, Sarah and me.'

'But not you and Clara Jean, huh?'

'No, not me and C.J., no. In the beginning, yeah, but not recently.'

'In the beginning, she just adored you, huh?' Ollie said.

'Yeah, we had a thing going.'

'That how you turned her out? Or was it smack?'

'No, she wasn't doing smack.'

'Just fell in love with you, that it?'

'More or less.'

'Easy to see why, you're so gorgeous.'

'She thought so,' La Paz said.

'Oh, *I* think so too, honey,' Ollie said, and waved a limp wrist at him. 'You fuckin little pimp, you turned the girl out as a whore, you realize that? Don't that mean nothin to you?'

'It didn't hurt her,' La Paz said, and shrugged.

'No, it didn't hurt her at all,' Ollie said. 'All it done was *kill* her.'

'Hooking didn't kill her.'

'What *did*?' Carella asked at once.

'How do I know?'

'Why are you hiding?' Carella asked.

''Cause I knew about the moonlighting.'

'Make up your mind,' Carella said. 'You just tole us you *didn't* know anything about it.'

'About what? I ain't followin you,' La Paz said.

'About the Wednesday night beach parties.'

'What's that got to . . . ?'

'He's talking about the *moon*lighting, you dumb shit,' Ollie said. 'The Wednesday night *parties*. The parties you don't know anything about even though you know the fuckin girl was *moon*-lightin. Now which is it? *Did* you know or *didn't* you know?'

'I knew she was moonlighting, but I didn't know what it was. I didn't know it was a steady party, anything like that. I just thought she was holding out on me.'

'How'd you feel about that?' Carella asked.

La Paz shrugged.

'Just didn't matter, huh?' Ollie asked.

'I had a choice,' La Paz said. 'I could've beat the shit out of her and risked her crossing the street to some other dude, or I could've looked the other way. What was she skimming, when you got right down to it? A bill a week, something like that?'

'Two bills,' Carella said.

'So even two bills,' La Paz said, and shrugged. 'Was it worth losing her for a lousy two bills?'

'How much was she bringing in?' Meyer asked.

'Fifteen hundred, two grand a week, somewhere in between there. So should I risk that for a lousy two bills?'

'All your girls bringing that in?' Ollie asked.

'Yeah, somewhere in there.'

'How many girls you got?'

'Four with C.J. Three now.'

'So you were making something like six, seven grand a week, huh?'

'Eight grand, some weeks.'

'You know how much *I* make a *year*, you fuckin shithead? I'm a Detective/Second, you know how much I make each year, you know how much me and these two guys standin here make each year, huh? You got any idea?'

'No, I got no idea,' La Paz said.

'Twenty-three fucking thousand dollars a *year*, that's how much we make, you little pimp.'

'Who told you about C.J.'s moonlighting?' Carella asked.

'Twenty-three thousand a *year*,' Ollie said, shaking his head.

'Sarah Wyatt,' La Paz said.

'But she didn't know it was a beach party, huh?'

'No, sir, she didn't.'

Carella and Meyer looked at each other. Carella sighed. Meyer nodded.

'Hey, you guys,' Ollie said, 'don't cry, huh? I hate to see grown men cry. You, you little shithead,' he said to La Paz, 'get your ass out of my precinct. I see your pimp ass up here ever again, you'll wish you were back in Mayaguez or wherever the fuck you came from.'

'Palmas Altas,' La Paz said.

'Same fuckin thing,' Ollie said. 'Out,' he said, and jerked his thumb towards the door.

'Let me get dressed first,' La Paz said.

'Make it fast,' Ollie said, 'before my friends here decide to bust you just for the hell of it.'

The moment La Paz reached for his shirt, Ollie turned and winked at Meyer and Carella. Neither of the men winked back. They were both thinking their case was as dead as all three victims.

13

The Elsinore County cops did not know they had a fourth victim in the tandem cases being investigated jointly by Midtown South and the Eight-Seven. The Elsinore County cops thought of *their* corpse as a first victim. They found the body that Thursday night at 10.00 p.m. The dead man's name was Wilbur Matthews. Before his demise, he'd been a locksmith living behind the shop he owned in the town of Fox Hill, previously known as Vauxhall after that district of Lambeth metropolitan borough in London – everywhere on the Eastern seaboard of the United States was the influence of colonial Great Britain still felt.

Fox Hill had been a sleepy little fishing village until as recently as thirty years ago, when an enterprising gentleman from Los Angeles came east to open what was then called the Fox Hill Inn, a huge rambling waterfront hotel that had since fallen into other hands and been renamed the Fox Hill Arms. The building of the hotel had also been responsible for the building of a town around it, rather the way a frontier fort back in the dear dead days eventually led to a settlement around it. Fox Hill was now a community of some forty thousand people, thirty thousand of them year-round residents, ten thousand known alternately as 'summer people' or, less affectionately, 'the Sea Gulls'. The locksmith Wilbur Matthews had been a year-round resident. A quick glance at the meticulous records he kept in his shop's locked filing cabinets showed that he had installed some three thousand locks in the past five years (his active records only went back that far) and had repaired another twelve hundred during that same time, some of them automobile locks but most of them locks on homes.

Wilbur Matthews was a well-liked man in the community. Lock yourself out of your car or your house at two in the morning, all you had to do was call old Wilbur, and he'd get himself dressed and come help you, just like doctors used to do. Wilbur's wife had died back during the last big hurricane, not from the hurricane itself, not from drowning or anything, but just natural in her bed, sleeping like a babe. Wilbur had lived alone since. He was a church-going man (the First Presbyterian on Oceanview and Third) and a God-fearing man, and there wasn't a person in all Fox Hill who'd have said a mean word about him. But someone had shot him twice in the head, and the Elsinore County cops just couldn't figure out why.

The cops out there were somewhat more paramilitary than the cops in the city; even the detectives had ranks like sergeant and corporal. The two men assigned to the Wilbur Matthews homicide were Detective-Sergeant Andrew (Buddy) Budd, and Detective-Corporal Louis Dellarosa. They crouched in the rain outside the bedroom window of the old man's house, looking for shell casings. The lab technicians weren't there yet; the lab technicians had to come all the way from the county seat in Elsinore. Budd and Dellarosa searched but found nothing. Inside the house, a man from the Medical Examiner's office was looking down at the dead man where he lay in his bed. There were two bullet holes in the wall behind the bed and another bullet hole in the pillow just to the left of Wilbur Matthews' head, and two more in Wilbur Matthews' head itself, one drilled through his left eye and the other through his forehead. The Assistant Medical Examiner turned to look towards the window because it seemed to him the trajectory had originated there, but he wasn't a Ballistics cop, and it would probably take the man from Ballistics just as long to get here as it would the lab technicians, both of them having to come all the way from Headquarters in Elsinore. The Assistant ME figured he'd best pronounce the man dead, and further figured he'd be absolutely safe in stating that the cause of death had been multiple gunshot wounds. He was beginning to write up his report when a flash of lightning illuminated the window he'd been glancing at not a moment before, followed by a thunderclap that scared him the way he'd once been scared on a vill sweep in Vietnam. He went out into the hallway at once, and asked a uniformed cop there if it was all right for him to use the bathroom.

The cop said, 'No, this is a crime scene.'

After forty-eight hours, you begin to get a little desperate. After seventy-two, you start praying for a break; it is amazing how many cops get religion after putting in seventy-two hours on a cold homicide case. After four days, you're sure you'll *never* solve the damn thing. When you hit the six-day mark, you begin getting desperate all over again. It is a different sort of desperation. It is a desperation bordering on obsession; you begin to see murderers under every rock. If your grandmother looks at you cockeyed, you begin to suspect her. You go over your typed reports again and again, you study your crime-scene drawings, you read homicide reports from other precincts, you search through the files looking for homicide cases in which the weapon was a .38 or the victim was a hooker or a singer or a business manager, you hash over homicide cases involving frauds or semi-frauds like Harry Caine's vanity-house caper, you rehash homicide cases involving missing or kidnapped persons – and eventually you become an expert on all such homicides committed in the goddam city during the past ten years, but you *still* don't know who the hell killed three people in the immediate past, never mind ten years ago.

It was now 9.40 a.m. on Friday morning, September 22, only fourteen hours short of 11.40 p.m. when exactly one week ago a concerned citizen dialled Emergency 911 to report two men bleeding on the sidewalk at Culver and South Eleventh. Fourteen hours short of a week. Fourteen short hours short. At twenty minutes to midnight tonight, George C. Chadderton would have been dead a full week. At 3.30 a.m. tomorrow morning, Clara Jean Hawkins would likewise have been dead a full week. Ambrose Harding, who was at present lying in a coffin at the Monroe Funeral Home on St Sebastian Avenue would be buried tomorrow morning at 9.00, by which time *he'd* have been dead almost four days. And the case continued to lay there like a lox without a bagel.

At 9.40 that morning, Carella went to see Chloe Chadderton at her apartment in Diamondback. He had called from home first, and was therefore somewhat surprised to find her wearing the same long pink robe she'd worn on that night almost a week ago, when he and Meyer had knocked on her door at two in the morning. It occurred to him, as she let him into the apartment, that he had never seen Chloe in street clothes. She was always either in a nightgown with a robe over it, as she was now, or else strutting half-naked on a bartop, or else sitting at a table wearing only a flimsy nylon wrapper over her dancing costume. He could understand why George Chadderton wanted his wife to get out of 'show biz', considering what she seemed intent on showing day and night to any interested viewer. Sitting opposite her in the living room now, Carella looked across at the long length of leg revealed in the opening of her robe and silently admitted that he himself was an interested viewer. Embarrassed, recalling Chloe's total exposure on the bartop at the Flamingo, he quickly took out his notebook and busied himself leafing through its pages.

'Would you like some coffee?' she asked. 'I have some on the stove.'

'No, thanks,' Carella said. 'I just want to ask you some questions, and then I'll be on my way.'

'No hurry,' she said, and smiled.

'Mrs Chadderton,' he said, 'I tried to fill you in a little on the phone about what we believe is the connection between your husband and C. J. Hawkins, the fact that they'd been talking about doing an album together.'

'Yes, but George never mentioned that to me,' Chloe said.

'Something called "In The Life". Do you remember in his notebook . . .'

'Yes . . .'

'The night we were here . . .'

'Yes, I remember.'

'That's what we think the title of the album was going to be.'

'Mm-huh,' Chloe said.

'But he never mentioned this album to you.'

'No.'

'Or Miss Hawkins. He never mentioned anyone named Clara Jean Hawkins or C. J. Hawkins.'

'Never,' Chloe said, and shifted her weight on the sofa.

Carella looked at his notebook again. 'Mrs Chadderton . . .' he said.

'I wish you'd call me Chloe,' she said.

'Well . . . uh . . . yes, fine,' he said, but instead skirted the name the way he might have a puddle on the sidewalk. 'In the appointment calendar you let me have, the name Hawkins and the initials C.J. appeared on the following dates: August tenth, August twenty-fourth, August thirty-first and September seventh. Those are all Thursdays. We know that Miss Hawkins' day off was Thursday . . .'

'Just like a cleaning woman,' Chloe said, and smiled.

'What?' Carella said.

'Thursdays and every other Sunday,' Chloe said.

'Oh. Well, I hadn't made that connection,' Carella said.

'Don't worry, I'm not about to start another racial hassle,' Chloe said.

'I didn't think you were.'

'I was wrong about you that night,' she said. 'That first night.'

'Well,' he said, 'that's . . .'

'Do you know when I realized you were okay?'

'No, when was that?'

'At the Flamingo. You were checking names and dates in your little notebook, same as you're doing now, and you asked me who Lou Davis was and I told you he was the man who owned the hall my husband . . .'

'Yes, I remember.'

'And you said "How dumb" or something like that. About your*self*, I mean. You were calling yourself dumb.'

'I was *right*, too,' Carella said, and smiled.

'So I decided I liked you.'

'Well . . . good. I'm glad to hear that.'

'In fact, I was very happy when you called this morning,' Chloe said.

'Well . . . uh . . . good,' he said, and smiled. 'I was saying that your husband's meetings with C. J. Hawkins . . .'

'She was a hooker, is that right?'

'Yes, always took place on Thursdays, which was her day off, Thursday. We've got reason to believe that some sort of beach party took place every *Wednesday* night, however, and I wonder if your husband ever mentioned any such party to you.'

'A beach party?'

'Well, we don't know if it was a party *on* the beach. We only know that C.J. went out to the beach someplace.'

'What beach?'

'We don't know, and got paid for her services out there.'

'Oh.'

'Yes, we think it was, you know, some sort of regular, uh, prostitution she was performing out there someplace.'

'With George, are you saying?'

'No, I'm not suggesting that. I know you had a good marriage. I know there was no trouble . . .'

'Bullshit,' Chloe said.

Carella looked at her.

'I know that's what I told you,' she said.

'Yes, more than once, Mrs Chadderton.'

'More than *twice*, in fact,' she said, and smiled. 'And it's Chloe. I wish you'd call me Chloe.'

'Are you telling me now that things *weren't* good in your marriage?'

'Things were rotten,' she said.

'Other women?'

'I would guess.'

'Hookers?'

'I wouldn't put it past him, for all his "Sister Woman" bullshit.'

'Then you're not discounting the possibility of a sexual relationship between your husband and Miss Hawkins.'

'I'm not discounting *anything*.'

'Was he ever gone from the apartment on a Wednesday night?'

'He was gone from the apartment almost *every* night.'

'I'm trying to find out ...'

'You're trying to find out whether he and this woman were together on Wednesday nights ...'

'Yes, Mrs Chadderton, because ...'

'Chloe,' she said.

'Chloe, right. Because if I can establish that there was something more than this *cockamamy* record album between them, if I can establish that they were seeing each other, and maybe got somebody *angry* about it ...'

'Not me,' Chloe said at once.

'I wasn't suggesting that.'

'Why not? I just told you we were unhappy. I just told you he had other women. Isn't that reason ...'

'Well maybe,' Carella said, 'but the logistics aren't right. We were here until almost three a.m. last Friday night, and C.J. was killed at three-thirty. You couldn't possibly have dressed, travelled all the way downtown, and found her on the street in that short a time.'

'Then you *did* consider it?'

'I considered it,' Carella said, and smiled. 'I've been considering *everything* these past few days. That's why I'd appreciate any help you can give me. What I'm looking for is a connection between the two of them.'

'Two of them? What about Ame?'

'No, I think Harding was killed because the murderer was

afraid of identification. He was even warned beforehand ...'

'Warned?'

'Warned. With a pink orchid called *Calypso bulbosa.* I think the killer wants to be caught. I think it's like that guy years ago who scrawled it in lipstick on a mirror. That orchid is the same damn thing. Otherwise why warn the man? Why not just kill him? He wants to be stopped, whoever he is. So if you can remember anything at all about any Wednesday night your husband was out of this apartment ...'

'I don't think you understand,' Chloe said. 'He was gone more often than he was here. There were times, this last little while, where I'd be sitting here talking to the four walls. I'd find myself longing to go back to the club. I'd get home some time around eight-thirty, nine o'clock, and I'd eat here alone in the apartment, George'd be gone, and I'd sit here wondering what the hell I was *doing* here, why didn't I just go on back to the club? Talk to the girls, have someone to talk to. Dance for the men, have someone looking at me as if he knew I was *alive*, do you understand? George was so involved with his own damn self, he never ... well, look at me, I'm a pretty woman, at least I *think* I'm a pretty woman, and he was ... do you think I'm pretty?'

'Yes,' Carella said, 'I do.'

'Sure, but not to George. George was so much in love with himself, so completely involved in his own projects, his pipe-dream record albums that never got made, his big-shot calypso singer bullshit, his search for his goddam brother who probably ran off and left him cause he couldn't stand him any more than anyone *else* could! George, George, George, it was all George, George, George, he named himself right, the bastard, King George, that's exactly what he thought he was, a fucking *king*! You know what he told me when he wanted me to quit the Flamingo? He told me my dancing there reflected badly on his image as a popular singer. *His* image! *I* was embarrassing *him*, do you understand? It never once occurred to him that maybe I was embarrassing *myself*, too. I mean, man, that's degrading isn't it? Squatting on a bartop and shoving myself in some man's face? You look nervous,' she said suddenly. 'Am I making you nervous?'

'A little.'

172

'Why? Because you've seen me naked?'

'Maybe.'

'Join the club,' she said airily, and waved one arm languidly over her head. 'Do you understand what I'm saying, though?'

'I think so.'

'There was nothing between us any more, is what I'm saying. When you brought me the news that night, when you came here and told me George had got killed, I started crying because ... because I thought, hell, George got killed a long time ago. The George I loved and married got killed more years ago than I can remember. All that was left was somebody running around trying to be the big star he didn't have a chance in hell of becoming. That's why I began crying that night. I began crying because I suddenly realized how long he'd been dead. How long *we'd* been dead, in fact.'

Carella nodded and said nothing.

'I've been lonely a long, long time,' she said, and then softly, so softly that it seemed a part of the whisper of rain against the windows, she said, 'Steve.'

The room went silent. In the kitchen, he could hear the steady hiss of the gas jet under the coffee pot. Somewhere in the distance, there was the low rumble of thunder. He looked at her, looked at the long length of tan leg and thigh in the opening of the pink gown, looked at the slender ankle and the jiggling foot, and remembered her on the Flamingo bartop.

'If ... if there's nothing more you can tell me,' he said, 'I'd better be going.'

'Stay,' she said.

'Chloe ...' he said.

'Stay. You liked what you saw that day, didn't you?'

'I liked what I saw, yes,' Carella said.

'Then stay,' she whispered. 'The rain is gentler in the other room.'

He looked at her and wished he could tell her he didn't want to make love to her without having to say it straight out. He knew a hundred cops in the department – well, fifty anyway – who claimed they'd been to bed with every burglary, robbery, assault, or what-have-you victim they'd ever met, and maybe they had, Carella guessed maybe they had. He guessed Cotton Hawes had, though he wasn't too sure about that, and he supposed Hal Willis had, and he knew Andy Parker had or else was lying when he boasted in the squadroom about all his bedroom conquests. But he knew Meyer hadn't, and he knew that he himself would rather cut off his right arm than be unfaithful to Teddy, though there were many times – like right this goddam minute with Chloe Chadderton sitting there opposite him, the smile gone from her face now, her eyes narrowed, her foot jiggling, her robe open clear to Sunday – when he would have liked nothing better than to spend a wet Friday in bed with a warm stranger in another room where the rain was gentler. He looked at her. Their eyes locked.

'Chloe,' he said, 'you're a beautiful, exciting woman – but I'm a working cop with three homicides to solve.'

'Suppose you didn't have all those homicides to solve?' she asked.

'I'm also a married man,' he said.

'Does that mean anything nowadays?'

'Yes.'

'Okay,' she said.

'Please,' he said.

'I said okay,' she snapped. And then, her voice rising, her words clipped and angry, she said, 'I don't know anything about George's Wednesday night parties, nor the whore's either. If there's nothing else, I'd like to get dressed now.'

She folded her arms defensively across her breasts, and pulled the robe closed around her crossed legs. She was sitting that way when he left the apartment.

The dog was sitting just inside the locked double doors, the keys hanging on his collar where she'd put them. She'd been late bringing Santo his breakfast, but she seemed happy and excited this morning, and her exuberance frightened him somewhat. As he spooned cornflakes into his mouth, he watched her pacing the room, and he remembered that she had been this way just before all the other times she'd done things to him. The time with the needles, and then when she'd burned him with the cigarettes and when she . . . when he woke up that time and . . . and the . . . the little finger of his right hand was missing, she had . . . she had

174

doped him first and then ... then had cut off his finger while ...
while ...

'Eat your breakfast,' she said.

She hardly ever doped him in the morning, it was usually
dinner, she usually put something in his food at dinner time and
then ... did what ... did whatever she ... she ... but this morning she was higher than he'd ever seen her, pacing the room,
walking back and forth from the locked entrance doors to the
closed bathroom door, passing Santo where he sat eating from
the tray on the coffee table in front of the couch.

'Drink your coffee, too,' she said, 'drink it while it's still hot.
I made you hot coffee. Why don't you ever appreciate any of the
things I do for you?'

'I appreciate everything you do,' he said.

'Oh, yes, certainly,' she said, and laughed. 'Which is why you
tried to run away.' She laughed again. 'And *did* run away, don't
talk to me about gratitude.'

'*Did* run away?'

'Well, you're never going to run away again, don't worry about
that.'

'Are you talkin about the time Clarence ...'

'No, no, no, no,' she said, and laughed too heartily, and a shiver
ran up his spine. 'Not dear Clarence – no, *stay*, Clarence – not
your good friend Clarence who pinned you to the ground that
time, do you remember that time, is that the time you mean? No,
not that time, I mean the *first* time, don't think I didn't *know* you
wanted to leave me, don't think I didn't realize it.'

'I told you I wanted to leave.'

'Be quiet!' she said. 'Drink your coffee. I made hot coffee for
you. Drink it!'

'Is there something in it?' he asked.

'Why? Are you afraid of what I'll do to you when you're
asleep?' she asked, and laughed again. 'Do you know what
happened to the old man in his sleep last night?'

'What old man?' Santo asked.

'The keeper of the keys,' she said, 'the man who fixed the locks,
do you remember the man who fixed the locks?'

'I never saw him,' Santo said.

'That's right, you were unconscious, weren't you? Someone put something in your food. You never met the poor man, did you? Clarence met him, though, didn't you, Clarence?'

The dog, at mention of his name, began thumping his tail against the floor.

'Yes, Clarence,' she said, 'good dog, you're the only one who knows now. You and Santo. The only ones who know.'

'Know what?' Santo asked.

She laughed again, and suddenly the laughter caught in her throat like a choke, and her face sobered, and she pointed her finger at him and said, 'You shouldn't have left me, Robert.'

'Robert?' he said. 'Hey, come on, I'm ...'

'I told you to be *quiet*! I should have hidden your clothes. You wouldn't have been able to leave without your clothes. Couldn't have left here naked, could you, Robert?'

'Listen, I'm ... I'm Santo. Now cut it out, you're ...'

'I *said* be quiet!'

He closed his mouth. Just inside the door, the dog growled.

'Take off your clothes,' she said.

'Listen, I really don't feel like ...'

'Do as I tell you. Or do you want the dog to help you? Would you like to help him take off his clothes, Clarence?'

The dog's ears sprang suddenly erect.

'Would you like to help Robert take off his clothes?' she asked. 'Would you, sweetie? Or shall we wait till he's unconscious, shall we wait for that?'

'You *did* put something in the coffee, didn't you?' he said.

'Oh yes,' she said, laughing merrily, he hated it when she laughed that fucking merry laugh of hers. 'Something in the coffee, and in the milk, and in the orange juice, something in *everything* this morning.'

'Why?' he said, and rose from the couch. He felt nothing yet, perhaps she was lying. Those other times, all the other times, he'd become dizzy almost at once, but this time he felt nothing.

'Why?' she repeated. 'Because you *know*, don't you?'

'What the fuck is it I'm supposed to *know*?' he said.

'That you're *here*. That you're here where you're supposed to be instead of running off leaving a bride of six months, you rotten bastard, I'll cut out your *heart* this time!'

'Listen, you're getting me mixed up with ...'

'Be quiet, can't you *please* be quiet?' she said, and covered her ears with her hands.

'You didn't really put anything in the food, did you?'

'I *said* I did, why can't you believe anything I *say* to you or *do* for you, I'm trying to save you, don't you realize that?'

'Save me from what?'

'From leaving here. From disappearing. You mustn't leave here, Robert. You'll disappear if you leave.'

'All right, I won't leave. Just promise me that if you put anything in the food ...'

'Yes, I did.'

'All right, then promise me you ... you won't do ... do anything to me while I'm ...'

'Oh yes,' she said. 'I will.'

'You'll promise?'

'Promise?' she said. 'Oh no, Robert, you mustn't leave,' she said. 'Not now. Look,' she said, and reached for her handbag and pulled the pistol from it, the same pistol she'd shown him long long ago, so long ago he could hardly remember, the cornflakes and orange juice she'd said, large black pistol in her hand, 'Look,' she said, 'I'm going to kill the dog,' she said, 'look, Robert, because the dog the dog knows you're here here, he'll tell them, Robert, they'll come take you take you away, Robert, I'm going to kill the dog,' the room going out of focus as he rose from the couch, hand outstretched to her, 'and then I'm going to take off your clothes, all your clothes, you're going to be naked,' she said, the gun coming up level. 'See the gun, Clarence,' the dog's tail thumping against the floor, 'strip you to your skin,' she said, moving towards her, his hand reaching reaching, his mouth opening and closing around words he could not form, 'strip your skin,' she said, 'strip you naked,' she said, and the gun exploded once, twice, and he saw the back of the dog's head splattering against the massive wooden door in a shower of gristle, bone and blood before he fell flat to the floor, trying to say don't cut me don't burn me don't hurt me don't please don't please.

It was a little after twelve noon when they reached Dorothy Hawkins' apartment. This time they had a search warrant with them. And this time, Dorothy Hawkins wasn't home. The building superintendent told them that Mrs Hawkins worked out on Beth-town in a factory that made transistor radios, something the detectives already knew, and something they might have remembered if the case hadn't reached the true desperation phase. Desperately, Carella and Meyer showed the super the court order, and explained that Bethtown was one hell of a way from Diamondback, and that finding Mrs Hawkins would necessitate a car trip all the way downtown to Land's End, where they'd have to take a ferry over to the island, or else go across the new bridge, but this would put them smack in the centre of Village East, the heart of Bethtown, and they'd then have to drive all the way over to the other end of the island where most of the factories were located, and if they had to drag Mrs Hawkins back here with them to unlock her door, she'd lose a day's work, did the super want the poor woman to lose a day's work? The super said he certainly didn't want a nice lady like Mrs Hawkins to lose a day's work.

'Then how about opening the door for us?' Meyer said.

'I s'pose,' the super said dubiously.

Under his watchful eye, they searched the apartment from top to bottom for almost two hours, but they could not find the slightest clue to where C. J. Hawkins had gone each and every Wednesday for the past thirteen weeks.

The girl who opened the door of Joey Peace's downtown pad was a tall redhead wearing nothing but a pair of red bikini panties. She had very long legs and rather exuberant breasts with nipples that peered at each other as though in need of an ophthalmologist. She also had green eyes and frizzy hair, and she looked and sounded somewhat kooky.

'Hey, hi,' she said, opening the door and peeking into the hall. 'Is there just the two of you?'

'Just the two of us,' Carella said, and showed her his shield.

'Hey, wow,' she said, 'cool. Where'd you get that?'

'We're police officers,' Carella said. 'We've got a court order to conduct a search of this apartment, and we'd appreciate it if you let us in.'

'Yeah, hey, wow,' she said, 'what are you lookin for?'

'We don't know,' Meyer said, which was close enough to the truth, and which caused the redhead to burst into paroxysms of laughter that jiggled her exhilarated breasts and caused them to look even more cross-eyed than they had a moment before.

The judge who'd granted the warrant had been reluctant to give them what he called 'a blind licence to conduct a search for will o' the wisps' until Carella pointed out that he had very specifically mentioned what the detectives were searching for, and what they were searching for, Your Honour – if you'll just glance here at heading number two – is *sand*, your Honour, to match sand discovered in the apartment of a homicide victim and already in possession of the Police Department and in custody at the Police Laboratory, in the hope of making a positive comparison, your Honour. The judge had looked at him askance; he knew the premise was utterly groundless. But he also knew that these men were investigating a triple-homicide, and he suspected nobody's rights would be compromised if they conducted searches of the apartments one of the victims had most commonly inhabited, so he'd issued one warrant for a search of Mrs Hawkins' apartment and another for a search of Joey Peace's rather more sumptuous pad on Laramie Avenue.

The redhead looked at the warrant Carella held in front of her face. She kept studying the document and nodding. Meyer, watching her, realized that her eyes were even more out of focus than her wayward breasts, and he decided that her natural kookiness was being aided somewhat by something that was causing her to float around on the ceiling someplace.

'You just shoot something?' he asked.

'Yeah, a tiger,' the girl said, and giggled.

'What are you on, honey?' Meyer said.

'Who me?' the girl said. 'Straight as an arrow, man, they call me Straight Arrow, man, yessir.' She peeked around the warrant into the hallway. 'I thought there was gonna be more of you,' she said.

'How many?' Carella asked.

'Ten,' the girl said, and shrugged.

'A minyan,' Meyer said.

'No, only ten,' the girl said.

'Which one are you?' Carella asked. 'Lakie or Sarah?'

'Sarah. Hey how'd you know my name?'

'My wife's name is Sarah,' Meyer said.

'Where's Nancy Elliott?'

'She split. She was afraid Joey was gonna hurt her. Hey, how do you know Nancy?'

'My grandmother's name is Nancy,' Meyer said.

'Yeah? No kidding.'

'No kidding,' Meyer said. His grandmother's name was Rose.

'Where's Lakie?' Carella asked.

'Out buying some booze. This is supposed to be like a big party today, man,' she said, and looked out into the hall again.

'At one o'clock in the afternoon?' Carella said.

'Sure, why not?' Sarah said, and shrugged. 'It's raining.' Each time she shrugged, her nipples demanded corrective lenses.

'You've seen the warrant,' Carella said. 'Now how about letting us in?'

'Sure, hey, come on,' Sarah said, and stepped into the hallway and looked towards the elevator bank.

'You'd better come in,' Meyer said, 'before you catch cold.'

'It's just they're supposed to be here by now,' she said, and shrugged.

'Come on inside,' Meyer said.

Sarah shrugged again and preceded him into the apartment. Meyer locked the door and put the chain on it.

'You're Joey Peace's girlfriend, huh?' he said.

'No, he's my big daddy,' Sarah said, and giggled.

'Go put on some clothes,' Meyer said.

'What for?'

'We're married men.'

'Who ain't?' Sarah said.

'Where'd C.J. sleep?' Carella asked.

'*All* over,' Sarah said.

'I mean, where's her bedroom?'

'Second one down the hall.' The buzzer on the door sounded. Sarah turned towards it, and said, 'There they are. What should I tell them?'

'Tell them you're busy,' Carella said.

'But I *ain't* busy.'

'Tell them the cops are here,' Meyer said. 'Maybe they'll just go away on their own.'

'Who, the cops?'

'No, the minyan.'

'I *told* you not a million,' the girl said. 'Only ten.'

'Go answer the door,' Carella said.

Sarah went to the door and unlocked it. A tall blonde girl wearing a soaking wet trenchcoat and a plastic scarf on her head came in carrying a bulging brown paper bag. She put the bag down on the parsons table just inside the front door, said, 'What took you so long to open it?' and then saw Carella and Meyer and said, 'Hi, fellas.'

'Hi, Lakie,' Carella said.

'They're fuzz,' Sarah said glumly.

'Shit,' Lakie said, and took off the plastic scarf and shook out her long blonde hair. 'Is this a bust?' she asked.

'They got a search warrant,' Sarah said.

'Shit,' Lakie said again.

They had scarcely begun opening drawers in C.J.'s room when the door buzzer sounded again. A few minutes later, they heard loud voices in the entrance foyer. Carella walked out of the bedroom and towards the front door. Six wet and obviously annoyed men were standing there arguing with Sarah, who still wore nothing but the red bikini panties.

'What's the problem, fellas?' Carella asked.

'Who the fuck are *you*?' one of the men said.

'Police,' Carella said, and showed them his shield.

The men looked at it silently.

'Is that a real badge?' one of the men asked.

'Solid gold,' Carella said.

'There goes the fuckin party, right?' Sarah said.

'Well put,' Carella said.

'Boy oh boy,' one of the men said, shaking his head. '*I* gotta tell *you*.'

From the bedroom, Meyer called, 'Steve! Come look at this.'

'Close the door behind you, boys,' Carella said, and wagged them out with his hands.

'This was *some* great idea, Jimmy,' one of the men said.

'Shut the fuck up, willya?' Jimmy said, and slammed the door shut behind him. Carella locked it and put on the night chain.

'So what am I supposed to do all afternoon now, huh?' Sarah asked.

'Go read a book,' Carella said.

'A *what*?' she said.

'Steve!' Meyer called.

'You guys come bustin in here,' Sarah said, following Carella down the hall, 'and we're gonna lose half a yard, that's what this party was gonna bring us.'

'What've you got?' Carella asked Meyer.

'This,' Meyer said.

'C.J.'s train schedule,' Sarah said, 'big deal. What the fuck good is it now? She's dead, she ain't gonna take no more trains *no* place,' she said, vigorously shaking her head and her breasts from side to side.

'Will you go put something on,' Meyer said, 'you're making me dizzy.'

'Lots of people say that,' Sarah said, looking down at her breasts. 'I wonder why.'

'Go put on a bra, will you?'

'I don't have any bras,' Sarah said, and folded her arms across her chest.

'Ever see her consulting this?' Carella asked.

'Only once a week,' Sarah said.

'When?'

'Every Wednesday.'

'Look at what she marked,' Meyer said.

One side of the schedule listed all trains from Isola to Tarkington, which was the last stop on the Sands Spit Line. The other side of the schedule listed all trains coming into the city from the opposite direction. C.J. had circled the name of one town on the return side of the schedule: Fox Hill.

'Listen,' Sarah said, 'would you guys like a drink or something? I mean, I hate to waste the fuckin afternoon, I really do.'

'Next train out is at three-oh-seven,' Carella said, and looked at his watch.

'I mean,' Sarah said to Meyer, 'you seem to dig the jugs, what do you say?'

'What's this?' Carella said.

'Where?' Meyer said.

'Right here,' Sarah said. 'My bedroom's just down the hall.'

'Here on the bottom of the schedule,' Carella said.

'What do you say, Baldy?'

'Some other time,' Meyer said.

'*When*?' Sarah said.

Scribbled on the bottom of the schedule were the numerals 346-8711. Unless both detectives were enormously mistaken, they were looking at a telephone number.

The harbour patrolman who took them out to the island in the Elsinore County police launch was a man named Sonny Gardner. What had been a steady downpour when they left the city an hour before had become here on the Spit a faint drizzle that was something more than fog but less than true rain, a misty cold wash that blew in off the water and penetrated the skin as if by osmosis.

'You picked a hell of a day to go out to Hawkhurst,' Sonny said. 'I could think of better days.'

'Is that what the island's called?' Carella asked. 'Hawkhurst?'

'No, that's the house. The island is <u>Kent</u>. But the names are connected, if you know what I mean? The guy who built the house used to spend his summers in Kent. That's in England, that's a county in England. When the British were here on the Spit, the commander of the fort on one of the islands was originally from Kent. He named the two islands Greater Kent – that's the one had the fort on it – and Lesser Kent, that's the one we're going to. Anyway, the guy who later bought Lesser Kent was familiar with England and when he built the house out here, he named the house Hawkhurst, which is a town in Kent.'

'Man named Parker, is that right?' Carella said.

'Nossir, not to my knowledge.'

'Phone company said the phone was listed to an L. Parker.'

'That's the daughter.'

'What's her first name?'

'Lily. The old man built the house for her when she turned sixteen.'

'What was *his* name?'

'Frank Peterson. Peterson Lumber, you familiar with it?'

'No.'

'Very big out here on the Spit. Started the business in Jackson Cove, oh, back after World War I some time, turned it into a multi-million-dollar enterprise. Built the house for his daughter when she was sixteen. Only child. A birthday present, you know? How'd you like to have a father like that?' Sonny asked.

'Yeah,' Meyer said, thinking the only thing *his* father had ever given him was a double-barrelled monicker.

'Though who knows?' Sonny said. 'People say the kid's nuts now, so who knows about things like that, huh?'

'The kid?' Meyer said.

'Yeah, the daughter. Well, she ain't a kid no more, she must be close to forty by now.'

'I take it she's married,' Carella said.

'*Was* married,' Sonny said. 'Husband left her practically on their wedding day. That's when she went bananas.'

'How bad was she?' Carella asked.

'Well, she couldn'ta been *too* bad,' Sonny said, 'cause they didn't put her away or nothin. Took care of her out there on the island. I used to see the old man at the railroad station picking up the nurses – when they changed shifts, you know.'

'But people still say she's nuts, huh?' Meyer said.

'Well, eccentric,' Sonny said. 'Put it that way. Eccentric.'

'Where's the old man now?'

'Dead,' Sonny said. 'Must be six or seven years now. Yeah, that's right, it was seven years this July. That's when he died. Left the daughter all alone in the world.'

The boat was coming in towards a small sandy cove on the southern end of the island. A fog-shrouded dock jutted into the bay there, its pilings standing like ghostly sentinels in the mist. Beyond, on the ocean side of the island, the surf pounded in against a long white sand beach.

'Only house out here, you know,' Sonny said. 'Hawkhurst. It's a private island. This one and Greater Kent. Both private islands.' He manoeuvred the launch into the dock, and Carella leaped ashore and caught the line Meyer tossed to him. He made it fast on one of the pilings, offered his hand to help Meyer ashore, and then said, 'Can you wait for us?'

'How else would you get back?' Sonny said. 'No ferry service here, it's private like I told you.'

'We may be a while,' Carella said.

'Take your time,' Sonny said.

The house stood stark and grey against a greyer, disturbed sky. Meyer and Carella came up a slate walkway to the front door. There was no bell and no nameplate, but a tarnished brass knocker hung on the door and Carella lifted that now and rapped it several times against the weathered wood. The detectives waited. A cold wet wind blew in off the ocean side. Carella lifted the collar of his coat, and then rapped again with the knocker.

The door opened only a crack, abruptly stopped by a night-chain. Beyond the door, beyond the crack was darkness. In the darkness, they could vaguely make out a pale oval that seemed to be a woman's face floating in space behind the door.

'Mrs Parker?' Carella said.

'Yes?'

'Isola Police,' he said, and showed his shield.

'Yes?'

'May we come in?'

'What for?'

'We're investigating some homicides back in the city,' Meyer started, 'and we'd ...'

'Homicides? What would I know about—'

'May we come in please, Mrs Parker?' Carella said. 'It's cold and wet out here, and I think we might be able to talk better in—'

'No,' she said, 'I'm busy,' and began to close the door. Carella immediately shoved his foot into the narrowing wedge.

'Take your foot away,' she said.

'No, ma'am,' he said. 'My foot stays where it is. Either you let us in ...'

'No, I'm not letting you in.'

'Fine, then we'll talk right here. But you're not closing that door on us, ma'am.'

'I have nothing to say to you.'

'We're here because we found your telephone number on a train schedule belonging to one of the homicide victims,' Carella said. 'Is 346–8711 your telephone number?'

Pinpoint pricks of light in the darkness beyond the cracked door, her eyes flashing. Silence. Then – 'Yes, that's my number.'

'Do you know anyone named C. J. Hawkins?'

'No.'

Long blonde hair, he could make that out now in the darkness. The eyes flashing again in the narrow pale face beyond the narrow open wedge of door and jamb.

'How about George Chadderton?'

'No.'

'Ambrose Harding?'

'No.'

'Mrs Parker, we know that C. J. Hawkins came out to Sands Spit every Wednesday, and was met at the Fox Hill station by someone driving an automobile.' Carella paused. 'Was that someone *you*?' he asked.

'No.'

'Ma'am, if you'd just open the door, maybe we could . . .'

'No, I won't. Take your foot away. *Move* it, damn you!'

'No, ma'am,' Carella said. 'Do you know anyone named Santo Chadderton?'

Again the eyes flashed in the darkness beyond the door. A brief hesitation. Then – 'You asked about him earlier, didn't you?'

'That was *George* Chadderton. This is his brother Santo.'

'I don't know either one of them.'

'Do you own a pistol?'

'No.'

'Have you left this island within recent days?'

'No.'

'Were you here on the night of September fifteenth at around eleven o'clock?'

'Yes.'

'How about three-thirty a.m. that same night?'

'I was here '

'Anyone with you?'

'No '

'Mrs Parker,' Carella said, 'I'd appreciate it if you took off this chain . . .'

'No.'

'You're not helping yourself—'

'Go away.'

'You're only forcing us to come back with a search warrant.'

'Leave me alone.'

'Okay then, that's what we'll do,' Carella said, and

pulled his foot from the door. It slammed shut at once. His goddam foot ached.

'Rotten bitch,' he said, and began walking down the path towards the waiting launch.

Beside him, Meyer said, 'We really going for a warrant?'

'In Elsinore County?' Carella said. 'It'll take us a month.'

'You thinking what I'm thinking?'

'I'm thinking we go in anyway.'

'Good,' Meyer said.

Sonny Gardner was waiting at the dock for them.

'We're staying a while,' Carella told him. 'I'd like you to head
back to the mainland without us. Make a hell of a lot of noise, rev
your engines, toot your fog horn, make sure she knows you're
going. You got that?'

'I got it,' Sonny said. 'When do you want to be picked up?'

Carella looked at Meyer. Meyer shrugged.

'Make it an hour,' Carella said.

'What the hell's *in* that house?' Sonny asked.

'Ghosts maybe,' Carella said.

'It sure looks it,' Sonny said, and rolled his eyes. He was starting
the engine when they heard the first scream. The scream was one
of terror and pain, it threaded the fog, it raised the hackles on the
backs of their necks. Carella and Meyer reached for their guns. At
the same moment, Sonny killed the engines and drew his own
weapon – but he did not move from the boat. The two detectives
came pounding up the slate walkway to the front door. Carella
kicked it in, and both of them fanned into the entryway, lighted
now with a Tiffany lamp that hung over a corner table upon which
were heaped magazines, newspapers and mail. Crouching, they
probed the empty foyer with their guns, and heard the second
scream coming from somewhere below and to the right.

'The cellar,' Carella said,   1 ran towards a door at the far end
of a corridor leading to a kitchen beyond. He threw open the door
and heard the screaming again, sustained this time, unrelieved this
time, this time a single piercing steady scream that paused only
long enough for whoever was screaming to draw breath, and then
continued again. He came down the cellar steps with Meyer close
behind him. Together, they ran through a finished room with a
pool table in the centre of it, and then past an enclosed furnace,

187

and then stopped just outside a massive, piano-hinged, oaken door that was open into the corridor. The screaming was coming from inside the room beyond that door, a pause, the gasping for breath again, and then the scream, steady, terror-ridden, agonized. There was a second door beyond the first one, also open, this one angled into the room. Carella stepped into the room and almost tripped over the carcass of a German shepherd dog lying just inside the doorway. The back of the dog's head had been blown away, there was a puddle of drying blood on the floor. Carella was moving around the blood and around the dog and around the second door when she came at him.

Sonny Gardner had told them that the woman who lived here was only forty years old, but the woman who came at Carella now was certainly older than that. Oh yes, she was tall and slender, and yes her body seemed youthful in the long black dress that covered it, her blonde hair greying only slightly here and there. But her face was the face of a sixty-year-old, lined and haggard, a ghastly pallor clouding it, the eyes sunken, the lips tightly compressed. He realized all at once that he was looking into the ravaged face of a madwoman, and felt a sudden cold chill that had nothing whatever to do with the incessant screaming that came from the other side of the room.

Lily Parker had a knife in her hand, and the knife dripped blood, and her long black dress was drenched with blood, and her long blonde hair was streaked with blood and there was blood spattered on her hands and on her face. As she came towards him – he had not yet seen what was on the bed – he wondered if the blood was why she had not opened the door; had she been drenched with blood standing there in the hallway beyond the nightchain? Her eyes were wide and staring as she came at him – he had not yet seen the man on the bed – the knife extended and flailing the air. He fired low the first time, at her legs in the black sheath of the blood-drenched dress, and missed, and still she came at him, and this time he raised the gun and pulled off two shots in succession, both of them catching her high on the left shoulder, and spinning her around, and dropping her to the carpeted floor.

He had not yet seen the horror on the bed.

There was blood all over the carpet around the bed. There was blood soaked into the bedclothes. On the bed, on his back, a man lay spread-eagled, his arms and legs tied to the four posts. The man was still screaming though Lily Parker lay wounded on the floor, where she could no longer harm him. The man had skin only on his face. The rest of his skin had been peeled away from his body so that he lay there a naked pulsing bleeding mass of unsheathed muscles and nerves.

Carella turned away at once, almost colliding with Meyer who was directly behind him. 'We'll ... we'll need ...' he said, and could not get the rest out. He looked for a phone, found none in the room, and went swiftly out into the cellar and upstairs to the kitchen where he found one on the wall. He dialled the local police then, and identified himself, and told them what they had here, and asked that they send an ambulance at once.

'It's very bad,' he said. 'I've never seen anything like it in my life.'

It did not stop raining until Sunday morning, September 24. The rain stopped all at once; the clouds would not dissipate for hours, but for now at least there was no rain. The first tentative rays of the sun filtered down through the overcast at 2.00 p.m. and by 2.15 the wet pavements were glistening with sunshine. At 3.30 that same afternoon, Santo Chadderton died in the Intensive Care Unit of the Fox Hill Hospital. That same day, in the Psychiatric Unit on the sixth floor of Isola's Buena Vista Hospital, a team of psychiatrists was interviewing Lily Parker to determine whether or not she was sane enough to stand trial. A transcript of the interview later found its way to Carella's desk. It was in the form of a standard Q and A. As he read it, he could remember nothing but the flayed body of Santo Chadderton in that basement room at Hawkhurst.

Q: Mrs Parker, can you tell us why you killed George Chadderton?
A: Because he knew.
Q: What did he know?
A: That Robert was with me on the island.
Q: Robert?
A: My husband.
Q: Was with you on the island?
A: In the basement room where they used to lock me up.
Q: Who used to lock you up?

A: Robert and my father.

Q: Mrs Parker, your husband left you almost twenty years ago, Isn't that so?

A: Well yes, but he came back.

Q: If he left you so long ago ...

A: Yes, but he came *back*, I just told you.

Q: Then it would have been impossible for *him* to have locked you in that basement room.

A: Yes, but not my father.

Q: It was your father who locked you in that room, is that it?

A: Nurse sitting outside the door. Giving me *shots* all the time.

Q: Your father did that to you?

A: *And* Robert. *Because* of Robert, don't you see?

Q: Because Robert left you?

A: Yes. That was when I got sick. When Robert left. That was when my father had the doors put in, and locked me up.

Q: Mrs Parker, when did your father die?

A: Seven years ago.

Q: What month, would you remember?

A: July.

Q: And when did you meet Santo Chadderton?

A: I don't know who that is.

Q: Mrs Parker, we have here a guest list for something called The Blondie Ball, a charity ball that took place on September eleventh, seven years ago.

A: Yes?

Q: Your name is on the list – we *assume* it's your name – L. Parker. Is that you?

A: Yes, Lily Parker.

Q: Santo Chadderton was one of the musicians at the ball that night.

A: I don't know anyone named Santo Chadderton.

Q: Isn't Santo Chadderton the man you were living with on the island?

A: No, no.

Q: Who was that man then?

A: Robert. My husband. He came back. After Daddy died. Robert came back to me.

Q: Where did you meet him again, Mrs Parker?

A: At the ball in September, fairy princess all in white, mask on my face, he didn't even know it was me at first. Silly Robert making music in a band.

Q: When did you take him to the island?

A: In the morning. We spent the night at the hotel, he was extremely apologetic, we made such beautiful love.

Q: And in the morning you went out to the island?

A: Yes.

Q: And he stayed there with you from then on?

A: Oh yes, why would he want to leave? I took very good care of him. He knew that. He finally came to understand how much he loved me.

Q: Mrs Parker, why did you kill Clara Jean Hawkins?

A: She was the one who told.

Q: Told what?

A: About us on the island. I brought her home to Robert one night because I thought he might be, well, stimulated by her, you know, by a third party. It wasn't fair, he never wanted to leave the island, I thought I'd bring him some outside stimulation, you know. I spotted her on the street downtown one day, in the city outside the railroad terminal, she seemed young and vivacious, I asked her if she'd like to come out to Hawkhurst with me. And of course she accepted, she could see I was a beautiful woman of good breeding, he always used to tell me how beautiful I was, my father, gave me Hawkhurst as a sweet-sixteen present you know, and C.J. recognized my beauty as well, licked my cunt, savoured my cunt, it was a shame I had to kill her.

Q: When you say she told ...

A: She told his brother, don't you see?

Q: Santo's brother?

A: I found out last Thursday when I was driving her back to the station. She told me she was going to do an *album* with him, songs! They were going to write *songs* about all her experiences, can you imagine? Songs about us! Songs about what we did together on the island.

Q: She said that? That the songs would be about you?

A: Well, what else *could* they be?

Q: So you killed her.

A: Of course. To save Robert.

Q: To save him?

A: Yes, to *save* him, to *keep* him.

Q: Then ... Mrs Parker ... why did you kill *him*?

A: I didn't.

Q: He's dead, Mrs Parker. We learned a little while ago that he's dead.

A: No, no. He'll come back, you'll see. *I* thought he was dead, too, for the longest time, but he came back, didn't he? Only this time I won't be as understanding, I can tell you that. I took all his clothes from him, you know. Stripped him naked. That was so he wouldn't run away again. But when he comes back this time, I'm going to be a bit harsher with him. I put needles in his cock one time, to keep it stiff. That was before C.J. started coming out to join us. Cut off one of his fingers, too. But that was because his cock wasn't stiff. A man has to have a stiff cock. If he hasn't got a stiff cock, what good is he? I kept telling him that. This time ... when he comes back this time ... well, he'll see, I can promise you that.

Q: What will you do this time, Mrs Parker?

A: Oh, he'll see. He'll see.

It was almost October when the report reached Carella's desk. By that time, Lily Parker had been remanded to the Riverhead Facility for the Criminally Insane. By that time, the city's skies were clear and blue, and there was a clean crisp bite on the air. Typewriters were clacking in the squadroom, phones were ringing. Carella rose from his desk and walked to the filing cabinets, and found the folder for Chadderton under C, and filed the report at the front of the folder. The case was closed, everything wrapped up neatly and tied with a pretty little bow. All the pieces in place, just like a phony fucking mystery novel.

But the phone on his desk was ringing again.